ZECHERIAH'S LEDGER

ZECHERIAH'S LEDGER

Hendrik Hoitinga

Zecheriah's Ledger

Printed in the United States of America
ISBN 978-1-967279-65-4 (hc)
ISBN 978-1-967279-66-1 (sc)
ISBN 978-1-967279-67-8 (e)

2026.01.12

This book is printed on acid-free paper.

Blue Ink Media Solutions
1111B S Governors Ave
STE 7582 Dover,
DE 19904

www.blueinkmediasolutions.com

TABLE OF CONTENTS

DEDICATION

For Mum
&
In memory of Dad

Thank you to Liz and Joan from Wick,
for their loyal support.

Author's favourite passage of Scripture:
'Trust in the Lord with all your heart,
And lean not on your own understanding.
In all your ways acknowledge Him,
And He shall direct your paths'
Proverbs 3; 5-6

Finally, a big thank you to Blue Ink Media Solutions
for their guidance, support and for the most memorable
experience of the International Book Fair in Frankfurt.

PROLOGUE

Antwerpen-Belgium

June 2022

Samuel Price was running. He didn't often run, having recently turned fifty, he left that activity for others, but now, he was running for his life. The cobbles on the dock were glistening as the rain came down. As he ran, he briefly thought about a time when he had been running across a road, had tripped and had slithered across the wet surface, to be stopped by a roadside barrier, preventing him from going over the edge and into a river far below. Crazy, why did that thought suddenly come into his head! Focus and run, he silently screamed to himself.

A storm had come in from the Atlantic, bringing much rain and despite the sound it made on the rooves of the building he unmistakenly heard the sharp whistling sound whizzing past his right ear. They were shooting at him! Sam veered a little to the left, he hadn't heard the shots, no doubt a gun with a silencer. The corner of the building was coming up fast, he reached it and turned around it. The end of the cobbled dock area was just ahead. There was no way out. Beyond the edge he could see the dark water and far beyond that, the lights of the city. It was after midnight. He kept running. Aware that his corduroy jeans were getting soaked, but thankful he had dressed for the impending rain, the lightweight jacket zipped up and dealing well with the heavy downpour. He was also glad his trainers had a reasonably firm grip on the cobbles, nevertheless he was fully concentrating on keeping his balance. Sam then eased up, slowing down as he neared the end of the dock. Though he knew the city a little, he knew these docks better for he had studied the layout. Knew there was no way out, but he had a plan. Knowing he was, at least for the moment, out of their line of sight, he reached the end of the dock. His heart was thumping loudly. The rain came down heavily and without turning, he jumped.

Three days earlier- Wednesday 1st of June

When the Royal Museum of fine arts began its ten-year renovation, there came a time when the basement had to be cleared. This in readiness for the installation of a new heating and air conditioning system as well as an updated security office. Whilst in the main body of the museum the art and sculptures would be able to be more easily moved and protected, the over two hundred paintings that were housed in the basement, had to be moved. A security storage firm was hired, and special fixtures were created. Thirty containers were specially designed and made. These were then transported when required, to the basement of the museum. Each container could store up to eight paintings which would be hung onto rails. Each work of art was photographed, then an opaque plastic sleeve would be put on and secured onto the rail by felt covered clips. A label was attached to the top left corner of each sleeve with a number, a description, measurements and who, if it was known, had painted it. There were many where the details were very limited, either totally unknown or in progress of being researched. Several days it had taken to achieve that part of the process and then the last stage was to take all the containers to the storage facility in another part of the city, to be retrieved when the reconstruction of the basement was completed.

It was the morning of the first of June, a Wednesday. The light breeze was from the north, and it was overcast. Rain was forecast. The trucks arrived, two of them, to move the containers back over to the museum. A team of six men and four women employed by the storage company worked the containers. Two women, the museum curator and her assistant checked each container as it appeared in the covered docking area, checking the details of each painting housed and ticking them off in a register before securing it and allowing it to be rolled into the waiting vehicles which had backed right onto the loading bay. All went well for the first fifteen. The sixteenth container was rolled before them. They opened the door and immediately spotted a problem.

Out of the eight, two sleeves were obviously empty. Emma Brood, the Belgian Museum curator and native to Antwerpen was astonished. She discovered that both sleeves had a cheap frame within each, which had then been clipped to the rail. The label on each sleeve showed the details of the painting that had been there but were no longer. She was puzzled and for several moments unsure as to what to do. Then, looking at her assistant, made her decision. She called a halt on the proceedings. She instructed her assistant to get the truck drivers to lock their vehicles and to close the loading doors, then to come inside, she herself instructed the other staff to also now come inside and then wheeled the sixteenth container back into the main building where it was more protected from the rain which had begun to fall.

She then told all the storage staff to remain where they were. She called the police first, then called her boss at the museum and finally made a call to the storage facility manager to get his butt down there. Many things were going on in her mind as she looked at the container. Looking at each label, she knew, which two painting had gone missing, but she pondered, why place a different frame into each sleeve, why not simply take the whole painting, sleeve and all, away? This was disturbing and most mysterious. She looked at her assistant who could only shrug in response.

Whilst awaiting the police and the storage manager, Emma scrolled through the phone in her hand, she saw the number she was looking for. The insurance company. She decided that she would await the police, then check the remaining containers before contacting the insurance company.

Samantha Price ended the call, switched on her laptop and scrolled for a few moments until she found the file she was looking for. The thirty-seven-year-old read through the file, then looked at her notes as the rain which had been forecast, beat against the windows of her apartment that overlooked the river Scheldt. A senior insurance consultant and investigator for Zwart Wit Verzekeringen, she mostly worked from home. For a while that home had been in Mexico where she had met Rico, this whilst on the trail of a fraudster. Romance had blossomed.

Standing her five-foot seven frame up she walked over to the window. Tucking a few light brown strands of hair behind her right ear, she gazed for a while, through the droplets on the glass and thought through the recent telephone call. She had been ready to go out and see Rico, who was now her soon husband to be, who was in hospital having had minor surgery the day before. But this case needed to be followed up. She had to go down to the storage company right away and speak with the manager of the storage facility as well as with the curator of the museum, Emma Brood, about the theft of two paintings. Looking out of her lounge windows that overlooked the River Scheldt, she decided that bringing an umbrella might be a good option. Then grabbing a notepad, checking her handbag that she had all that she would need, she donned a long lightweight beige coloured trench coat and left the apartment.

For some reason, as she walked from her apartment to catch a tram to where the storage facility was situated on the southeast side of the compact city, she cast her mind back to when she had set out for Rotterdam that day to meet her name- sake. Sam Price. She smiled as she thought back, already nearly three years ago, having originally decided on a brief meeting to see what this man might know about the circumstances of a theft she was investigating. It turned out that he had uncovered far more, and a partnership developed that proved very successful, moreover a good friendship grew as well. Even more important, she thought, that it was during that case, that she met Rico. The reminiscing brought a smile to her face. The clouds, though still threatening, released no more rain for the moment as she boarded the tram.

Forty minutes later she had made her way to the storage facility, had spoken to the manager, had taken several photographs and had listened to his account of what had happened, or rather, what had been discovered. She had then set up an appointment with the curator, with Emma Brood, who had, at that time, finished with the police and had returned to the museum. After another tram journey back into the city centre, she was now sitting in her office. Samantha, though preferring it to be addressed as Sam, saw that she was still visibly shaken and pale.

'I know this must not be an easy day for you, but I do have to do my own investigation, you will hopefully understand' Sam said, pen and notepad in hand.

'Yes, of course....' Emma replied, 'it's just, that, well, I can't understand it, it is all so, well, very strange...'

Sam looked at the woman across from her. Figured her to be in her fifties, her dark hair neatly tied up in some kind of swirl. She wore minimal makeup and wore a smart dark blue dress with a floral white blouse underneath.

'So, please tell me, these paintings were transported from the museum here, to the storage place, what, ten months ago?'

'Yes, I oversaw the move, all the paintings, there were a total of two hundred and twelve, were all photographed, catalogued and labelled once they were secured into the specially designed sleeves, which, as you will have seen, were then secured to a rail and hung into the containers. The police are going through cctv footage from the storage building, but according to the logs at the facility, once all the containers had been locked away, all rolled into one chamber, twenty-seven in all, the chamber room had not been accessed until this morning.'

'Once you discovered that two paintings were missing, did you then also check the remainder of the containers?'

'Yes, I felt it best to call the police in first, they could check for fingerprints and so on, they were very efficient, then my assistant and I checked the remaining twelve containers, but they were all in order, all the contents accounted for. There are just two paintings that have gone, it's then when I called you' Sam made some notes, then saw the photographs on the curator's desk and asked, 'These are the ones that are missing?' nodding towards them

'Yes, these are copies, the police also have a copy, these are for you' Emma replied, still so confused and stumped as to how this could have happened, handing them over to Samantha.

'Thank you' Sam said, then looking on the back of each where the details had been written. One of them was by an artist called Jacob Leyssens and the scene was that of some buildings and a river that looked to be, Sam thought, in Rome. The other had the title of the work, both in Dutch and English written down, and the artist being Rubens. The dimensions, she saw, had also been noted as well as a very brief description on the type of frame it was in. Both paintings, Sam saw, were the same in dimensions, ninety-two centimetres by sixty centimetres. Also, the frames of both were listed as neo-classical with beaded surround.

'Okay' Samantha said, then looking across at Emma, asked, 'who were present here, when all the paintings were labelled and placed into those containers?'

'Myself, my assistant, miss Kaplova, and…' Emma said, then shuffling some papers, pulled a sheet from a pile, handing this over, 'this is the list we made at the time, it shows those present when recording the paintings and putting the relevant labels onto the sleeves. And here' the still shaken curator said, handing over a further five sheets of paper' A complete list of all the artwork and into which container each painting was stored.' After a brief pause as Samantha perused the papers, she then said, 'The missing ones were in container eleven. I also see a value beside each of the paintings listed, I take it that these are the figures estimated for insurance purposes?' Having not dealt with that insurance quote herself, she wondered how they had arrived at these figures, calculating that the two missing paintings were insured each for fifty thousand euros.

'Yes, many of the stored paintings are still being researched, a value was difficult to be precise on, but we felt it was prudent to be generous, for insurance purposes' The curator answered.

Samantha looked up from the sheets, smiled briefly, then said, 'Thank you, and I notice that this was done over a period of four days?

'Yes, it was a lot of work, but at night we had special security on the premises, o, the names of the security personnel during that period are also on that list, they were from the same company that would house the containers.'

'I see, that will be all for now, I will follow up with the police, who I believe have security footage of both the storage facility and the museum?'

'Yes, and this man,' Emma said, writing down a name of a slip of paper, 'is leading the investigation'

'Thank you,' Samantha said, taking the note, 'and I'll get back to you if I need anything else' Standing up, she offered her hand.

Emma stood up and shook it,' Thank you, I will see you out' then asked, 'Now that the police have done their things, and you have been and seen the setup, can the paintings be released and come back to the museum?'

'Yes, you have a team of people brought together for that purpose today, so yes, carry on' Samantha answered, given the curator a comforting smile.

Fifty minutes later, she was armed with a full police report and a promise that she would soon receive a copy of all the security footage. Together with the notes she had taken when having gone to the storage facility and the museum, Samantha walked home, passing by the very bench, where she recalled, as she walked by, she had sat when she last had seen Sam Price. She smiled at the memory, and recalled his words when he had parted, saying that he would look forward to the invitation. Her wedding. Her plans had been put on hold for a moment, it now seemed more likely, she thought, as she rounded the corner and walked towards the entrance to her apartment, that it might be Sam and Chrissie who would marry first, less than two months away. Entering the foyer, she decided she would give him a call, whilst she was confident of her own investigative abilities, Sam was good at specific research, and she would enlist his help, for this seemed to be a rather baffling case. After that she would change and visit Rico in the hospital. Moments later, keys at the ready, she walked up the path to the front foyer of her apartment building. She entered and took the lift to her fifth-floor apartment.

T H E   P A S T

Period 1: 1655

Rotterdam

The little girl, ten years of age, bounded up the short narrow path, reached the green door, and as she reached for the doorknob, it opened and there stood her grandfather. She loved her grandfather, and he loved her, embracing the dark-haired little girl he looked up to see her mother coming up the path.

Bibiana pulled herself free from him, passed by him and went into the house to find Salee, her grandmother. Karel Maas smiled but then noticed the look on his daughter in law's face.

Farah, the woman his son Pieter had met and taken from her homeland, from a city named Bandar Abbas, in Persia, spoke no Dutch. She also barely spoke her own language, in fact, she hardly spoke at all. Stopping about five feet away from the door, she placed a large holdall bag on the ground, then gave a brief nod, before turning around and walking away.

Karel sighed and understood. He then stepped from the doorway to retrieve the bag.

Closing the door, he thought back, back to a time when he and Salee were still in Surabaya, in Java, where they had run a vast trading post. One he had set up, having decided to stay after the storm that had sunk the ship he had been on and had resulted in the death of his master. He recalls visiting the grave where Pietro Esposito lay buried, close by the little village, where Salee had lived, close by the shore, at the grave that he himself had dug. It was a place he visited every year, and every year he would stand by the grave and look out over the waters to see, still sticking above the water line, the remains of the ship that had been taken by the storm. The ship he had been a ship's boy on for four years. A time when he had learned so much, every day, from the captain, from the master, who had hired him that day in the port of Amsterdam where he had travelled to from Rotterdam seeking work and adventure.

As Karel entered the lounge, seeing his granddaughter sitting in her lap, Salee, he smiled at the recollection that went through his mind. She had been the villager who had spotted the ship in danger when the rains and winds had unleashed their strength. She and the other villager had been so helpful. Still smiling he walked further into the room, one of two main rooms in the small house, and sat down in his chair, knowing that soon she would come and cuddle up to him and demand another story to be told.

Thirty years after the death of the master from which he had learned so much, he and Salee were at his grave together. It would be the last time he would visit, the last time he would speak and pray over the grave. Their eldest son, who they had named Pieter, in memory of the captain, had become a sailor, a seaman, had already travelled far and wide and they had received news that he had met a woman, when calling in at a port in Persia, had then stayed in the city of Bandar Abbas for nearly three months and had then travelled with her to where he now lived in a town called Middelburg. A letter had come, to announce the birth of a baby girl. Bibiana.

This had been the main reason that Karel felt it was time to return to his homeland. This they did in the year 1647, when young Bibiana was just two years old. Finding a house near the dock district of Rotterdam, called Haringvliet, this is where they settled, he was back in his hometown, and close to the docks, where, as a young boy he had often spent time. It was where he had made up his mind to make his way to Amsterdam, to see if he could secure work as a cabin boy. And to experience the thrill of travels over the seas. A decision he had never regretted.

Sure enough, the young girl left her grandmother's lap and jumped into his. Karel noticed Salee looking around to see Bibiana's mother, but Karel shook his head and just gave her a look, then nodded to the large bag he had brought in and placed by the door. She noticed, understood and got up.

Smiling, Karel teased Bibiana by saying that he had no more stories to tell, but she was having none of it and the severe look she gave him, was amusing and he cuddled her tight before beginning another tale. Meanwhile Salee took the bag, opened it up and could see what was inside and could also see that new arrangements were to be made.

Less than six months ago, their son Pieter, had not returned from a voyage. Word had reached them about a storm, about the loss of all hands. They had felt and observed that Farah was not handling this well. The visit was no surprise. But it was so hard for them to communicate with a woman who didn't communicate. Karel often wondered about why their son had decided to take her away from her people, take her to a strange land, and then often leave her quite alone.

Salee looked at where Bibiana was intently listening to another story. She smiled, she loved Karel very much, they would bring the girl up as their very own.

Outside, Farah stood for a moment by the gate, then, without looking back she left. There was a determination in her face, in her eyes. She strode confidently towards the docks, though she hardly uttered a word, she was very capable of communicating, but only when she chose to do so. She had not wanted to leave her home in Bandar Abbas, but her family had decided to ban her, because she had lain with a foreigner. Leaving then was the only option, Pieter had treated her well enough, but also not well enough. After a while he was often away longer and longer. Bibiana was born, this, at least was good. But Farah became more and more homesick. She found herself more and more alone, had not bonded with her daughter in a way that mother and daughter should. Also, she had met another man. A man from her country. A man who spoke her language, a man who was interested in her and made a promise that he could get her home.

When the news of Pieter's death came, it had not affected her much at all, eight year old Bibiana, having not seen much of her father, had not felt a love from him when he had been home, often spoke and longed for visiting Opa Karel and Oma Salee, whom she had been able to see a few times, each time having received such love and attention.

Farah made her decision. She would drop Bibiana off at their house in Rotterdam. They would no doubt look after her better than she could. Then, have decided a meeting point, she headed for the docks. Later that evening she would sail away, a voyage that would take her home.

At the end of the lane that led to the cottage, Farah did stop briefly, turned around and looked, then turned and walked on. Thirteen years later, her daughter Bibiana, would do exactly the same, leaving the cottage to begin a new life.

Eight weeks later Farah became increasingly more worried. The man she had met some years ago now, the man she had fallen for, the man she had lain with, changed. He was no longer as attentive as he had been. He was often remote and angry, and Farah could see, as they were getting closer to their home country, that he was looking worried, even afraid, she thought, and began to wonder why.

One afternoon, when all men were on deck, when all men were busy battling some heavy winds, the ship rocking quite dramatically, Farah decided to take a good look around the small cabin which she shared with him. The rocking motion did not worry her, recalling her voyage away from her homeland when Pieter had brought her to Holland, a journey also fraught with severe weather on two occasions. There was a place in the small cabin, where she noticed a panelling in the inner wall, was not flush, and studying this, despite being caught off balance twice due to the ship's movement, she could see marks, from a tool of sorts. Using her fingers she managed to find a grip and pulled a panel towards her. It came away suddenly, once more sprawling her on the floor. What she saw, once having regained her balance, stunned her.

What caught her attention straight away, was a large painting. A rural landscape. It had quite a wide and ornate frame around it and after some scrutiny, she even noticed the name of the artist. A bit of a scrawl, but she read it to be, Pieter Bout and a date beside it, 1653. Deciding that it was nicely painted, Farah began to wonder why it was here. There were also several small bags in the space behind the panel but feeling that the ship was not heaving as much, thought it better to replace the panel, as he could come back at any moment.

Though rarely speaking, and very good and maintaining an air of innocence and ignorance, Farah knew more that she led on. She knew things. And what she had seen, she figured, was a very nice oil painting by a Flemish master. She was troubled by what she had discovered and was opening the top drawer of a narrow chest of drawers when she heard him come back.

THE PRESENT

Wednesday 1ˢᵗ June—Boston USA

Opening a drawer, she took out a knife from the utensil box, then turned and walked over to the work island in the kitchen. Christina Small, known to her friends as Chrissie placed two slices of bread in the toaster and was in a reflective mood. Thinking back to that time, in this very kitchen, when her rival for Sam's affection had spoken to her. A tense and yet tender moment, when Alison had relinquished her pursuit…

Closing her eyes, she brought the scene to mind, almost three years ago.…

.…She stood by the sink and sensed there was someone behind her. Turning, there was Ally. They stood, facing each other, some six feet apart, each fixing their eyes on one another. Like two gunslingers in the old wild west. How can she look so beautiful at six in the morning? Chrissie was thinking. Sam was safe, he was asleep. The search was over. Was she now, once more, looking at her rival?

It was Ally who broke the silence. 'You are very much in love with him,' she said, walking towards Chrissie. Reaching her, she placed her hands gently on Chrissie's shoulders. Chrissie could find nothing to say. She looked up into Ally's eyes.

Yes, she said to herself, yes, I do love Sam.

Ally broke her gentle hold, turned away and spoke, 'I love him too.' Then turned and again faced the other woman, 'The man saved my life. He risked his and goodness knows how, but he pulled me to safety. If it wasn't for him, I would be dead Chrissie, so yes, I love Sam'

13

Then walking towards her again, taking hold of Chrissie again, she said 'But my love is different from yours.' Then again releasing the hold she stepped back, still holding her gaze on Chrissie, 'Do I want to be with him? Sure, yes, I do, but I can't. I can't be with him knowing how much you love him, and, you know, Sam, I believe, would choose you, should choose you'

Chrissie could still find no words to say. Her eyes were tearing up. Ally stepped forward again, this time she embraced Chrissie. They hugged each other for a moment. Then again it was Ally who spoke 'Sam needs you Chrissie, he won't hurt either of us, he probably won't make a decision just now, he is still so vulnerable. I need to be with my daughter. I'm going to be with her, and you, my rival, Ally said, smiling and reaching forward to wipe a tear from Chrissie's face, you need to be with Sam'…

Chrissie smiled at the recollection, felt a tear welling up, then sniffed, looked at the kitchen clock and headed for the lounge. Entering the front lounge, she looked out of the window. A sunny and bright afternoon. Again, thinking back, she brought to mind, the very first time she met him. He had pushed the doorbell. He was on the trail of a painted miniature on ivory, had discovered it had been purchased by her grandfather which had brought him to this address. This had started a renewed search for her grandfather who had gone missing not long after the second world war, A romance had not begun then. Not then.

Upstairs in the old brownstone house in Boston, Sam Price was busy scrolling through pages on his laptop computer in search of what Samantha had asked him for. She had called, less than half an hour ago. Fortunately, he was an early riser, for Samantha had not calculated the time difference correctly and it was six-thirty in the morning. She had told him, after having suddenly realised the time difference and apologised, of the burglary, of the missing paintings, of the suspicious circumstances that she was determined to investigate. She also told him that Rico, the man she was to wed soon, was in hospital, he had fallen awkwardly, ruptured his appendix and broken his leg and had surgery done to fix both appendix and leg. They had earlier postponed their wedding due to family circumstances, it now seemed to be that he and Chrissie would marry before them, because Rico did not want to get married wearing a plaster cast.

Sam, briefly looking up from the screen and out of the window, smiled when recalling how he had sat with her on a bench in Antwerp and had said that he better get an invitation to their wedding.

Back to the screen. She had asked him what he could find out about two paintings, one by Rubens, the other by Jacob Leyssens, and why it might have been these two paintings only, that had been stolen.

With music playing softly in the background, for he found he could focus well with his favourite music from the sixties and seventies accompanying him. A couple of things seemingly happened at once. The first was a lovely scent of food hit his nostrils, Chrissie was downstairs preparing breakfast, then he saw something on the screen drew his attention but before even closer investigating this, Chrissie appeared and said for him to come down and have breakfast, knowing that once he was focused on something it would be hard to drag him away from his research. 'Sam?'

Sam turned and looked at her, smiled and complied. Moving his slim six-foot one frame out of the swivel desk chair he followed her downstairs, he thought of how it had been, in that search that he started in partnership with Samantha, that he had come across Chrissie. Smiling as he watched her lovely figure as she headed for the kitchen, he thought that it wasn't too far away now, a couple of months in fact, when would marry her. A little later, whilst tucking into toast and coffee, Sam knew he had to contact Tammy, for she had knowledge of something he needed. It was the very thing that had caught his attention when Chrissie called him away to have breakfast.

Two hours later; New York

Tamara Wilson, known to her friends as Tammy, placed her smart phone on the kitchen counter and recalled the recent conversation in her mind. Walking over to the window, she looked down onto Central Park, twenty-eight floors below. Frowning, some other thoughts crept into her mind, but she shook them away and once more focused on what Sam had asked her to do. It was mid-morning and after having re-organised the team at her restaurant, which was only a few blocks away, to cover for the lunchtime service, she set about to follow up on this assignment. Leaving the kitchen she walked to the connecting dining room, opened a few drawers to find what she was looking for and placed several items on the long table, that could easily seat eight. This was where, during the covid time, she had spent many hours of research on tracing her roots, her family line, the history of the Quintons. This had come about after receiving an enormous heritage from her grandmother, Rosemary, who's journey she traced through a letter she had received, one which revealed her to be the grandmother she never knew and the quest that was contained therein, asking her to find out what had happened to a man that her grandmother had known, a quest that had taking her to France and Italy.

Rearranging some papers, she flicked through some sheets and found what she was looking for. Sam had asked her to find out more about Zecheriah's ledger which she herself had come across when researching her ancestry. She had sensed an urgency in Sam's voice, had made a note of what he was searching for, but couldn't help thinking that he sounded somewhat puzzled. She made a mental note to call Chrissie soon, a woman she had bonded with when both had been in search of the same man, for the man in her grandmother's request turned out to be Chrissie's grandfather. Reading the notes she had made on the sheet, she got up to retrieve her laptop from her bedroom and less than twenty minutes later she audibly said, 'Yes!'

Tammy got up, arched her back, ran her fingers through her short cropped blond hair and picked up her phone, scrolled down and pressed a button, then walked, barefooted, back to the kitchen.

'Hi Tammy' Chrissie said, realising who it was that was calling but before being able to say anything else, it was Tammy who spoke, 'Okay Chrissie, what's going on? Sam sounding excited and a little puzzled about the research he is doing for Samantha?'

'Oh Tammy, yes, yes he is, but then, not long after he called you, we had a call from Rico, he is the guy she is about to marry, the one from Acapulco, anyway, he was concerned, told us that he had received a text from Samantha, which simply said, and I quote, I think I'm in trouble, call Sam. '

'Goodness!' Tammy interjected.

'Goodness indeed, well, you know Sam, he got into action straight away and is, as we speak, on his way to the airport.'

Tammy thought back to when she had met this Samantha in Belgium, just over three years ago, she had helped her contact a man who knew about a chap who had been her grandmother's boyfriend, a man she felt could well be her biological grandfather.

'So, any idea what has happened, is this to do with what she asked Sam to do?' Tammy asked.

'Don't know, but I guess, quite likely. Rico tried several times to call her, but failed, as she had asked him to call Sam and not the police, Rico did just that, and without hesitation, Sam, well you know Sam, he's about to board a flight across the Atlantic, left shortly after calling you to find out what you can about those paintings, he mentioned…'

'I have information on that, but, but what now? Is this to do with these paintings? Surely it must be…' Tammy asked, sensing the concern also in Chrissie's voice.

'He said he would call once he is in Antwerpen and has spoken to Rico' Chrissie said.

'Shall I forward the information I have found to him?' Tammy asked, have returned to the dining room and was looking at the screen of her laptop.

'About Zecheriah's Ledger? Yes please, do, thank you.' Chrissie replied, thankful for her friend.

'Hey, listen' Tammy said, 'With Sam away, would you like to come up here, or I could some up to stay with you?'

'You know what, that's a great idea, but I'll come up to you, you've got a restaurant to run, I'll make the arrangements, thanks Tammy…'

After chatting for a while longer, Chrissie then ended the call and sent off a text to Sam, before arranging a flight to New York'

Two hours later

Chrissie was heading for the airport and meanwhile, levelling out at the cruising altitude, the plane carrying her fiancé was crossing the

Atlantic. Not long after take-off, Sam, having managed to secure a seat on a flight to Amsterdam, called his friend Martijn, a detective on the Rotterdam police force, gave him the details of what he knew, and they arranged to meet. It would be after midnight when he arrived at the apartment, his apartment, which now was occupied by Martijn and Sophie.

It was Sophie who opened the door, warmly embraced him, planted a kiss on each cheek, then looking into his face said, 'I see your concern, and you're tired, a quick chat, then off to bed!' she said, then throwing a telling look at Martijn who had joined her in the hallway. The men embraced and the three of them went into the lounge.

Two hours earlier

As Chrissie, at that point un beknown to Sam, was heading for the airport to catch a flight to New York, Sam contacted his friend, Martijn, in Rotterdam where it was mid evening. Sophie, wearing a light pink coloured nightdress, appeared in the lounge and waited expectantly watching Martijn in deep conversation and writing some notes now and then. She looked at the man sat on the couch and leaning forward where he had placed a notepad on the coffee table. She smiled as she thought about this man, how much she was in love with him, though at one point she had wondered about a relationship with the man who was calling. With Sam, who had come to her rescue that evening, some three years ago now. It had been Sam who had introduced her to Martijn, then still with the police force of Amersfoort. Finally, he put his phone down, looked up at Sophie and said, 'I guess you probably know that was Sam'

'You look worried, what's happened Martijn?'

'Do you remember a woman called Samantha, the insurance lady from Antwerpen and the case of the missing item, the ivory, that Sam was involved with, it was how I first met him, right here in fact in his apartment.?

'Something has happened to her.? Sophie asked, having picked up bits of the conversation.

'She contacted Sam this morning, asking him to help in the research of a couple of paintings by Flemish Masters, which had been stolen, anyway, not long after she had spoken to him, Sam received another call, this time from Rico, Samantha's boyfriend, actually, they're due to be married, anyway, he is in hospital at present, just had an operation. He told Sam he had received a text, from Samantha, that simply said, I think I'm in trouble, call Sam.'

'Gosh!' Sophie said, sitting next to Martijn on the couch, 'so, what now?'

'Well, Sam figured that as Samantha had asked Rico to call him, not the police, he immediately arranged to fly over, in fact, he called me just now, already well across the Atlantic, he's coming here.'

'This then has to do with whatever Samantha is investigating?'

'Very likely Soph, better get the guest room ready, Sam will be here, around midnight'

Present time, well after midnight

'All this doesn't sound good Sam' Sophie said after having listened to all that was known at this time, and that there had been no word from Samantha, no texts to Rico, nothing, 'anything I can do?'

Martijn got up from the couch, stepped over to her, hugged her, kissed her briefly on the lips and said, 'As you are a curator, perhaps you could speak to the curator of the museum in Antwerpen, this is where the burglary has happened, maybe get some info that might be helpful? I will contact the police there in the morning.' Martijn looked at Sam, still sitting in the armchair, and looking tired, 'and you, my friend, nothing more to be done now, get some sleep.'

'Yes, you're right, though I will call Chrissie first' Sam answered getting up, then giving Sophie a hug and a nod to Martijn, he then went to the guestroom.

It was nearly one o'clock in the morning, when Sam called Chrissie and gave her an update. Pleased to hear that she was now with Tammy in New York. 'And thank her for the information she has found so far, it's most intriguing, perhaps you two could dig a little deeper, see what else might come up? Ending the call, he then stripped, got into bed and within seconds had already entered a deep sleep.

THE PAST

Period 2: 1763

Philadelphia-Trading Post—USA

He entered the port's Trading Post.

Never before had he seen such a set up as this one. Not only was there a vast array of goods, from food and ingredients to clothing, from leather goods to woollen blankets, but there was also riding gear, and you could buy a horse, purchase a cart or wagon, or even hire one complete with drivers.

The man who ran this little empire was a short fellow. His name was Zecheriah Strauss, and as well as being able to barter or purchase any goods, he also dealt in gold and silver, copper and jewels to be bought or sold. He had a crew of over twenty, spread across the several buildings he occupied in the busy port.

Christopher Rosenborg was an astute man, an observant man, a learned man. Born in Copenhagen, Denmark, into a wealthy family, he was well schooled, but, at an early age decided that, as the youngest of the children and certainly unlikely to inherit any of the family's estate or fortune, he wanted to be an adventurer. He wanted to discover the world, but not just discover, also to journal his travels, write about the things he would see, the people he would meet, the different cultures. In his early teens he would frequently be found in the dock area. Watching, observing, taking notes, speaking to the dock workers, to the customs people. He could get about easily and the people knew the lad and that he came from an important, and influential family, an observation that didn't go amiss for Christopher, and he used it well. Over the next couple of years he befriended several Dutch merchants, learned about their vessels, their cargoes and their trade routes.

When he was seventeen, he sailed away on his first journey, to the port of Amsterdam. With finances at his disposal and family backing, he stayed in the Netherlands and continued his studies at the university of Leiden. So it was that three years later, at the age of twenty he joined the VOC, better known as 'The Dutch East India Company'. He had knowledge of trading and bartering, knew about loading cargo and weight distribution, had a grasp of trading routes, map reading and navigation and he now spoke several languages, for as well as his native Danish, he could speak Dutch fluently and could comfortably converse in French, English and Spanish.

He was taken on as a negotiator, with responsibilities for the loading and unloading of cargo. Furthermore, he would journal his voyages, document procedures and contacts, in fact, be a correspondent for the company. Now, some sixteen years later, he stood in the large trading post in the port of Philadelphia.

Christopher, having taken it all in, was now looking at the leather wide brimmed hats that were displayed against a far wall, next to the saddles, riding gear and boots. Still giving some thought to the headwear he was looking at, he noticed a man who entered. Ever observant, he studied this man as he, after briefly glancing around, made his way to where the silver haired Zecheriah stood behind a large wooden counter, beside which stood a glass encased display unit.

Zecheriah was busy writing in a big ledger book. Already, in the short time he had been inside the trading post, Christopher had seen the little man at work, going about his business and had found him to be a likeable man. He was witty, had a sense of humour, his blue eyes behind horn-rimmed glasses were bright and quite piercing. He was obviously a sharp operator with a knowledge of many things. The man who had just entered, Christopher presumed off a ship that had docked about twenty minutes or so ago, headed for the counter. The jacket the man wore was of good quality, but seemed a little tight, the trousers were a much poorer quality, as were the boots he wore, Christopher noted. The two satchels he carried were again of good quality, but the cap he wore over his ruffled and unkempt hair was old. It was certainly a strange mix of clothing, and the man was somewhat nervous.

Deciding to keep an eye on this newcomer, he took the hat he was holding and headed for the counter, circumnavigating several racks and boxes of goods, to where the man was now placing the bags on the floor and heard him say to Zecheriah, 'You buy things?' his voice low.

Christopher stopped by a rack of denim jeans and pretended to look through them, all the while watching the scene by the counter not far away as he was a little suspicious of this rugged looking newcomer. Just then two men came from another part of the store, chatting amicably in French, nodded a greeting to Christopher as they passed by, and one of them, noticing the hat, asked him if he was going to be a cowboy now. Christopher smiled and replied in French that he felt the hat would appeal to the ladies, recognising them as seamen on the ship he had recently arrived in. They both laughed and carried on. Turning his attention back to the counter he saw Zecheriah hand the man a few coins.

Zecheriah had also been suspicious when he spotted the man coming towards him. But having asked him for and perused his shipping paperwork, he studied the item the man wanted to sell and shaking his head a little and shrugging his shoulders a bit, produced a few coins which he handed over to the man. Pleased that he accepted them and collecting his bags turned to leave the store. Then studying the piece more closely was pleased with the purchase. He placed the item in the glass case and looked up as Christopher approached placing the hat on the counter and looking at what he had placed on a shelf in the glass display unit.

A quarter of an hour later Christopher exited the trading post, heading along the dockside and passed by yet another ship that had docked and was unloading. He nodded to a man who was standing by a selection of crates, reminding him of not that long ago when he himself had arrived in this part of the world, in Boston, from where he had now come from, also with a selection of crates and boxes.

Bartolo Acosta nodded in return to the man that past by him, then returned his focus to his belongings. A little later, having found a secure place for the goods he had brought with him, he set off for the trading post, where, he was informed, he needed to speak to a Zecheriah.

It was early evening when the trading post closed its doors. Zecheriah stood behind the large wooden counter and reflected for a moment. It was the first year of the business he had started along with his brother, who sadly died in an accident only a month after the trading post opened. Zecheriah had since then given all his energy and time to make the business a success. And it was a success, with over twenty staff members and a healthy turnover, business was good. Today had been a good day. Three ships had arrived in port. Zecheriah closed his big ledger book. The fate of three men who had been noted in the book, would be so very different. The Danish man, Christopher Rosenborg, who had purchased a hat and the painted ivory, would find voyage to Caracas in Venezuela, where he would fall in love. The rugged looking man, who, according to the papers he had with him, was John Robert Powell, from Plymouth, from whom had purchased the painted ivory, would, less than three months later be found dead on a sidewalk in New Orleans. The Spanish man, who had arrived from Antwerpen, was Bartolo Acosta, and from him Zecheriah had purchased three paintings and had sold him several clothing items and food supplies, along with a horse, cart and the use of a driver that would take him to a place some ten miles to the south. One of those paintings, that of a regal gentleman standing beside a horse, would, some eighty years later, be won in a poker game by Tucson Joe, the proprietor of the White Parrot saloon in Tucson Arizona.

As Zecheriah was preparing to shut up shop and go home, he glanced at the three paintings he had purchased, one of them, he felt was painted by an Italian, the other two were most assuredly done by Flemish masters.

Four months later; Plymouth England

William Quinton stood on the starboard side of the old galleon and watched the goings on as the ship was being loaded. Not much earlier he had stood on the quayside and observed the ship. It was a weatherworn three master, originally built in Portugal but now owned by a Plymouth based company, it still bore its original name, 'Golfinho Azul', which, he was told, meant blue dolphin. Taking a deep breath, he looked at the surroundings, then decided to head for his cabin, wondering if he would ever return to his hometown.

Once back in his compact cabin, William took out the sheet of paper from a worn satchel and studied it. It was a police sketch of a man. A rugged and quite mean looking man. Four months ago, this man, known to the police as the Oxman, was described as a hardened criminal and murderer. Originally from Oxford, he moved around a lot, couldn't read or write, spoke only in gruff grunts of barely recognisable English and survived by robbing people either in the streets or by breaking into homes. William put the sketch away. It angered him.

Four months ago, his cousin, though more like an older brother, John Robert Powell, had been so excited to set off for America. But the Oxman had targeted him, had lain in wait, had clubbed him to death, disposed of the body and had taken several belongings, including passage on board this very same ship, and had sailed away to Philadelphia. William sought revenge, he would cross the Atlantic and find this rogue who had so brutally killed John Robert. He heard shouting and felt movement. The ship was loose from its moorings, and they were on their way.

And so it was, that, a little under seven weeks later, young William Quinton, armed with the sketch, entered the large trading post. First of all, he looked around in awe at all the goods on display, then, struck by the hive of activity as he slowly walked about, taking it all in, William eventually spotted a man who seemed to be in charge. Approaching the silver haired man, he asked him if he was.

'Zecheriah Strauss, at your service young man, just off the ship from Plymouth?'

'Yes sir, I wonder...' William began, then showed the man the sketch he had in his hand, 'do you recall a man who looked like this, coming here? Earlier this year?'

Zecheriah studied the sketch, then, handing it back, said, 'Sure do, he was here. Strange fellow sold a miniature painting to me. Painted on ivory. Nice piece, I sold it on the very same day, I recall. He didn't look the smartest tool in the box, if you know what a mean, but I had no reason to be too suspicious of him, his papers were in order. What's the story?'

William tucked the sketch away, 'A bad man, killed my brother, well, cousin really, but more a brother, stole his papers and sailed on the same ship that I have just arrived in. Any idea where he went?'

Zecheriah thought for a moment, then said, 'I recall some folks heading down to Louisiana around that time. Might be he went along.'

'Thank you so much, at least you've confirmed that he came here, on John's ticket, and with his possessions, particularly with that piece of ivory.'

Then William, having started to turn, turn back to face the proprietor of the large trading post, asked, 'I don't suppose you could tell me who purchased the miniature, could you?'

Zecheriah thought for a moment, then looked at the young man before him, and headed for the counter, where he took a ledger from a drawer and opened it. A few moments later, having thanked the silver haired proprietor of the trading post, Wiliam left and having now also an address where to stay for a few nights, apparently within walking distance, young William set off. Thinking as to how he would go about getting revenge on the man who had so brutally killed his cousin.

The port was a busy place and the smell that continuously hit his nostrils, was that of fish. It reminded him of his hometown, Plymouth, and that he had better write a letter soon to tell his folks of his safe arrival.

THE PRESENT

Thursday 2nd June

Antwerpen

Samantha stirred. An unpleasant smell hit her nostrils, and she quickly realised that it came from the old mattress upon which she lay. She also realised that her right hand was in some sort of shackle and as she slowly worked her way to a sitting position, in the dimness she noticed it was attached to a chain. The other end of the chain was secured to a steel pipe. The room was small. The early morning light finding a way to penetrate through the cracks of a wooden shutter that mostly blocked the only window. Her head hurt and for a moment she thought she was going to be sick. With some effort she stood up. The chain was long enough to allow her to walk around most of the room and she walked slowly toward an old copper sink that was bolted to the wall below the shuttered window. A single tap. With her left hand she tried it. It worked. Leaning forward she carefully tried the water. It was cold but fine. To the right of the old sink there was a bucket, and beside that what looked to be an old wooden orange crate, the labels faded but she could make out the logo of the Valencia brand. On top of the crate was a toilet roll. Samantha took a deep breath and easily figured out what this area was meant for.

Turning, she looked at the worn mattress, then at the door, the only door, which looked sturdy, and no doubt locked. She looked down and for some reason was glad that she had changed before going out, her feet still into her tan coloured ankle boots, her trousers were navy blue having changed out of the pencil skirt she had worn earlier, the top she now wore was pale blue over which she wore a lightweight pale red pullover. The leather jacket she had been wearing when setting out to visit Rico, this after having first headed for the museum, was totally gone. The museum. That was as far as she had gotten. That's where it had all gone wrong, not long after having made that discovery. Yesterday, it all happened yesterday.

Taking in a deep breath, Samantha headed for the sturdy door, the chain allowed her just to reach it. She tried the round knob. No movement.

Making her way back to the sink, she turned the tap on, cupped her hand and gathered some water, she drank a little, then with a second handful, she managed to sort of wash her face, take the sleepiness away and then, making her way back to the old mattress, she sat down, leaned her back against the wall, closed her eyes and thought back.

Yes, she had gone home, had changed her clothes and had then spoken to Sam in Boston, giving all the details of the missing paintings. Then, she remembered, having read through all the notes she had made, took a decision to follow up on a hunch, a feeling she had. Putting her short leather jacket on, which was now nowhere to be seen, and deciding this time to leave her umbrella at home, she walked back to the museum. Initially she had wanted to go and visit Rico in hospital, but something was nagging at her and so, after giving him a quick call, she made her way back to the museum. She had seen the storage facility, but, she realised, she hadn't in fact seen the basement of the museum where the paintings had been sorted, catalogued and placed into the containers. She wanted to get a picture in her mind.

She nodded to the man at the reception desk whom she had met earlier. Though the museum was now closed to the public, the main foyer doors were still open, he didn't question her arrival and nodded back. Without hesitation Samantha walked towards the entrance to the basement, having seen a plan of the museum, she knew where to go, opened the door, took the stairs down and began to wander around the large area. Of course, it was so much different now from ten months earlier when the paintings had been here. She could see the new equipment, the generators, the new air conditioning system, then there were the new security offices, though there was some equipment in there, this area was not yet operational.

Samantha reached the area where the new aisles had been built to accommodate the overflow of artwork and paintings. Then there were the containers, all twenty-seven of them. The police had done their forensic thing, and the curator was told that they could commence the work of restoring the paintings into the new racks.

Samantha took a close look at each container. Each with a number, each with a taped-on label showing the contents. She felt strongly that it had to have been here, that the paintings were taken, not at the storage facility. The focus being on two specific paintings, meant, according to how she was thinking, that it must have involved someone, who knew exactly where these two would be. Knew the container. Four days it had taken, Samantha figured that it must have been in that period, that the thieves had taken them, but how?

Walking along the length of the containers, checking to see whereabouts the security cameras were, she then spotted a door. Squeezing between two of the metal containers, fortunately the wheels rolling smoothly to allow her through, she reached the door. It was an old door, yet, still painted now in the new colour that had been applied through the basement area. She checked the position of the security cameras again, then tried the handle of the door. It opened towards her and feeling around in the darkness of the room, she located a switch. Two sets of fluorescent tubes flickered on. The room was not large, it contained several metal shelves, there was an array of cleaning equipment, tins of paint and equipment, several ladders, two old vacuum cleaners, and hung on a coat rack were about half a dozen dust jackets.

She was about to leave when she noticed something else. The coat rack was attached to a door. Moving the dustcoats aside she felt for and located a knob. Turning it, the door opened towards her and what she saw took her by surprise. For there, she could see by the light that was penetrating the room, stood a metal container. The same type of container that had been used for the move, and moreover, she noticed the number on the label. Number eleven. Suddenly things began to make sense in her mind, but then she heard a noise coming from somewhere. Someone was coming. Thinking quickly, and with her heart suddenly beating faster, she reached for her phone, then sent a text to Rico. 'I think I'm in trouble, call Sam.'

About to head back out of the room, the light suddenly went out. Samantha felt her heart thump in her chest as she turned, quickly shoving her phone into a pocket of one of the dust coats that hung on the hooks. then, turning around again, a beam of light hit her face. She was dazzled. Next something stung her neck…

Samantha felt her neck. She had been drugged. Getting up from the old mattress, she walked about a bit, rattling the chain that confined her movement. Who was behind this? And where was she now?

Samantha tried to manoeuvre the crate to a position just by the small sink, hoping to be able to stand upon it and see through the cracks in the wooden slats that covered the small window. Working slowly and carefully, not wanting to slip and fall back onto the concrete floor, she managed it. Though not able to see much, after a moment of concentration and trying to picture the city in her mind, taking into consideration what sounds she could hear, she figured it out. Stepping down and placing the crate back where it had been, she took a closer look at the chain that held her. She knew, or at least felt quite certain, that she was somewhere in the old docks. Whilst she was quite a fit woman, the chain was made of links of steel, and she knew they would be virtually unbreakable. The iron clasp that bound her ankle was equally solid, with a lock that she knew she would not be able to pick, even if she did have something that would be of any use to try and do so. Which left only where it attached to the wall, secured to a steel ring. This was, she was sure, the weakest part of her chain. She thought about how to lever the chain free from the ring, and running things through in her mind, wondered if anyone would find her phone, or had her captors seen her hide it.

Meanwhile, Samuel Price was on board the high-speed train enroute to Antwerpen. Martijn had dropped him off at the central station, had then headed for his office. He was now a senior detective in the Rotterdam police force. He was worried, something had obviously happened to Samantha. He thought back to when he had first come across Sam and Sam, the coincidence of it all, both known as Sam Price, and both involved in the same case. Having not known each other prior, they met and then successfully worked together to solve the case of the missing Ivory painting. During that case he had also come across Sophie, the former manager of a Parisian Auction house. Martijn afforded himself a quick smile, recalling another case they were all involved in when he had travelled to Cologne with Sophie, a woman he knew he was now very much in love with. But the brief smile turned back to concentration. Find Samantha.

Back at the apartment, Sophie checked the clock in the kitchen, then set about to again read some notes she had made and questions to ask the curator of the museum in Antwerpen, whose name she had discovered, was Miss Emma Brood. Sam had also asked her to monitor any messages that might come from either Chrissie or Tammy.

She had not, as yet, met Chrissie personally, but had spoken with her when she and a woman named Alison Hudson, were looking into the disappearance of Sam. Tammy she knew, and quite well, having met her and Alison's daughter, Terri, when following a lead on the portraits of the three monks, which had taken them to Florence. Checking the time on her watch she would soon make the call.

It was busy as usual at the Antwerpen central station. A beautiful building, designed by the architect Louis Delacenserie it is regarded as one of the world's greatest buildings. Three floors down, the high-speed train that connects Amsterdam to Brussels pulled in smoothly. Moments later as Sam was on the escalator riding to the top, his phone rang. It was Martijn. Sam listened intently as he crossed the main foyer of the station, with its high dome above. It was often referred to as the Cathedral station because of it. Sam spoke little, thanked Martijn and stopped for a while to pull up a map on his phone. Martijn had been busy and successful. Armed with Samantha's telephone number, he had managed to almost pinpoint as to where it was at present. Looking at the map on his phone, and the radius that Martijn had given him, Sam felt sure as to where he needed to go.

Meanwhile Martijn in Rotterdam, had, by checking a map of the city, and seeing the area where, according to his equipment, Samantha's phone should be, also worked out as to where he was sure Sam was headed. He called Sophie.

'Hi, have you spoken to the curator at the Antwerpen Museum?'

'Yes, a few minutes ago, got the low down on all that has happened, why?'

'Can you call her back, Sam's on his way there, ask her to meet him, Samantha's phone, it seems, is in the building somewhere.'

'I'll call her straightaway, shall I then call Sam?'

'Yes please, thanks, I'm following up on some leads from here about the thieves.'

Emma Brood put her phone down and sat back in her chair. Everything was sure moving fast, she thought, still feeling a little shaken after all that had occurred. Someone, named Sam Price, was coming. Trying hard to gather her thoughts and put the sequence of events in her mind, she closed her eyes briefly, and then a shiver ran down her back. Taking in a deep breath, she sat upright again, determined to focus and to resolve this mystery.

THE PAST

Period 3: 1770

Plymouth

The man and the woman took in a deep breath.

The grave had been dug. Earlier four men had lowered the coffin. Evonie Dupois Quinton was laid to rest.

For some moments, Rene and his wife Virginia, stood by the graveside. Both still a little shaken as the death of Rene's mother had been quite sudden. Other mourners and the officiating vicar moved away. They held onto each other, on a chilly April morning. Then, when they at last turned to head back home, they noticed the man. As they passed him, he nodded a greeting but said nothing.

Rene and Virginia headed for their home. Passing by the docks of the port city, Rene thought back to when he had first arrived here, all those years ago. He and his mother had landed here, from Le Havre in France, in the year 1729. Sadly, his father had been imprisoned as the Catholic and Protestant war had been raging in mainland Europe. Fights, skirmishes, destruction of buildings, destruction of churches, chaos.

They had managed to flee, had reached Plymouth safely. Years passed. His father had never reached them. Though there was no official news, it was without doubt, his mother had accepted, that her husband had perished. He and Virginia walked hand in hand by the dockyard, heading for their cottage not far away, each with his and her own thoughts. Seven years earlier, they had waved goodbye to their only son, William, as he had set off to find the man who had so brutally killed his cousin and had taken his travel documents to sail to Philadelphia. A letter they had received two months later informed them that he had not been successful in finding this man, whom the police had referred to as the Oxman, but that he had met a lovely young girl and was getting married. Sadly, they had not received any more letters since. Virginia looked across at her husband as they walked up the path to their cottage, earlier, as they walked through the graveyard, they had passed the marker where John Robert had been buried, her brother's son, who, it had been discovered, had been so brutally killed by the Oxman. She then thought about the man they had seen at the cemetery. He did look sort of familiar.

Anton Pique, after having nodded to the passing man and woman, whom he knew to be Evonie's son and wife, waited a few more moments, then walked over to the graveside. He had been in love with her. But although she knew her husband had most likely been killed, she honoured his name and her vows and would not consider any other relationship but that of friends. He stood there for some time, then, hearing the towns church clock chime the hour, he closed his eyes briefly, then bowed, put his cap back on and walked to the port. He was the captain of a two-master and due to sail later that day.

Several days later, somewhere on the Atlantic Ocean.

The sky was a vivid blue. Not a cloud to be seen. The swell on the ocean was gentle, there was no wind. It was hot, oppressively so, he thought. A change was coming, a storm was likely. He looked up at the mast. A young lad sat in the crow's nest. Though pirates usually operated along the coastlines, picking on smaller coastal schooners, it would not do to be complacent. A watch must be kept. The two masts were barren of sails. They had been lowered, an opportunity for inspection and repair. Sixty-five-year-old Anton Pique nodded up to the boy who gave a wave back. Then, taking a last look around the empty ocean, he retreated into his quarters.

Against a wall, secured with some rope, was the panel. He knew it to be the right-hand side of a triptych. He didn't much care for it, but had come by it, all in the quest to win the heart of the woman he loved. It was a love which would now never be returned. Captain Pique sat in the wooden armchair upon a cushion she had made for him. He thought back, back to when he had first seen her, had first been taken by her beauty. Over forty years ago, he half smiled to himself, thinking back. He was a first mate then, on a small schooner, preparing to set sail. He had been informed of some passengers coming on board, passengers who needed to leave French soil immediately, for they were in danger of being captured by religious zealots, he was told.

The captain was ready, he was ready, the crew was ready, the tide was right. Two horses, pulling a cart came trotting up. A woman and a boy emerged. Men quickly escorted the woman on board, took care of the luggage she and the boy had, took care of the driver of the cart who promptly turned the horses about and left. When the captain, a few moments later, introduced them, Anton could find no words to say. His voice seemed to have been completely lost. Moreover, his feet were firmly anchored to the floor, and all he could do was manage a nod and half a smile.

Evonie Dupois Quinton and her son Rene. She spoke in rapid French to the captain, thanking him, then, and he recalled the moment, she turned to him and gave him a smile. That, he now thought as he sat in the chair, the ship so very gently bobbing on the swell of the ocean, was the moment he fell in love.

He threw another look at the painted wood panel. The monk it portrayed he knew to be a brother Ignatius. It was of no use now, she was gone. He would sell it when they reached the port of Philadelphia. Taking some tobacco from a tin, he filled his pipe, lit a match and then sat back upon that cushion she had so lovingly made for him. The painting would go, the cushion never.

The wind eventually grew stronger, and it was only a few days later that the ship docked in Philadelphia. Anton was pleased that the ports trading post owner, Zecheriah, liked the painting and purchased it.

However, it would be over thirty years later when he sold it to Rudolph Meyer from Cologne who was surprised to learn that it had not been the portrait of a monk he had been looking for. Zecheriah studied the German for a few moments, wondering what had puzzled him about the portrait of a monk. Then, seeing his new customer as a learned man with a knowledge of art, Zecheriah made a decision. He asked the man to wait as he had something he wanted to show him. Rudolph, already very pleased with the acquisition of the wooden panel, upon which was painted the monk, and which Rudolph knew now to be the right-hand panel of a triptych, agreed. Ten minutes later Zecheriah returned, holding two paintings, the ones he had taking a liking to and purchased from the Spaniard, more than three decades ago, back in 1763. He had hung them on the wall of his residence, which was adjacent the Trading Post. As he was now about to retire, it was time to move them on.

Rudolph Meyer studied both paintings, felt he could easily sell these back in Germany, knowing them to be nice works by Flemish Artists, and agreed a price.

And so, these paintings, having originally been acquired by Bartolo Acosta in Antwerpen and taken to Philadelphia, were now heading back to mainland Europe. Zecheriah made the notations in his ledger. 'Battle on the coast' by Rubens, and Italian city scene, by Jacob Leyssens.

Rudolph studied both paintings. He particularly liked the Rubens painting, the details were well defined, it was a stirring battle fought on the beach.

THE PRESENT

Thursday 2ⁿᵈ June

Antwerpen

On her desk in her office, two photocopies were placed. One showing the landscape scene, thought the be in the vicinity of Rome, and painted by Jacob Leyssen when he was in Italy, the other the vivid scene of a battle on the beach, by Arnold Frans Rubens. She was still totally perplexed as to why these two were of such importance. Shuffling the copies together, she placed them in a file and got up.

Emma Brood took the stairs one floor down and reached the reception area of the museum, when a man, she felt was sure the person she was expecting, walked in.

'Mr. Price?' she asked walking towards him.

'Yes, Miss Brood, I take it, and please, call me Sam, did Sophie fill you in as to why I am here, and to what has happened?' Sam said, shaking the offered hand.

'Yes, and please, I'm Emma, it was your policeman friend, Martijn, from Rotterdam, who also called a few moments ago, he asked me to not share anything with regard to the disappearance of Miss Price, oh, is she your sister?'

Sam smiled at her as she led them to where the access to the basement was. 'No, quite the coincidence, but no relation, I assume we're heading for the basement?'

'Yes, I discovered that Samantha was here yesterday, I'm not sure about informing the security team here at present…'

'If Martijn has asked you not to share anything, then let's not do that just yet.'

Moments later Sam stood in the same place where the day before Samantha had stood. Somewhere here, he felt strongly, is where her phone just had to be.

'Wait, 'Emma said, 'maybe in there?' pointing in between two of the metal containers to a door.

Sam wriggled through the gap, opened the door, walked in and found a light, he then turned to look at Emma who was right behind him, then took out his phone and scrolled to find the right number. He pressed a button.

Not far from where they were, they heard a ringtone.

Sam recognised the tune, it was the song, Loco in Acapulco, a Four tops hits from the late eighties. Sam smiled, he loved his music, specially from the sixties through to the seventies and even into the eighties, he even recalled that it had been Phil Collins, the drummer from Genesis, who had written the song and also played the drums on that track.

'Definitely Samantha's' Sam remarked and headed for where a rack of coats hung on hooks. Feeling through the pockets he found the phone and switched it off. 'She lived in Acapulco for a while' he explained.

'There's a door here' Emma remarked, having noticed the knob whilst Sam had been searching through the pockets of the coats.

The curator tried the handle and opened the door. She gasped after she had barely entered, for there, gleaming in the light from the storage room, stood a single container.

'Samantha found this' Sam said, 'then was disturbed, had time to text Rico and hide the phone. Someone knew she was here.'

For a moment Emma stood by the container, noted the number on it and her mind was whirling, it was here where the paintings were switched and taken. But who was behind it all?

'I hope she's alright' Emma said, her voice only just above a whisper.

'Me too, but I feel she is, she was taken from here, we need to check security footage,' Sam replied, seeing that the curator had lost colour in her face.

Sam put Samantha's phone in his pocket, then using his own he rang Martijn, as they left the storeroom Sam felt sure that any security footage would by now have been erased. Martijn answered, and Sam gave him an update as he and the curator headed back through the basement.

Sam's suspicions turned out to be correct, for together with the security team that operated in the museums opening times, it was clear that security footage had been tampered with. Emma, looking at Sam, still quite pale from all that was going on, dialled a number for the police and gave them the details of the night security team that had been on duty.

Emma Brood was quiet, still quite pale, she was trying to work out when it had been, that the containers were switched. Thinking it through, she began to wonder when it was that the extra container had even arrived. Was the storage company involved? They must be, the container was identical, then, the number, the references, all down to the very detail, identical. But again, that question foremost in her mind, when had the container been switched, and when had the two paintings actually been removed from the museum, and why? Why those particular paintings. But however she thought it through, nothing seemed clear.

For a while neither had spoken, each with his or her own thoughts. Someone had brought them coffee, and they were informed that a detective would be here soon.

'Oh, goodness' Sam said, remembering, taking out his phone, he found the text that Tammy had sent, 'A friend of ours in New York has done a little research, a while ago she came across a ledger, written by a Zecheriah Strauss, he ran the trading Post in Philadelphia for about forty years or so, he and his brother had set it up, anyway, this ledger is a quite detailed account of things either purchased, traded or sold, other than the ordinary things, like clothing, footwear and foodstuff, anyway, it helped us in research a while back, so, I asked her to see what she could find out about the two paintings that are missing, and…let me read to you what she found out…

"So interesting, Zecheriah's ledger is a great source of information, now take this in, back in 1763 he purchased three painting from a Spanish guy named Bartolo Acosta, one was a Spanish painting, the other two, according to his notes, by Flemish masters, now, surprise, thirty three years later, he sold two paintings, to a German, a Rudolph Meyer, from Cologne, this was now in 1803, and this is the amazing bit, one was titled, Battle on the coast, by Rubens, and the other, an Italian scene, by Jacob Leyssens!"

What Tammy had written was not all that Sam related to the curator, for Tammy had reminded him that this was the same German man, who, at that same time, had purchased the portrait of a monk, something she had discovered when they had been researching a portrait that had been sent to Sophie, this being a bequest by the late forger, Roberto Solari. A small world indeed, Sam was thinking, as he related the relevant information to Emma.

Emma sat in awe behind her desk, not able to say anything for a moment. She took the two photocopies out of the file she had earlier put them in and showed them to Sam.

Then she said, 'wow, that's, incredible, so, the two paintings that were stolen, these two, once went over to America, then came back? So, this Rudolph chap, any idea who he is, the name doesn't ring a bell, the only provenance I have on these two paintings just goes back to an auction, oh, about seven years ago, I think, I haven't even had the chance to investigate, it is all happening so fast, it is why the paintings were in storage, more provenance was being researched.

'But does the time fit in as to when they were painted?' Sam asked, placing the photocopies on her desk.

'Oh, yes, perfectly' Emma answered, then the phone on her desk rang.

'It's the detective.' She said, having answered the call, 'he's on his way up'

Just as the detective, a detective sergeant Schenk, entered the office and Emma, who had dealt with the same man before, introduced Sam, Sam's phone buzzed.

'Excuse me a moment,' Sam said, taking the call, then' Hey Martijn...'

Only a few moments later, 'yes, as a matter of fact, he has just arrived...' Sam said, then, handing the phone to the sergeant, said, 'This is my friend from the Rotterdam police...'

The sergeant nodded, took the phone, listened for some time, then handed the phone back after saying he would put some men on it straight away...'

Both Emma and Sam looked at the detective sergeant quizzically. He looked from one to the other, then spoke, 'Your friend, Martijn, I spoke with him earlier today, has viewed some footage, he says he has sent the relevant segment to your computer, Miss Brood...'

Emma frowned, then, half wondering how this friend of Sam's had found out about her computer, pressed some keys, found the sent clip and opened it.

Sam and detective sergeant Schenk both went around to her side of the desk, with each standing on either side of the curator, they watched the footage on her screen.

'Oh No!' Emma exclaimed, not far into the footage showing a side entrance to the museum, though the lighting wasn't the greatest, and the figures, two men and woman, were rather grainy, Emma recognised someone. The sergeant paused the film clip and both he and Sam looked at Emma.

'That woman, on the left there, with the long coat, that's Crystal, that's my assistant, Crystal Kaplova. Then, suddenly remembering, she said, 'Crystal hasn't come in today...' Emma said, her face now even paler than before and quite obviously shocked by this revelation.

The sergeant pressed play, and they watched. A van had pulled up, two men and a woman had exited the vehicle, then the door opened at the rear of the museum, and a man came out, then all three went inside, only to appear again moments later, the two men carrying a woman between them.

'Samantha' Sam said, immediately recognising his friend.

'Yes,' Emma agreed, 'she, she looks drugged, can hardly walk' she observed.

Moments later the van drove off, the third man went back inside the building.

'Inside job' the sergeant said, 'obviously your assistant, this Crystal Kaplova is in on it, do you recognise the security man?' he asked Emma.

'I think it might be one of the night security people, but I don't know'

The detective sergeant got on the phone and spoke to a colleague, giving the description of the vehicle used, and also that of the security man, who was likely in his fifties and of large stature. Sam called Martijn.

Emma, still pale and feeling a little embarrassed that this had all happened under her nose, once more sat back in her desk chair and tried to make sense of it all.

THE PAST

Period 4: 1782

Shropshire- England

Lady Evangeline Powell-Hunter sat in her favourite chair. A silk covered gilt wood armchair, one of a pair that were in her bedroom. Placed by the sash window she would often sit and read. The room was situated on the first floor of the magnificent manor house that, with hard work and diligence, she had kept in the family, along the with the grounds of nearly two hundred acres comprising of woodland, farmland a couple of small lakes and several outbuildings and a farmhouse.

It was the middle of the morning. The sun shone brightly in a clear blue sky. It was a day of reflections, for it was thirty years ago, to the day, that she had sat in her room, had sat in her favourite chair, and had, after having received that devastating news, had cried and cried. Thirty years. Where had the years gone? She recalled the trip she made to the boarding school to tell their twin girls, just eleven at the time.

Looking out the window she smiled. The girls, twins, so much alike, so like each other, up until they were in their teens, then, they changed. Began to have different interests. Rachel, the slightly elder twin, by about ten minutes, dark hair, dark blue eyes, very much like her father, an adventurer, inquisitive. Joanna, slightly fairer hair, but the very same dark blue eyes. Loved animals, loved the farm, loved to stay home. It had been Joanna who had married, had given her two grandchildren, had worked and managed the estate. Managed the farm and had, seemingly, kept everything running whilst having babies. Her husband a gentle and quiet man.

Joanne had taken on the running of the estate in her late teens and had since been successful in maintaining and developing the many facets of it. Sitting in her chair, Evangeline turned away from the window to look at what she held in her hand. She was grateful to her daughter, thankful for Joanna and her husband, for despite the challenges, they had kept and improved the manor house and the estate. She had her own wing, her own bedroom, a lovely lounge and a small kitchen, all on one side of the first floor of the house. All to herself.

Rachel had started travelling, she had not wanted any of the responsibilities of running the estate, had gladly given it all over to her sister and had left for London not long after her seventeenth birthday. Since, she had sailed over to America, had, for a time, worked for the same newspaper as her father had done, and had, ignoring the warning of the dangers, traversed the interior of the United States. Fortunately, she coped well and returned to England to celebrate her thirtieth together with her sister.

Evangeline looked at the diary in her lap. His diary. It had been returned to her by the same men who had called that day, that morning, much like today, a morning when the sky was blue, and the sun shone brightly. He had been killed in rioting in the country of Yemen, the city of Mocha, where he had travelled to cover the uprising there, being the adventurer and a keen and prominent journalist that he was. Though he had retired from that work when her parents had died, and she had been left to run the estate. He proved to be a wonderful help, as well as a doting husband. But someone had called, someone had asked if would be willing to cover the troubles in Mocha. She had seen the glint of adventure in his eyes and had insisted he go. Holding the diary lovingly, the worn leather covering smooth with wear and which she often just held to her nose, as she often just read a few pages, it wasn't the diary that she focused on this morning. Looking at the wall above the bed, she looked at the painting which she herself had hung there.

It had been the strangest thing. Nearly four months after his death, a parcel was delivered. From him, from her husband. There was a letter. Now folded and tucked into his diary, a letter written when he was in Mocha. A letter describing a little about the riots and the dangers, but more about something else, more about the contents of the parcel. A painting. An oil painting, by a Flemish Master.

'My dearest Evangeline,' the letter began,' I wasn't going to write this, but the situation here is rather tense, word is, it is going to get worse, but in the midst of chaos, I found a little peace. I was inside an old barn, on the outskirts of the city. Having my little book of Psalms with me, I chose to rest and read. Opening it up, it fell to Psalm 62, let me share with you my darling, you who have given me such a new lease of life. It reads, 'Truly my soul silently waits for God, from Him comes my salvation, He only is my rock and my salvation, He is my defence, I shall not be greatly moved'. Well, my love, this calmed me down, for I had been very disturbed and considered that it had not been a good thing to come here. I miss you. Then, as I reflected on that reading, I noticed a corner of what seemed to be a wooden frame of sorts, tucked behind several sacks of wool. I investigated and low and behold, there was a painting, slightly damaged, dusty and dirty, but I saw that the frame was solid, ornate, beautifully made. The scene was that of a rural landscape. I held it, studied it, looked at it for long moments and it brought you to me. Do you remember, I'm sure you do, when, at your birthday party, you tried to trick me in saying if I liked the Rembrandt your father had just purchased? Having a little knowledge, I knew the painting to be a Vermeer. I can still picture your face, your beautiful face. I miss you, I feel I should not have come here. The elderly owner of the barn came in, saw me admiring the painting. I was helpful to him and his family amid earlier riots. He insisted I have it. So, my lovely, this will be a great feature in our house. He will make all the arrangements to send it, along with this letter, to our home. I myself will endeavour to make arrangements to travel back as soon as I can. Give my love to the girls.

With all my love, your Thomas.'

The date on the letter was two days before he was shot and killed.

Lady Evangeline got up from the chair, tears welling up behind her eyes, stood at the foot of her bed and looked at the Painting. The rural scene was peaceful. There was some damage to it and the solid frame had several gashes in it. It was a little dirty and could do with a clean, but she decided that she wanted it left as it was, the way Thomas had seen it, when he found it. She did find out who the artist was, a Flemish painter called Pieter Bout, who created this scene nearly a hundred and thirty years ago. But how on earth did that painting ever find its way to an old barn in Yemen?

Reaching for a lace handkerchief that was tucked into the sleeve of her blouse, she blew her nose, left the room and headed downstairs.

THE PRESENT

Thursday 2nd June

Antwerpen

Frustratingly, with no further leads at present, Sam took the stairs to the ground floor and left the museum. He made his way to the hospital. Having bade farewell to Emma and arranged to re connect with Detective Sergeant Jan Schenk, later in the day.

He knew he would have to inform Rico of what he knew so far. He also had to come across as positive and calm, so as not to add too much stress to the man he had not actually met, though it had been Sam who had located him in Acapulco and had then persuaded Samantha to call on him. This all happening when he and Samantha were on the trail of the missing ivory. It had been a journey that had changed so much for both of them. For Samantha in particular, for it was then when she fell in love.

Sam had phoned Rico, told him he was on his way. Taking the lift to the third floor, he was mentally preparing himself for a difficult conversation.

Meanwhile in Rotterdam

Martijn was busy, working in co-operation with the Belgian police force, he was combing through shared camera footage of the streets around the museum, hoping for a break in the locating of the van that had taken Samantha. He spoke to Sophie earlier, asked her to maintain a connection with the curator at the museum and he asked her to find out as much as she could about this woman, the assistant, Crystal Kaplova. He frowned after ending the call. Kaplova, he knew that name, but from where?

Whilst in New York

Chrissie ended the call, looked at Tammy, then said, 'Sam's on his way to talk with Rico, don't envy him, bless, poor Rico'

'He'll know what to say' Tammy replied, seeing the concern in her friend, then' Sam asked for something else?' she prompted.

'Yes!, of course,' Chrissie said, then holding Tammy by her shoulders and looking into her eyes, 'you are such a good friend, I'm so glad I came, now, Sophie is talking with this Emma lady from the museum, trying to find out as much as she can about the woman involved in this whole thing, Crystal Kaplova, Sam feels this is a plot that has been planned over some period of time, so, let's see if we can't find out anything about this woman, and, why those two paintings might have been so important.'

Back at the hospital

Rico lay back and stared at the ceiling. To have finally met Sam, was good, to have met him under these circumstances, was bad. But he resolved to the fact, that he could do nothing. His body was recovering from the operation and there was no way he could be of much use with a broken leg either. Sam had been brief, had been specific in the details, had clearly outlaid the plans that were on going as to locating Samantha. There had been a positiveness in his demeanour, in his voice and most certainly in his eyes. Knowing a little of what Sam was capable of, this gave him some peace.

Rico closed his eyes. He thought back, back to that time in the café, his café, the one he had set up, the one he had established and turned into a good business. He was almost at the point of thinking about how he had come to be in Mexico in the first place, how he had reinvented himself, how he had changed his name… but he stopped himself, and instead thought back to when he had first seen her…

...at first, he hadn't taken a lot of notice, had looked at her, thought she was attractive, knew for sure she wasn't from around the neighbourhood, a visitor, a tourist perhaps. She ordered a latte, and for some reason he felt that she was a little hesitant. He then told her to find a seat, that he would bring her order over and watched as she chose a table by the window. A clock on the wall showed it to be a little after nine-thirty in the morning. Already the sun was high. It was when he brought her the drink and when she asked him if he was Rico, that he focused on her. His eyes meeting hers. 'I am' he had answered, a questioning look on his face. 'Do you think we could talk?' she had asked, her eyes never leaving his, then added, 'please.'...

Rico opened his eyes, realised he was tearing up, then took a deep breath and told himself to be positive... his thoughts went back to that day...

...A little later, after he had organised some extra staff to cover the café, he had taken her upstairs. To the balcony that faced the sea and how he had leaned on the railing and had gazed out over the ocean, so many things whirling around in his head. How had he been found? How was his sister involved? And who was this lovely young woman from the insurance company?...

Opening his eyes again, Rico smiled. She stole his heart. Again, taking a deep breath, he pushed any negative thoughts from his mind and began to think how he could achieve what Sam had asked him to do. He wasn't sure how important it was, or whether Sam was just trying to get him to focus on anything other than where Samantha had been taken, but he was determined to follow up on the request.

He was to obtain a detailed map of the city and surrounding areas and think about possible places they that could have taken her, he was to receive information from the police if they had any sighting of the van and the location in order to help with this task. The first of those calls came only twenty minutes after Sam had gone.

One of the nurses had purchased a map for him and Rico noted the position on the map, marking it with a pen, and drawing a line from the museum to that point.

In Rotterdam

Martijn marked the position on a map he had on the wall in his office and called Sam. He studied the map as he waited for the call to be answered. Thinking back to when he had first met Sam, in the very apartment where he and Sophie now lived. Only three years ago, but in that time a good friendship had developed. Sam's connection with the chief of Police in Rotterdam, had ensured a positive result in a case he was working on, furthermore, through that same connection, he was now a senior detective.

Sam answered the call and Martijn gave him an update, Sam then informed him that he would update Rico who could help to work things out from his hospital bed.

Ending the call Martijn stepped over to the window of his office, the sky was dotted with clouds, and it was already well into the afternoon. He had not met Samantha personally but sighed and prayed that she would be alright.

With a six-hour time difference it was mid-morning in New York.

'Okay, so, here we have Zecheriah's ledger' Tammy said, showing it on the monitor to Chrissie sitting right beside her.

'Right, wow, that's quite neat writing, Chrissie observed, so this is how you found out about how the item was purchased and sold, when we were all on the trail of its journey?'

'Yes, this Zecheriah character was very organised, though, the ledger was only used for special items he either bought or sold' Tammy replied,' not ordinary stuff, like clothing, food and basic tools and equipment, no, this ledger he only used for things that were out of the usual, like paintings, jewellery, sculptures, special old books and so on, it makes for interesting reading, by the way, I found out that the original ledger is on display at the Seaport museum in Philadelphia'

'Really? That sounds interesting, wouldn't mind seeing the actual book' Chrissie said, turning to her friend.

'We should' Tammy replied, returning the look, then, facing the screen, said, 'right, let me show you the entry for the year 1763, 'scrolling to the right place with her mouse. 'Here we are, now, see, here we have that entry when Zecheriah purchased the ivory from a guy named John Robert Powell... And., He sold it on almost immediately to Christopher Rosenborg, it's that information that helped Sam and Samantha in the search... gosh, I do hope she is alright...'

Chrissie squeezed her friend upper arm, 'Let's be positive, I'm sure Sam and Martijn are doing all they can...'

Tammy turned to smile at Chrissie, then nodding silently, she turned back to the screen and continued scrolling. 'Right, this is the chap, came in on a ship from Antwerpen, but says he's Spanish, see, he sold Zecheriah three paintings, and all noted in detail, oil painting of man in red robes standing by a black horse, likely Italian, and then, coastal battle scene by Rubens and Italian city scene by Jacob Leyssen'

Chrissie read the notations, marvelled at the details and still quite amazed that here, written down, in 1763, are the very two paintings by Flemish masters that were now missing from the museum collection.

'Then, look' Tammy said, scrolling further down on her laptop, 'see, here we are, now in the year 1803, and, this is where we found out that Zecheriah sold the portrait of the monk to Rudolph Meyer, who, we discovered later, had come across on a ship from Spain, but actually lived in Cologne, this was of great help, but, what we didn't know,' Tammy continued, Chrissie looking intently at the screen as she sat close beside her, 'was that this Rudolph chap, also bought two more paintings, and voila!, see here we have them, the very two paintings that are now missing from the museum'.

'That's just so incredible! Has Sam replied yet to this find?' Chrissie asked, 'and have you heard where he is at present?'

'He was on his way to speak to the curator, Emma something or other, and no, he hasn't commented on this discovery yet, but he must be quite busy, with all that is going on, well, you know Sam, not quick at forthcoming with the events!'

Chrissie looked at her friend and smiled. She was not wrong. Sam would often keep things to himself for a while.' She sighed and hoped he was alright, and of course Samantha, poor woman, where had they taken her?'

At the docks in Antwerpen at this very time

The door had been unlocked, it opened slowly. Samantha sat on the mattress, back against the wall and watched. A hand appeared, placing a tray on the floor, then pushing it further into the room. The door closed and locked, she distinctly heard the click as the key was turned. She didn't see anything other than the hand and arm of her captor. She was sure it was a male.

Waiting a little longer, she then got up and walked over to the tray. The aroma coming from the food was pleasant. She was hungry!

Less than three hundred metres away Sam realised he hadn't eaten much, and his stomach was complaining. He had, with the help of the detective sergeant, Jan Schenk, gained entry into the upper floor of an old warehouse. Thanks to the vigilance of Martijn in Rotterdam and to the local police, sifting through footage from traffic and other cameras, they had plotted a timeline and with further help from Rico who was working in unison with them, they had been unanimous in their findings. They had taken Samantha to the old docks, but there were several buildings there, all in a row.

It would be far too risky to even contemplate going there in the daytime, there were various buildings in close proximity strung along one of the dock sides. Too many variables. The detective sergeant, feeling very much part of this team with Sam and his counterpart in Rotterdam, realising that he too was getting hungry, said he would go out and get some food and also bring back a more detailed map of this particular dock area.

Sam nodded his thanks. What had been so special about those two paintings? He wondered as he was left to his own. He also just then remembered he had not replied to Tammy and thank her for her findings, nor sent a text to his lovely Chrissie, giving her an update on the proceedings. Once he was focused on something, he knew that he kept others in the dark. He smiled, thinking, and certainly hoping, that Chrissie and Tammy would understand. Whilst the information that Tammy had gleaned from the Zecheriah Ledger was most useful, the most important thing at present, was to secure the safety of Samantha. He hoped the detective would get back soon for he really was rather hungry!

THE PAST

Period 5: 1859

Tucson, Arizona

Jeremiah Prudence owned the stables and a blacksmith operation on the edge of town. His wife had just brough him a large slice of pie which he was happily consuming, as he was rather hungry. Jeremiah was in his late fifties, had a barrel chest, strong arms and a weather-beaten face. His eyes were a piercing blue and his smile was infectious. Though at present his face showed concern. His watched as the rider that had paid a brief visit, kicked up the dust as he headed back to town. He was Joseph Calhoun, a wealthy rancher with a mean streak and he had sought out the young man that had recently arrived from Fort Yuma and was working for Jeremiah as a blacksmith.

At six foot three, Juan Castagnet was taller than the average man. Also, as he was solidly built, not many would care to even think about crossing him. His tanned, clean-shaven face was handsome, his brown eyes deep and warm, his hair combed back and almost black. As he grew older, he became more and more like his father in appearance. He knew that he attracted women to him but still had to meet one that touched his heart. Hopefully, whilst in Tucson, this might happen, as he was beginning to think about settling down and raising a family.

The 'Golden Nugget' was the most popular tavern in town, according to Jeremiah, but not the friendliest. He suggested a better one to check out would be The White Parrot' on account of the white parrot owned by 'Tucson Joe' who acquired it from a passing traveller.

And so, it had been this tavern he had sought out, and it had been there, when he saw her. Juan watched the rider head back into town and heard Jeremiah behind him.

'One day here, and already making enemies?' Taking another bite of his lunch time pie.

Juan noticed his smile, then, continuing to work on the horse he had been shoeing before being interrupted asked, 'Who is he?'

'Rancher, wealthy, nasty. Name's Calhoun, Joseph Calhoun.'

'And who does he think his woman is?' Juan asked, releasing the front left leg and standing up, for that had been the man's threatening utterances when arriving.

'Guess you must have met Joe's daughter, Magdalena, he has designs on her'

When Juan didn't answer, Jeremiah added, 'be careful'.

When Juan strode towards the tavern that evening, he was smiling to himself and felt confident in what he had discovered a few hours earlier when he had travelled to a nearby garrison. Entering, he greeted Joe and ordered a drink. When the drink was placed before him, Joe caught his eye, the said, 'Watch your back'. Then moved to another part of the bar to resume his conversation with three men there.

Juan watched the mirror behind the bar. In it, he could see a mirror that was above the piano by the staircase, and it that he could see the swing doors. Less than ten minutes later he saw the doors open and watched the man enter, the same man that had called upon the stables earlier. Juan noticed that he wasn't very tall, the two men who followed and came in behind him, were both almost a foot taller. The talking stopped and there was an immediate tension in the air.

The rancher, Joseph Calhoun, strode up to the bar and spoke, 'How about that deal Joe,' he said, his voice, raspy and thin, 'wouldn't want you to lose any more customers now would we'.

Then looked at Juan, smiling.

'There will be no deal,' the voice soft, and yet strong.

She had appeared from somewhere and had answered before her father could, standing beside him behind the bar and looking at the man directly.

'Now honey, you know how I feel about you. Wouldn't want your pappy to get hurt now, would you?'

'Sounds like a threat there, mister' Juan said, finding his voice was calm, and as he looked at the short man, felt confident of what he could achieve.

'Ain't none of your business son,' came the reply, almost a snarl. The two men who had followed the rancher into the saloon, now placed themselves either side of Juan. Joe said nothing.

Juan was wary and again looking into the mirror, he could see that there was a shotgun of sorts tucked underneath the counter. Joe was close by and ready for trouble.

'That black mare you were riding this morning, mister Calhoen' Juan said, his eyes once more fixed upon the man.

'What of it' came the curt reply, the voice again raspy and without depth.

'I know horses, mister Calhoen, and that mare, I know its markings. I know, who it belonged to, I wonder, there is a garrison close by. I worked at Fort Yuma. I have contacts, do you really want me to get in touch with them? They don't take kindly to horse thieves you know.'

Joseph Calhoen coloured bright red. He tried to stare intently at Juan, but failed, then turned and stormed out of the saloon. His two henchmen following quickly.

For several moments there was a stillness. No one spoke. 'I'll have another, Joe, please,' Juan said, breaking the silence and smiling at Lena. Recalling a brief conversation, he had with her the previous evening, when she had challenged him, that he had better be good if he wanted to capture her attention. Juan leaned forward across the bar, and almost in a whisper, spoke to her, 'Might not be good enough yet, but it's a start, right?'

She looked at him, her cheeks ever so slightly coloured, then found her composure and answered, 'It's a start'. Then giving him a nod, she turned and disappeared from where she had moments earlier appeared.

Joe brought the drink, then reached out his hand to pump Juan's hand vigorously. He had no words to speak. Not much later, Lena showed herself again, caught Juan's eye and gestured for him to follow her. Up the stairs she went, up the stairs he followed. Stopping by a door, she opened it and entered. He followed, she shut the door, then walked over to one of the two windows in the room, which was furnished as a lounge. There were three old leather armchairs, a small table, some old cupboards, a couple of oil lamps.

She spoke, 'He'll not stop for anything now. He's riled, he'll want revenge, who are you?'

The colour had crept back into her cheeks, he could see she was concerned. Moreover, he could sense that she was angry.

'I can handle Joseph Calhoen,' she went on to say, her voice strong with a hint of fearless determination. 'The situation, though not ideal, was balanced. You've rocked the boat mister, all in order to win me over?'

Staying standing by the door, he looked directly into her eyes as she glared in anger at him, then, trying to keep his voice calm, he spoke.

'He came to see me this morning. Warned me. I didn't like him, I found out who he was, I have a few contacts in the area, so I learned more about him. Know your enemy. He threatened your father. He was menacing, but no more than a bully. You might accept a situation that is balanced, but I do not. You let folk like that take an inch, they'll take a mile. I understand he frequents the Golden Nugget?'

'He owns it' she said, quite stunned by his response.

'Right then, I'll go and find him, and make a deal to leave you and your father alone'

Juan was about to leave, but she said, 'Wait, please'.

She waited until he had turned around to face her, and found her heart was suddenly racing. She felt her anger subsiding quickly and realised that no man had ever spoken so strongly to her.

'Are you sure?' she asked, her voice no longer with an edge, but once again soft.

Juan looked into her eyes, noticed they were no longer glaring, but thought he detected a sparkle, and he could feel his heart beating in his chest. 'I'm sure, after all, as you suggested, in order for me to capture your heart, I better be good.' He said, smiling. It was then, as he was about to turn and leave the room, that he noticed the painting.

It was around eighteen inches wide and probably three foot in height. The frame was gilded and ornate wood, surrounding an oil painting showing a man standing next to a black horse. Juan strode over to it and took in the quality of the painting.

'Pa won it, poker game,' she said, slightly puzzled by his interest.,' a traveller, Spanish guy, former soldier I think, more than ten years ago now'

'It's a very good painting,' Juan said, admiring the horse, then, looking at the man whose coat was a magnificent red in colour, but it was not the uniform of a soldier, or a conquistador, but, seemed regal, perhaps a dignitary, a king even…,'

Three years passed

Lena sat on a cane chair on the front porch, lovingly rubbing her tummy. She was expecting their first child. Having only moments earlier kissed and waved goodbye to Juan, she'd sat herself down in the chair. Taking in the early morning sun, she reflected how it all came about that they were now here, in the smaller, but lovely town of Silver City, around two hundred miles from Tucson. The mine attracted many from far and wide and though a fair-sized camp was set up nearby, the miners would regularly come to town and visit one of the four saloons. Juan had sourced and purchased a set of stables on the far side of town, in the direction of the mine and had already, in a short time, established a regular clientele.

The house they were in, had belonged to her mother, who had long parted from her father but had not forgotten her only daughter. She passed, strangely on the night of the big fight, a messenger had arrived several days later with this news, as well as armed with documents to state that she was now the owner of the house and its land. It added to their wish to move, especially after the big fight in the Golden Nugget saloon. Closing her eyes Lena thought back to that evening and rubbing her knee she could feel the scar beneath her cotton dress.

The sun was getting warmer by the minute as she smiled at the memory. Though it was sad that Joseph Calhoen had died. But the town settled down after that, the atmosphere changed, the fierce rivalry between the White Parrot and the Golden Nugget turned to a friendly competition. It was just over a week later, that Joe walked Lena down the aisle to marry Juan. Lena got up, the sun was getting a bit too warm on her face now and she went inside.

Meanwhile at the stables he now owned, Juan was a happy man. Married to the beautiful Lena, a child on the way. He was also glad that, not long after their arrival in Silver City, they had decided to bury the gold. It had become a burden in a way and with Lena suggesting they use the mosaic tiles she had found in the house to create a marker and bury it along with the gold not far away from the stables, this is what they then had done.

It would be a Professor Emily Parker, an archaeologist, who would discover this treasure over 126 years later, which eventually would end up in a museum in Albuquerque.

THE PRESENT

Thursday 2nd June

San Francisco

At the home of Alison Hudson, in the Bay area of the city a phone rang.

'Hey mum, just had a call from Tammy, she would like some help with something, are you able to help me?' Terri asked, ringing from her office at the museum.

'Of course,' Alison answered. 'What is it she wants us to do?'

'I'll send you an email with all the information, I have a couple of task here at the museum to complete, which is why I am asking for your help, Sophie and Sam are also involved in all of this, I'll send it now, then I'll get back to you as soon as I can, probably in about half an hour, is that okay?'

'Of course, I'm intrigued, talk to you later then...'

Alison Hudson, forty-six years of age, walked her slim frame from the lounge into the kitchen and noticed the time on the clock. Eleven minutes past nine, she figured Tammy must have called Terri at her work only minutes ago. Pouring herself a cup of coffee, the second of the day, Alison, though preferring to be called Ally by her friends, returned to the lounge. Her laptop was already open, placed on a small writing desk in one corner of the rectangular room. Glancing through the window she could see that it was going to be a warm day, the sun already well up in the sky which seemed devoid of any clouds at present. Thinking she had chosen the right outfit for the warmth, a pair of lightweight white trousers and a deep pink sleeveless blouse, he long blonde hair in a ponytail, she sat down, placed her cup on a coaster and checked her email.

Meanwhile at the museum of art, Alison's daughter, having recently turned twenty-one, assistant curator, walked into the boardroom for a business meeting, that, hopefully, she thought, wouldn't last very long. Trying to focus on the current meeting, she found it hard to shake away the conversation she had with Tammy from New York, who had contacted her just as she had sat down behind her desk in her office. Sitting down at the boardroom table, she opened the folder she had, had her notepad ready and smiled as others entered. But found it hard to focus as she thought about the phone call…

She adored Tammy, had so quickly connected and become friends, along with the French woman, Sophie, who, like her was a curator in a museum. The three of them had travelled to Florence, following the mystery of the three monks.….

Someone spoke to her and Terri snapped out of her thoughts and made herself pay attention.

At her home on the northwest side of the city, Alison realised she had totally let her drink get cold. Though brief, there was a lot of content in the email her daughter had sent. She also found out that her good friend Chrissie was currently with Tammy in New York. Getting up, returning her cold drink to the kitchen, Ally picked up her phone, calculating that with the time difference it would be just after lunch time.

'Hi, it's me' she said as the call was answered.

'Thought you might ring, since Tammy sent that email to Terri, I take it that's why you're calling?' Chrissie said.

'Yes, of course it is always nice to just chat, so, you're in New York, what's happened? Terri sent me some stuff, not much, but all about two paintings and a chap named Bartolo Acosta?'

'Yes, I was going to call you Ally, what Tammi sent to your Terri, was the request for information on those paintings and helping to find out more about the Bartolo chap, so, let me get you up to date…'

'And you've not heard from him, since when?' Ally asked, after digesting all that Chrissie had told her.

'It's early evening over there,' Chrissie answered, 'he is working with Martijn and with the local police, also, though in hospital, Samantha's beau has been helpful, the last news I had was that they have an idea where they might have taken Samantha, but are still looking to pinpoint the exact location, having of course, to tread carefully.'

'Okay, well, keep me posted and Terri and I will do the research that Tammi has asked for, by the way, I suppose she is at her restaurant now?' Ally asked, trying not to let on that she was worried about Sam, as well as Samantha, whom she had never met.

'Yes, doing the lunchtime shift, she could have organised some extra staff, but felt it was good to clear her head and focus on something else for a few hours, I'm glad I'm here, her company is helpful, we must get together again soon though,'

'Absolutely, we must, okay, I'll get cracking over here, take care' Alison said, and ended the call.

Making herself a fresh drink of coffee, Ally then sat herself down behind her desk in the lounge and started her research. Find out about the Italian man, Bartolo Acosta, that was her task, Terri would delve into the trail of the two paintings.

The meeting had finished, and young Terri made her way to the archive room in the lower regions of the museum. She had been here, not all that long ago, when doing some administrative work on the many paintings that were housed here, in order to further establish the exact amount of works that were down there, as they hadn't been catalogued and cross checked for quite some time. She had been here that day, when intruders had come, when she had been held at gun point and one of the paintings had been stolen. Terri smiled to herself as she headed down the stairs, recalling how that event had triggered such an adventure.

She crossed over the large room and headed for a blue door on the far side. She had, more or less, claimed this area for her own, as she would often come down and research the many items which still needed to be investigated and researched. She entered the blue door and walked towards where she had set up a small desk. Many sheets of paper were strewn all over it. Organised chaos, she called it, smiling as she thought about it. Then sat behind the desk on a fold away type of chair, opened her extra laptop that she had down here specifically for research, and typed in her password.

THE PAST

Period 6: 1867

Venice, Italy

The winter weather was harsh. The coldest temperatures for decades. The wind from the north was biting. Eva and Isabella Umbrego sat side by side in the old library on St. Mark's Square. It was warm and it was quiet in the old building as they sat behind an oak table, taking a break and having something to eat.

Books and papers were strewn around them....

Three years earlier, in Monaco, just after the girls had celebrated their seventeenth birthday, they were walking towards an old stone building which had at one time been the main house. In the past this had stood at one end of a cobbled courtyard, with several outbuildings lining the other sides of the square. The outbuildings had been torn down and the materials used elsewhere on the vineyard which had been established nearly three centuries ago. The cobbled square had also been taken up to form a new courtyard for the recently completed main house a few hundred yards away. The old house was the only building from the past still standing. It was dilapidated and used mainly for storage.

Eva and Isabella were twins. Eva having come into the world full of life and vigour with a strong set of lungs and a healthy weight. Isabella, on the other hand, was only about half the size of her sister, struggled with breathing and for a few days it was touch and go whether or not she would survive. But survive she did, but it soon became clear that she had been born blind.

'This is where you took the boy?' Isabella, though known just as Bella, asked.

Eva looked across at her sister. Growing up had been difficult at times, but, unlike her, Bella was extremely quiet, patient and placid. She walked alongside her sister, not holding hands, for Bella's hearing and sense of smell was incredible, and she kept pace by listening to the footsteps.

'Carlos, yes, we had some fun,' she answered, 'but when I was there, I discovered something, that's why we are going there now'…

Eva smiled, briefly recollecting that time, when they had opened the trunk that she had found. The trunk that had a false bottom, something that her blind sister had discovered through the different sound it made when she had dropped a tool. The discovery of that painting and those scrolls.

Not long after having moved to Venice, it had been Bella that had come up with the idea of writing a children's book. They had left the painting of the monk behind but had taken the three scrolls with them. Using that information, with Eva reading it all once again, very carefully, and with Bella retaining it all in her memory, they put together this story. Whilst it was all factual, drawing the crucial facts from the scrolls, no-one suspected, all believing this to be a made-up story. *'Once upon a time, there was a princess. Her name was Anna, and she rode a white horse…'* the story began. A tale of three brothers who protected their sister, a tale of a crypt, a tale mentioning secret levers, inner chambers and hidden doors.

Often the girls would giggle as they compiled the story. It would be ninety years later that a woman would read it, picking up on the clues and figuring out, that this was not just a children's story. But what they didn't know, was that whilst they were sitting there, most days, for several weeks, preparing their little book, someone was observing them.

He had been coming to the library for a few days, had observed the twins, had noted that one was blind, but had been so impressed how they worked so well in unison. Whilst he had initially no intention of finding out exactly what they were doing, that changed the day before.

Two names, two names he picked up, though barely whispered in the quiet reading room. But he had sat close enough to hear snippets of their conversation. Two names, almost used in the same sentence. He was intrigued and puzzled. The first was the mention of a Petrus Kastanje, then seconds later the name Father Dominic.

Putting aside the document he was working on, he wrote the names down and sat back to try and bring to mind, how he knew these names. Luigi Cantoni was a scholar. The very first time he had seen the twins, arriving with scrolls and writing material he had been intrigued for he himself was also working from old scrolls. He also noted that they mixed their languages, sometimes they would be whispering in Italian, if fact most of the time that would be the case, but from time to time, they would speak French. Luigi focused on what he was studying, only every now and then glancing at them. The fourth day they had already been present when he arrived and he gave them a courteous nod, which was replied by the slightly taller of the twins with a brief smile.

And so, the days past and Luigi focused on a scroll he was translating, from Old Hebrew into Latin. But when he picked up those two names, he sat back and thought about why they had piqued his attention.

It was the following day, which turned out to be the last time he would see the twin women, when he picked up more on a conversation they were having. They mentioned they would travel to Florence and seek out the house one day. Though little could they know that that day would be quite sometime in the future, when both were married and both mothers to daughters.

It was that bit of information that helped him in his research, for after nearly four hours of searching, by which time the twins had already left, and it was getting dark outside, Luigi found what he was looking for, details about a certain Father Dominic from Florence. Though not at all from a source he had expected.

Taking the book back to where he had been studying the Hebrew Scrolls, he studied it, it was written in Italian and the title of it was 'Sacerdote Che Svanisce' meaning the vanishing priest, this intrigued him, more so where on the back of this old book, which was in rather poor condition, he saw the name, Sacerdote Dominic, Father Dominic. Could this be the same one he overheard the women talking about?

Luigi noted that the old book, quite a thin book, had been written in the year 1610, by Nikolai Wenschelburg, but the story began thirty-two years earlier, for Luigi began to read,

*'My aunt Alexandria and I travelled from Trieste,
making our way to Florence, it was the year 1578...*

Luigi was soon absorbed in the story. Occasionally he would stop reading to make a few notes. He learned that there had been an outbreak of sickness, many of the city's inhabitants had perished, including the authors other aunt, Alexandria's sister, and her husband, Petrus Kastanje. Nikolai had written that he was seventeen at the time. The story, a personal account of the events, mentioned that a little girl, his cousin, was believed to have survived. They had called upon the residence to be met by a Father Dominic, who informed them that the little girl, daughter of Petrus and Odette, had also died from the disease that had taken several hundred of the city's population at that time.

Luigi learned that although at first, as the young man had travelled with his aunt, he had thought there was a concern for the welfare of the little girl, now an orphan, but when they arrived at the house and met Father Dominic who informed them of the little girl's death, she, his aunt, became quite irate and suspicious. Nikolai wrote as to how he felt, how he suddenly saw a nasty side to his aunt, a greedy and selfish side.

She had insisted to be shown the bodies and Father Dominic had taken them down the steps into a small crypt where three coffins were laid out. It was then that the strangest thing happened, was written, but Nikolia would, at this point of his tale, not relate to what that was. Luigi smiled as he read, thinking this man, who would have been nearly fifty, knew how to spin a yarn, how to create suspense in the account he was writing.

He writes about his aunt searching through the house, almost out of control and furious to discover that there were no riches left. No jewellery, no furniture, no paintings, nothing of great value that she knew had been here. All gone. His aunt had asked him to check the coffins, a task that was not easy to do, and confirmed that indeed three bodies were there, a man a woman and a child.

Other than mentioning this, Nikolai wrote that he said very little, that he was disturbed by this side of his aunt, her greed and selfishness, and realised that it had not, been for the little girl's welfare than she had come, but to claim the riches she knew her sister had. He then returned to the point where they had been in the crypt, the point where Father Dominic had, with the aid of a lantern, shown the coffins, and when, both he and his aunt turned to speak with him, he had vanished.

The lantern had been left at the bottom of the steps. They had returned upstairs, but, much later, Nikolai writes, he had himself returned to the crypt, had thoroughly checked the area, but found no clue as to where, Father Dominic had so suddenly vanished to. Promising himself to, at some time in the future, discover the truth about this, he set about to think what he would do next.

His aunt found out that not only were there no items of value left for her to claim, but also that the house now belonged to someone else, the paperwork and details worked out and nothing she could do about it. This of course made her even more furious, and it was three days after first arriving in Florence, that she set off for Rome, for she had found out that it had been likely that Father Dominic had gone there. He himself decided to stay, he wanted nothing more to do with her. And he never heard from or about her again.

Less than an hour later, Luigi put the book down, studied the notes he made. He was now certain that what bits of conversation he had overheard from the twins, related to this very scene, to the very house and the very crypt, and Father Dominic was the priest who they had referred to. Luigi now had some additional, information, thanks to the book written by Nikolai. He knew to which house they were referring.

It was by now the middle of the evening, gathering up his papers and writings and the scroll he had been translating, Luigi set off for home, thinking about what he had learned, thinking about how he might follow up on this.

Returning to the old library the following morning, he first set out his scrolls, the ones he was reading and translating, set up his writing equipment and was set to continue, when he came across an anomaly. For a moment he didn't understand what it meant. Briefly he sat back and pondered on whether he should leave this work of translating for a while and seek to follow up on the clues he had overheard and discovered the previous day, about Father Dominic, about Nikolai and about the house in Florence. On his way home, he had a thought about leaving Venice, about travelling to Florence. But he had work to do, he had to earn finances, decided that, certainly at present, he could not afford to be sidetracked, finish the work he was paid to do, translating two scrolls from Hebrew, into Latin.

So, setting up his equipment, it was back to work, he looked across to where the twins usually sat, in fact, they had never placed themselves anywhere else in the library, which, was often very quiet. There was an emptiness. They were no longer there. Luigi sighed, then re-focused his attention on a part of the scroll he was working on and read it over again. He had studied the Hebrew language, not an easy task to come to grips with, often a phrase could mean several things, depending on its context. Nearly five years now, since he began. But the knowledge had paid off, his current work would be well rewarded.

After having read through the part of the scroll three times, having then read further down and checked what he had translated to that point, Luigi came to an astonishing conclusion. There were two lines, that made no sense, two lines that were not part of the flow of the document, two lines that shouldn't be there, reading further on, he was sure, that the scroll continued correctly, it was as if these two lines, came from a different story, a different tale, a different part of the Hebrew Script that formed passages from the Tanakh, including passages from the Torah.

For the next twenty minutes, Luigi read through the scroll he was currently translating, then turned to the second scroll and quickly scanned through this, and yes! He was right, there it was, another part where there were two lines, most definitely not part of the passage, but why, who had inserted them and, when he compared the two, what he now was sure were inserts, he discovered something else, they were identical, the very same two lines.

Focusing on these lines, Luigi set about to translate them, in the hope of them making sense in some way. Frustrated, he got up and walked about a bit, thinking through what this could mean and why had the scribe inserted these two lines? Not only that, but why were these same lines inserted in another document as well?

Time passed. Twenty-eight years passed.

The year was 1895. The place was Boston.

It was a warm morning. Despite it being the beginning of November. The sun filtering through the branches of the trees as she walked through the park. Smartly dressed in a dress that reached the ground, had a ruffle of sorts at the bottom as well as on the three-quarter lengths' sleeves. A lovely, scalloped lace collar and her feet in dark brown shoes which had a chunky heel. Unlike many women who wore tight fitting corsets, Caprice was not inclined to restrict her breathing and cared not for the fashion. She wore a pale green jacket over the top of her dress and her hair was neatly tied up and she carried a parcel, wrapped in a small blanket under her right arm.

Whilst not having an extremely thin looking waist, she nevertheless had an hourglass figure with a bust line that many women would be envious of. She had arrived nearly a week ago. How long would she be here she wondered, would she finally settle down, would she find the right man, would she have children. All these thoughts were running trough her head as she made her way to the Franck Huysen & Son auction house. She smiled to herself as she remembered the day she left home, her parents, such loving people, giving her their blessing as she set out on an adventure. She wanted to explore. She had heard of course of the tales of her mother and Father, particularly her father who had journeyed from far, and whose father had come from South America. The auction house was only a block away now as she smiled back at several men who looked at her admiringly.

She had left the family home in Silver City, when aged twenty-two, ten years ago already, she thought, again reflecting on her journey that brought her here to Boston. She had lived in Oklahoma, Indiana, Ohio and New York state. She had been romanced. She had been courted but had not fallen in love. She had read many books, she had studied, she had worked, not afraid of labour. She was good with horses, obviously a trait she had inherited from her father, and was fit and strong.

She reached the auction house. Several minutes later she was inside one of the offices where a mister Moshe had taken her. She handed him the parcel which he carefully unwrapped. Caprice could see that the man was impressed, though trying to hide it, she felt, and after a quick look at her, studied the painting carefully. It had been a farewell gift from her parents. They had been given it as a wedding present from her mother's father, her grandfather Joe, whom she had never met.

Franck Huysen, his wife Anje and their twelve-year-old son, Joachim had arrived in New York just over four months ago and had from there travelled by horse and wagon, on to Boston. They had fled Europe. Fled their hometown of Ghent and had sailed from Antwerp. Anje was Jewish and all over Europe, tension was mounting.

Although he initially thought to start life anew in New York, on the voyage over, Franck had met a fellow refugee, a Dutchman. They had bonded and after only a few conversations, had decided to work together. The Dutchman, his name Moshe, had worked for some years at the Weeskamer, an auction house in Amsterdam. Franck was a dealer in art. It seemed provident. They shook hands and agreed to start a business in Boston because Moshe had contacts there, mainly in the shipping industry. And so it was, four months after their arrival, that the business was set up. Though Joachim was only twelve, his father was determined for the boy to take over one day, hence naming the company Franck Huysen & Son.

Moshe knew art, knew artists, had studied books. Not letting anything show, or at least so he thought, he examined the piece. It was canvas, stretched over a light piece of wood, it had no frame. He studied the painting for some time, then turned to look at the back before again studying the art. There was a little damage around the edged, he surmised this had been done when the frame had been carelessly taken off. But the painting was good, he was sure he knew the artist. This was a work by Tiziano Vecelli, better known as Titian. The vibrancy of the red coat, the use of the almost purple blues. The face of the man, whom Moshe felt was Charles V, was full of expression. The horse was beautifully painted, though Moshe was unaware that Titian had painted animals before. Figuring this work was painted in the early fifteen hundreds, he was sure that this was indeed a work by Titian.

Finally, he looked at the woman, 'Where you get this piece' he asked, his English, though much improved since coming to Boston, was still broken and sharply accented.

'It originally belonged to my grandfather, Joe Wheeler, who won it in a card game, about thirty-five years ago, from a Spanish guy travelling in the area, this was in Tucson, Arizona., 'she answered. Then went on to say, 'It was given to my mother as a wedding present, now it belongs to me, I was given it about ten years ago.'

'Interesting' Moshe said, then once more looked at the painting, he then propped it up against a wall and stood back for a moment. 'The Spanish connection is good,' Moshe said, without taking his eyes of the painting, 'very nice piece, very good artist, will sell very good price.'

Caprice thought through what the man was saying, as he intently looked at the painting. She observed him studying the work. Her eyes wandered around, taking in the vastness of the auction house. There was a shelf, next to where he had placed her painting. Two scrolls were placed upon it, and she read the sign that was in front of them. Frowning, she read what it said. 'Ancient Hebrew scroll translations, by renowned scholar Luigi Cantoni.'

Moshe turned around, caught her eye and repeated what he had said earlier, 'Very nice piece, very good artist, will sell very good price'

Fifteen minutes later Caprice stepped outside and headed to where she was staying. She was happy. The auction would be in nine days' time, never having been to an auction before, she was looking forward to it. The fact that it would most likely sell well was also good news. For some reason she thought about the scrolls she had seen, interesting, but why, she wondered. Then she left the building, entered the street and the sun was still warming a November morning, still thinking about those ancient scrolls.

Little could she even imagine that four generations later, a descendant would discover more.

THE PRESENT

Thursday 2nd June

San Francisco

Chantal drove the rental car into the street, slowly, checking the house numbers. She stopped. Checked the writing on a slip of paper she had lying on the passenger seat and then shut the engine.

The afternoon was gradually turning to evening. Chantal sat for a moment, thinking back to, what was it, over fifteen months ago now? When she had attended the opening of a special exhibit at the Albuquerque Museum of Art. For some time now, she had focused on tracing her lineage, finding her roots, looking to gain information on her heritage, where she came from. She had married Charles Marcus Brewer nearly twenty years ago. The marriage was solid. She gave birth to two children, Arnold, now eighteen and attending the university in Boston, and Chloe, almost seventeen, who had decided to be a musician at an early age and was now part of a small orchestra, playing both the violin and the saxophone. They were popular and travelled around the country. She was happy and that was what mattered most to Chantal. Often wondering where her daughter's musical talent had come from, it was that which spurred her on to trace her roots. Charles Marcus was a Bostonian, through and through, a successful corporate manager, he was now the C.E.O. of a large retail outlet which in the past had been part of the Parker Empire, in fact he was related to Charles Parker through his mother's family.

But then, tragedy struck the family. It had happened when she had returned from the exhibition in Albuquerque. She had been so inspired, had so much wanted to chat more to the Hudson woman, find out more as to how the gold coins, once belonging to her ancestors, had found its way to silver City where they had been uncovered by the archaeologist Professor Emily Parker, co-incidentally also related to the Parkers from Boston. But she had come home to find her husband had collapsed at work. He had been taken to hospital and was subsequently diagnosed as having had a stroke. He was still this side of fifty.

Chantal sighed. She opened the car door and got out. Taking a deep breath, she crossed the road and headed for the house. To focus on something had been, and still was, most helpful. Charles Marcus, affectionally known as CM, had suddenly slipped into a coma, then just stopped breathing and died. All very sudden. After the funeral her son had returned to his study, her daughter had rejoined her little orchestra and was currently touring around Florida. Chantal had purposefully refocused on her family roots. Walking quickly up the path, she reached the door and rang the bell.

Meanwhile in another part of the city

Terri had finished the second meeting of the morning, having reluctantly left the archive room to head for the boardroom. Afterwards she went to her own office and once she had made some notes on the recent meeting, she checked her work roster, saw that all was up to date and headed back down to the basement to continue her search on the Flemish painters.

As she bounded down the stairs, she smiled as she recalled a memory of her new friend from New York. Tammy, what a close bond they had formed in such a short time when, together with Sophie, the three of them had solved the clues relating to the three monks. She was also drawn back into being concerned as she headed for the blue door. about the reason Tammy had called her, that a lady called Samantha had been kidnapped, that it was al to do with two paintings and any clues to find out why, would be most helpful.

Giving her mother the task of researching an Italian named Bartolo Acosta, she herself would follow up on what Tammy had already discovered.

The paintings had come across the Atlantic in 1763, and had then returned to Europe in 1803, all this information she had to hand. But why had these two pieces of art been targeted, why these two artists? Terri decided she would need to delve a far back as she could, when these painting were created and where, this might help as to why they had been stolen. Sitting once again behind her small desk in the vast archive room, she continued to work her way through the list of the many items that were housed here, to see if she could find any connection or any references to a painter named Jacob Leyssen or to the other Flemish master, Arnold Frans Rubens, not to be confused with the more famous Pieter Paul Rubens. She had searched for the paintings in question and had printed a copy of each to help her in her investigating, though a quick study of both did not offer any clues as to why these might be of significant importance.

Back across town

Alison Hudson frowned as she wondered who was at the door.

'Hi, I hope I am not disturbing you, I should have rung, but lost your number, still had your address, so…'

'Chantal, no, it's fine, come in, come in…' Ally said. 'Tell you the truth, I had at some point wanted to call you, but also couldn't find your number, crazy, come in, would you like a drink?'

Chantal smiled, asked for a coffee and both women were quiet until Alison brought the drinks into the lounge, seeing the expression on Chantal's face, she realised then, that something was not right, she sensed a sadness.

'Has something bad happened?' Ally asked, sitting down in the chair opposite her, 'I just sense…'

Chantal gave a brief smile, 'you sense right…' then after a pause as Alison waited for her to speak, she then said, 'Meeting you at the exhibition was very interesting, the whole exhibition was very interesting, however, when I got back home, back to Boston…'

Without hesitation Alison got up and was immediately beside her on the couch.

There was an instant bond between them. Alison sensing a definite sadness and Chantal recognising a genuine concern. Alison reached out, took hold of Chantal's hand and looked at her. Taking a deep breath, Chantal clasped the hand tightly and began to speak…

Alison listened to the story that unfolded.

Whilst in the museum Terri was totally focused on her research, particularly on the history of the Flemish masters, discovering, as she went through a vast list that ranged from the 13th to the 17th century, that surprisingly, they had two paintings right here, in the archive room, deemed to be by one of those that were on that list. Terri made a note to research these further but kept her focus on the ones she was looking for, on Jacob Leyssen and on Arnold Frans rubens.

There in the windowless archive room, the young Terri scrolled through the list and every now and then made notes. Thinking to herself, wondering, and every now and then looking again at the copies she had made, why it was that these artists, or these paintings, were of such interest.

Period 7: 1897

London

Samuel Wilfred Price was twenty-seven years old and had a great interest in old masters and their oil paintings. He already owned several thank to the wealth his father had left him when he had so suddenly died and Samuel had been just twenty years of age. His studies at Eton College were going very well and he was already a part of the diplomatic corps and was informed that next year he would get his first appointment as ambassador.

Feeling pleased with himself, and very much looking forward to his first appointment, wherever that might be, which he would find out about in five months from now, he walked his almost six-foot frame towards the auction house. Several paintings had caught his eye, always looking to extend his collection, as long as the price was fair and, always thinking ahead, that it would hold or better in price when at some point down the line he would sell them. There was one however, that drew his interest, not so much about the painting itself, nor the artist who he knew very little about, but because of its provenance, it had an interesting history. The previous day he had viewed the items that would be in the auction, had then discovered this work by the Dutch artist, Pieter Bout, and noticed the story surrounding it. He had sat down and read it thoroughly, the very detailed account had drawn him in, taking him into the story...

It was in the year 1804 that Lady Evangeline Powell-Hunter died. She had been married to a Thomas Powell, a journalist who had at one time worked in America, but who sadly had been killed when he was reporting on the violence in Yemen, back in 1752. According to the report, it had been he, who uncovered the painting, in a barn, and had sent it to his wife, a day before he was killed in the riots. Eventually the painting was handed down the family, first to one of their daughters, Joanna, who, again reading the detailed report, was running the large estate in Shropshire. She in turn handed it down to one of her children. Eventually, due to financial difficulties, the estate was sold in the year 1876, the painting was one of three that were bought by a Belgian gentleman, keen to collect Flemish masters. He died in 1892. It was then donated to an art studio and workshop in the city of Antwerpen, who then cleaned and restored a little damage and reframed the work in a lovely detailed and beaded frame that had been sourced from South America. Deciding that London might fetch a better price, the work was taken over and put up for auction. Titled 'rural scene by Pieter Bout' and it was signed and dated 1653…

Samuel loved the story and was determined that it would look good in his collection. The following day he was there, among many gathered in a large room. The auction was about to begin. He couldn't help but think of the story he had read the previous day, however, there was a huge gap in the provenance that no-one seemed to know. The painting was signed 1653. It had been this journalist, Thomas Powell, who discovered it in a barn in Yemen, in the year 1752, that's over a hundred years later. How did it end up in that barn in Yemen. Deciding that he might try and research the missing years, Samuel listened to the bidding and caught the eye of the auctioneer, giving him a nod which was understood.

It was late evening when Samuel returned to his digs. He was pleased with his purchase and had, thanks to some further information that had come to light, found out a little more about the Pieter Bout painting, which had originally first been sold in 1654, to an unknown buyer in Rotterdam. Thinking about where he might be posted for his first appointment as ambassador, and picturing in his mind how he would arrange his collection of fine paintings, it was nearly midnight when he fell asleep.

THE PRESENT

Friday 3ʳᵈ June

Antwerpen

It was after midnight. He kept running then slowed a little. Though he knew the city a little, he knew these docks better. Had studied the layout. Knew there was no way out, but he had a plan. Knowing he was, at least for the moment, out of their line of sight, he reached the end of the dock. His heart was thumping loudly. The rain came down heavily and without turning, he jumped.

His heart thumping like a jackhammer, Sam landed on the narrow wooden decking, made up out of two heavy timbers that extended beyond the dock. But it was less than two feet wide, a buffer to protect the dock from the mooring barges that frequented this part of the harbour….

One such barge had only moored earlier today. Along with the detective Sam had seen it arrive, and both had wondered if the barge was in any way connected to the robbers and the kidnappers of Samantha. But despite keeping a close eye on the proceedings, it seemed not. What it did do, they figured, it eliminated a section of the buildings that made up the warehouses on the dock. This left only two possibilities. With the help from Martijn in Rotterdam who had managed to find a very detailed map of the area, the detective, whose name was Jan, together with Sam, worked out a plan of action.

It began to rain just as Sam headed for the building on the dock that they figured to be the correct one, where, hopefully, they would be able to find and rescue Samantha. It was midnight and raining quite hard, when Sam tried the door handle.

It opened. When the rain had started, he had taken his glasses off, placed them in the top pocket of his jacket. Again, he recalled a time when, also in a rescue attempt, he had taken his glasses off when they had steamed up from exertion, he had then seriously wondered whether or not to get contact lenses, something he still, to date had not done. Hoping that the layout of this building, now clear in his mind, was correct, Sam entered. It was dim, but light was coming from a wall mounted lamp about eight feet away. He put his glasses back on, ran his right hand through his hair to clear the moisture as the rain thundered on the metal roof. At least the noise would be helpful to move about silently.

Ahead was a corridor, to the left a set of wide sliding doors that would lead to a large space, on the right were three smaller single doors, then, at the far end, a fire escape door. Sam moved quickly towards it. Felt quite sure that it wasn't alarmed, and as quietly as he could pressed down the metal bars and opened it. He was relieved. Not only did it come out where he had hoped, but he saw that the barge that had earlier arrived, was moored well away to the left of where he stood. He focused for a moment as to where he needed to be later, the pulled the door so that it almost closed.

Sighing a relief, next came the difficult part, find Samantha. Walking back along the dimly lit corridor, he now tried the handle of the first door. Locked! But he smiled when he noticed that there was a key, a large iron key, on a ring with two other keys, hanging from a hook on the wall beside the door. Whispering a thank you to above, Sam moved on, feeling sure that this was where Samantha would be kept. Sam moved along the corridor to the second door and listened. He heard nothing. Then along to the third door, here he picked up voices, it sounded like a television.

So far, so good. Sam went back to the first door, took the keys off the hook, picked what he felt was the right key and inserted it. Carefully he opened the door, then whispered, 'Sam?'

'Sam?' came a reply.

Entering the room, he saw her, she saw him, even in the dimness with only the light from the corridor making some effort to break through the darkness, he noticed her broad grin.

Sam walked over to her, saw her predicament and the chains and locks, then said, 'Take these keys, one of them must unlock those chains, then wait until I come back, don't let anyone in, got that?'

'Samantha took the keys, merely nodded and wondered how on earth Sam, all the way from Boston, had not only crossed the Atlantic, but had located her in such a short time. She wanted to hug him, wanted to speak, wanted to ask questions, but knew that now was not the time. She focused on what she was asked to do, seeing Sam already leaving the room. Closing the door behind him, he then got out his phone, pressing some number, he then spoke softly. 'Got her, going into phase two, don't know how many, are you ready?'

'Ready'. Came the short reply.

Sam put the phone away, headed for the third door, then taking a deep breath, he entered, with a loud voice, saying' Okay, where is the woman?'

Two men, young men, in their mid-twenties sat on a large well-worn couch, watching a small television. There was a small kitchen in the room, a low fridge, a wooden table, and an old standard lamp gave some light. The overhead tube lighting was off.

Whilst initially surprised, one of the men reacted quickly, and jumped up from the couch, reaching for a gun. A gun that Sam only now just noticed lay on a nearby small table. He turned on his heels, hoped that detective Jan and his men were ready and ran, taking off the way he had come in. Back outside and into the rain, Sam turned left, headed towards the end of the dock. Hopefully making the pursuers think he was going the wrong way. But, despite his speed, the young man behind him was faster. It was then, still hearing the rain pound upon the roof, that he felt a bullet whizz past his ear. But then he turned around the corner of the building, raced towards the end of the dock and jumped.

His forward momentum nearly took him beyond the timber decking and into the dark cold water, but somehow, he managed to turn, grip the edge of the dock and steady himself. With now his head and shoulders above the dockside, Sam bent low, then carefully, but as quick as he dared, moved to the corner, turned it, and headed back alongside the dock on this side, heading for where he had opened the fire door.

He heard commotion, but ignored it, ignored the rain that was still coming down heavily, nearly slipped twice, but managed to stay on the wooden timbers. Reaching the point that he had calculated would be the spot he wanted to be, Sam stood upright, reached up to the main dockside, pulled himself up and was relieved to be in exactly the place he wanted to be. He raced over the fire door, opened it, hoping that detective Jan was now in control of the situation on the other side and was thankful that the corridor was empty. Three strides took him to the right door, 'It's me, Sam, coming in' he said, still struggling a little to regain his breath.

THE PAST

Period 8: 1963

Istanbul -Turkey

She inhaled deeply, through her nose, as she stood there. She felt tense, though was determined not to show it.

The room was large, situated on the first floor. It had five windows, all overlooking the Bosporus from the European side of the city. A massive Persian rug covered the entire room in colours which ranged from muted oranges and reds through to soft shades of green and yellow. A set of double doors, in a dark wood, gave entry to this room from the hallway. A single wooden door, of the same dark wood, was at the far end. The three walls completing the rectangular shape were covered in dark green wallpaper and adorned with several paintings. The drapes which hung from a high ceiling, flanking each of the five windows were a dark maroon in colour and made of heavy velvet. The most unusual feature of this room was that there was no furniture.

The woman who stood by the middle window, looking out and observing the sun dazzling its light upon the water, was angry. Much like her ancestor had been, over four hundred years ago. An ancestor she had only learnt about, six years ago. A woman whose name was Alexandria Wenschelburg. She allowed herself a brief smile, thinking that she had obviously been named after her. One of the double doors opened and a man softly walked in and approached her. He stopped about ten feet away and observed her. Her stance was upright, her chin tilting slightly upwards, showing her lovely neckline. Her hair was dark, almost black, and cut quite short. He noticed her pearl drop earring and spoke to give her an update.

The man, in his late sixties, born and bred in Istanbul, left the room the same way he had come. Closing the door softly behind him, Youseff Turan, stopped for a moment, then walked over to his desk.

In the large room Alexa stood silently. Then finally taking a deep breath and turning, she threw a quick glance around the room. The multicoloured and soft pile rug that covered the entire floor, the wallpaper, the finest money could buy, the three ornate crystal chandeliers that were suspended from the high ceiling. And the paintings, there were ten in all each with a soft tube light set in a brass fixture above each one. A varied collection, from local artists to Italian, French and Flemish painters. But in that quick glance, Alexa didn't see any of that, instead she was angry and concerned as her plan had thus far not gone to plan. She headed for the single door and left the room.

It was four and half hours later, when she walked back into the large room. Lights were lit above each painting. The three chandeliers that were suspended from the ceiling, were lit. It was dark outside as Alexa walked over to the centre window, her favourite spot. Hugo was right behind her.

Hugo Visser. His mother was Italian, his father Dutch. His mother was volatile, animated, passionate. His father was placid, yet stern, quiet, yet commanding. For a moment he reflected on his childhood, of the tug of war between his father and mother, of his own decision to ensure that he was number one, his life, his terms. He briefly looked around the room and watched her as she stopped by the window and looked out into the darkness, the Bosporus a gleaming black ribbon. His mission had been successful, the rewards of it placed on the desk in her office. Though she looked pleased, there was something niggling at the back of his mind. His heart rate was a little faster. As he approached her, she turned, smiled, then drew close to him, snaked an arm around his neck and pulled him towards her, her lips connecting with his, but with her other arm, she drew the pistol and shot him.

Hugo stumbled back one pace, then collapsed onto his knees, his face registering shock, but only briefly, as he began to fall backwards, his left arm reached behind his back. Then, looking up at her, smiling, he said, 'I pulled you from the plane that day' It was Alexa's turn to register shock as she took in what he had said. Her jaw dropped and her eyes widened, for she could see now, that he had pulled a gun from behind his back. He pulled the trigger with the last breath he had, then went limp and died.

The bullet, in an upward trajectory, entered her chest just below her heart, the power of the shot almost lifting her off her feet tearing through her. The bullet exited her back and imbedded in one of the heavy velvet curtains. The sound of the shot reverberated around the room as Alexa hit the floor and died only seconds later.

Neither would ever know the significance of two of the paintings that hung on the wall. One by Rubens and the other by Jacob Leyssen.

Youseff Turan entered the room but stopped as he saw the bodies. The loud shot has alerted him. Taking a deep breath, he then carefully made his way to the centre window. For a while he stood by the bodies. They were both dead. He looked at the man, Hugo, noticed the bullet mark. Small calibre, straight into his heart. Saw the big gun in his limp hand. This was the shot he had heard. Looking at his employer, Madam, he saw the damage was severe.

He concluded the following, she must have shot him first, then he, collapsing, somehow must have shot her. He looked at the blood on the beautiful rug. That would take some cleaning.

There were things to be done, and Youseff worked quickly, still pondering as to why Madam had shot him. After he was satisfied that he was now ready, he called the police. Then, sat behind his desk, he started to write down some notes.

It was well after midnight, when he turned off the light and left his office, glancing at the double doors to the large room, he saw the police tape. He was told not to enter that room until it was fully processed. Suddenly feeling rather tired, he turned off the light and left the building via the back stairs. In his mind he tried to work out what to do next. He had some more notes to write, but, after the police were done, Youseff decided that it was time for a change, he would leave the city behind, he would go.

THE PRESENT

Friday- 3rd June

Antwerpen

'She was gone, left the day after they took Samantha' Sam said, back in his hotel room, talking on the phone with Martijn. 'She left the two young men to look after her, feed her, but not to harm her in any way, but to release her chains and let her go, once they had heard from her'

'Did they know where she was going?' Martijn asked, glad his friend was not hurt, knowing that he had been shot at.

'No, she took the paintings, which had been stored there awaiting further instructions, left those young men at the docks, then drove the van to the Sint Nikolaas shopping centre, the police found some footage, she changed vehicles, still looking for that one'

'Okay, well, I guess Rico will be relieved, as am I, you better get some sleep, Sophie sends her love, once she knew you were alright, she promptly fell asleep.'

Checking his watch, Sam saw that it was nearly two o'clock in the morning now, still towelling his hair as he walked about the hotel room. 'Thank you so much for what you managed to do, very grateful… you best get some sleep to, I must ring Chrissie next'

Throwing the towel on the end of the bed, Sam walked over to the window, pulled the curtain aside and looked down onto the area that was called the Groeneplaats. The cobbles gleamed in the streetlights from the earlier rain. It was quiet, the rain had stopped, and it seemed the city was asleep. As he should be, Sam thought, sitting on the edge of the bed, he pressed a key on his phone and heard the ringtone.

Moving himself into a more comfortable position on the bed, Sam could never know, that a little over three years ago, a woman named Petra Leyland, was in this very room, delighted that she had her jewellery back, which had been stolen from her seven years earlier. Petra Leyland, who had, for a few days, also stayed with Sophie in Paris, the two of them working together to find that very thief, whose real name was Lucie van Doorn but was going by the name of Steffie Baertjens. It had been this same woman, who, later, had been responsible for Sophie being stabbed which had in turn brought Sam to the rescue.

Sam heard a familiar voice on the other end of the line.

New York a little before eight o'clock in the evening, still Thursday.

'Are you okay? did you find her? What has happened, haven't heard from you for ages!' Chrissie said, answering the call, knowing it to be Sam.

'I know, I'm sorry, got so focused and working with Martijn and the local police, as well as with Rico in the hospital, but, yes, I'm fine, and yes, we have got her, Samantha is fine, despite the hour, it's two am here, she is with Rico at the hospital'

'Good, great, sorry, I was worried,' Chrissie said, calming down a little and smiling at Tammy who stood nearby.

'Well done, Sam' Tammy called out.

Suddenly feeling very tired and quite relieved after all the activities of the evening, Sam finished the call and sat upright on the bed, running through the events of the day in his mind. He sighed, lay down and recalled when he had entered that room, when he then knew that Samantha was alive. He smiled, thinking how much trouble he might be in, when he would tell Chrissie that he had been shot at. Then, turning slightly, he noticed the digital clock on the bedside table. It was already early morning. Sam closed his eyes and then promptly fell asleep.

THE PAST

Period 9: 2005

Istanbul

It was early morning. Driving in the rental van through the city, thankfully with good direction at hand, she focused on the traffic and thought back.

Recalling the story that had unfolded after the discovery she had made, she reached her destination, this was the right door, the right place. She stopped the rental van and got out.

Thirty-five-year-old Danielle Vitali unlocked the roller door of the old garage and lifted it open. Despite it not having been opened for some time, the door rolled up smoothly. Nearby a train rumbled across an iron bridge, the noise momentarily distracted her. She then looked once more into the garage which seemed to be stacked with all sorts of things. Taking a step inside, she found the light switch. Three tube lights flickered for a moment, made a buzzing sound, then settled to bring plenty of light all around.

Where to start she wondered, taking in all that she could see. Dressed in dark blue jeans and a red long-sleeved sweatshirt over a white blouse, feet into dark brown leather ankle boots with a small square heel, she was ready to get her hands dirty. Her long auburn hair tied in a ponytail, she was ready to sort through, what had been described to her, as a garage full of junk. Standing still for a moment, arms folded, she pondered her options. It was early morning and already quite hot. She heard another train rumble across the iron bridge adjacent to the garage.

Her mother had recently died after a long illness. She didn't know who her father was, and her own marriage had failed after less than five years. She had no children. It was when sorting through her mother's belongings, hoping to perhaps find more on her childhood, that she made several discoveries. Standing there, in the old garage, ignoring the traffic that went past and still with her arms folded, many miles away from her home in Trieste, Danielle thought back…

Having, not long after her mother's passing, taken the bull by the horn, so to speak, she had begun to sort through her mother's belongings. It hadn't been long before she had found something that totally stumped her. Her mother had been adopted.

How had she not known that? Sitting on the edge of the bed she looked at the papers in her hand. She had never known her father, her mother had brought her up and Danielle acknowledged that she hadn't always been that close to her. She had been a good mother, had provided, but there had been times, after Danielle had turned seventeen, when she had often gone away. At the time, and Danielle smiled to herself at the recollection, she had been a tough teenager. She had moved into her own place when she was nineteen, had travelled, had many times been away for months before even writing or making contact. Her commitment was poor, she knew that. She had married because she fancied him and knew that he was popular. It was a conquest, a victory. It was no surprise when the marriage failed. It was then that she had finally come home again, only to find her mother was poor in health.

It was a turning point then, to not be so selfish, to not make everything a competition. She focused on helping her mother, got a new job, settled and grafted at work and did all she could to make her comfortable and happy. Sitting on the edge of the bed that day, having discovered those documents, was another turning point. She made a promise to herself, to dig, to discover, to unearth the truth.

Danielle unfolded her arms, clapped her hands together and made a start to clear the garage. Starting on the left-hand side she worked her way from the front to the back and then from the left to the right. A little over two hours later, she rubbed her back, wiped the sweat from her brow and decided she needed a break and something to eat and drink.

Across the road from the garage, in an upper apartment, a teenage girl stood by the window. She was munching on a chocolate bar, after having only just got up and showered. She had a part time job in a nearby restaurant in the evenings. Watching from the window she noticed the woman, loading all sorts of stuff into the van that was parked right outside the old garage. In another room her grandfather was drinking strong coffee, she could smell it throughout the apartment. He was watching television. Severely damaged in a car accident many years ago, he got about on a pair of crutches but didn't get about a lot. He mainly sat in his small lounge, watching the television and drinking copious amounts of strong coffee.

He didn't mind his granddaughter living there. She cleaned house and made sure he had some meals. Did his washing and bought him magazines and newspapers. They hardly spoke to each other. The girl, just sixteen now, was about to turn away from the window when she spotted something. It was a portrait, she could see that, just a glimpse before it disappeared into the back of the van. She remained at the window for a little longer, thinking, the portrait was familiar, but why, it seemed to be an old painting, a painting of a monk. Then she recalled where she had seen it before.

Rushing into her bedroom, she found pen and paper, then came back to the window, wrote down the name on the side of the vehicle, then taking out her phone, though an older model now, it could still take pictures, and she took several of the woman who was continuing to load goods into the van. Satisfied that she had information she needed, she turned away from the window. Crystal Kaplova began to wonder how that painting had got into that garage.

Unaware that she was not only being watched, but photographed, Danielle, having been replenished with a slice of fruit cake and a hot chocolate, continued loading the van. Upon returning she had discovered that there was an upper shelf at the back of the garage. Here she had discovered the paintings, ten in all that were, at least in her opinion, lovely oil paintings, and then that panelled oil painting of a monk which she found most unusual, along with some other items seemingly related to it.

Just over two hours later she closed the doors to the vehicle she had hired, rolled down the garage shutter, locked it and got into the van. Quite some researching to be done and then what to do with all her findings. Driving to the airport she headed for the cargo centre where the previous day she had arranged to have the items packed and shipped. She hadn't appreciated how much there was in that old garage, but, whatever the cost, she would ship it all to her home in Trieste. It was time leave Istanbul. Checking her watch, she noticed that it was just past midnight. She made arrangement for an early morning flight, then took the rental back and checked into a nearby hotel. It had been a physically tough day, she felt it in her muscles and was relieved to finally get into bed.

THE PRESENT

Friday 3rd June

New York

After the call, Tammy and Chrissie looked at each other, then, seeing the relief in Chrissie's face, Tammy moved towards her, and they hugged.

'That was Sam being Sam' Tammy said, 'don't you think? Getting so involved in things and not communicating to anyone! Men!'

Chrissie smiled, 'I know, what is it about them! They test your patience!'

'How about you come with me, go over to the restaurant, give me a hand in closing up' Tammy suggested.

'Yes, get some fresh air too, but, before we go, I'll give Ally a call, let her and Terri know the latest' Chrissie said, thankful she had a good friend in Tammy, but also in Ally.

In San Francisco

It was a little after six o'clock in the evening when the silence in the room was broken as Ally's phone chirped. Answering the call she said 'Chrissie! What……'

Chantal looked across from where she sat on the two-seater, where earlier she had broken down and had shared her grief with Alison, who she already considered a new best friend. She picked up on the fact that it was her friend from Boston, who's boyfriend, or soon to be husband, had set off for Europe as another friend had been kidnapped, all to do with a couple of paintings that had been stolen. Knowing already the circumstances surrounding Alison and her daughter Terri, Chantal was thinking of the turmoil and danger that her new friend had faced in the past. But seeing her face register relief, the phone call was all about good news.

The call was short, and Ally smiled at Chantal as she ended the call. Then said, 'I have to let Terri know'

Chantal nodded and smiled back. She was glad she had come. It took her away from her home in Boston, thinking that perhaps, at some point she might well have come across either or both Chrissie and this Sam Price, having now learned of where they lived. Sitting back, she also gathered some information together in her mind. She had heard of various titbits of stories, relating to the Parker family, of which her husband was a descendant, heard about a man called Percivald, about three paintings, all seascapes that now hung on a wall in New York, in the apartment belonging to the New Yorker, Tammy, who, she had also learned, was very much involved in the various adventures with Ally, her daughter Terri, and a lady called Millie, whose mother had been Professor Emily Parker, again, related to her husband's family, a lot of pieces of puzzle, a lot of gaps too, she was keen to know more. It all would help her to focus on something other than the loss of her husband.

She too thought of her own research thus far, the auction in Boston, the painting by Titian, the scrolls her ancestor had made a note of. So much to properly research and record. Ally had gone into the kitchen, Chantal heard her talking, then, armed with a bottle of white wine and two glasses, she came back into the room.

THE PAST

Period 10: 2015

Paris - 19th of January

He decided to go in.

Only a few streets away from both the Gare Du Nord and Gare de L'est railway stations was the Paris Fine Arts Auction House. A set of three wide marble steps led to the entrance. The foyer was warmly decorated with various paintings and posters hung on the walls. Through a door to the left was a gallery where one could view the various items which would be auctioned later in the day. This space had by now been cleared. Through another door leading off from the foyer gave entrance to the auction room itself. It was spacious, well-lit and could comfortably seat around a hundred and twenty people, with room at the back for extra standing places.

The podium was around ten metres wide and close to four metres in depth. A large monitor was hung high above the right-hand side. The rostrum was in the centre and to the left two women were sat behind a desk keeping an eye on their computer monitors tracking on-line buyers. On the side of the podium, below the large monitor, a woman sat behind a desk, also watching her own monitor. Sophie Pontiac, the manager of the auction house, with various sheets of paper and some books also to hand, watched the crowd. She was ready for the auction to begin and to monitor the proceedings. It was not a full house, around eighty or so, she estimated.

The auctioneer came on stage and positioned himself behind the rostrum. He sorted out various sheets of paper, checked to see that the large monitor was working, then checked his microphone with a few taps from his finger. He then checked the big clock that was on the far wall, turned to look at the Miss Sophie, who gave a nod. He was no longer a young man, well into his seventies, was of very slight build, had thin grey hair and wore a pair of glasses that were perched almost at the very end of his nose. He began to speak. His voice did not at all match his appearance. It was clear, deep in timbre and rather voluminous.

Sam Price glanced at the programme, the catalogue, then up at the auctioneer, who, after welcoming the guests spoke first in French, then immediately in English. He was clear and fluid in both, though originally from Prague, Sam had picked up from the brochure he had read. The crowd settled and the first item was brought out.

After several quick sales a painting appeared on the big screen. Sam read the catalogue, an oil landscape, featuring a wooden bridge, the artist, a well-known Turkish painter, Hikmet Onat. Seated five places along from Sam, was a woman. Her brunette hair was cut short, exposing a slim neck. She wore glasses and her brown eyes were focused on the auctioneer. Danielle Vitali wore a white blouse under a soft pink cashmere pullover and the beige trench coat she had worn upon arrival now lay folded on the seat next to her. She wore a long skirt with predominantly burgundy tones and her feet were in calf-high leather boots.

She was pleased she had come. The price of her painting was going up and up. It was the first of two which she had offered to be auctioned. Danielle thought back, shaking her head a little, realising how the years had passed. It had been nearly ten years ago. Ten years had passed since she had travelled from Trieste to Istanbul. Ten years since she had opened that old garage door. The auctioneer banged his gavel down. She smiled, well pleased with the sale of her first lot.

Two rows directly behind Danielle, Crystal Kaplova, now nearly twenty-six years of age, watched the proceeding. Though she had registered to be a buyer and had her number on top of the catalogue on her lap, she had no intention of purchasing anything, but mainly to observe. She was waiting for Miss Vitali's second lot. An oil painting by a Flemish master, Jacob Leyssens 1661-1690, listed as 'Scene of Rome'.

Crystal recalled that morning, when she had first seen the Italian woman. Her grandfather, for whom she was a carer, had not been well during the night. She had kept him comfortable, administered the correct medicine and by the time she herself had gone to sleep, it had been almost dawn. No school today for her. They knew, knew her responsibility of looking after her grandfather. Understood when she called, she would stay home today.

Her observation from the front lounge window had been only a little curious, that is, until she saw her with that painting of the monk. Then her curiosity sharpened, she focused, she thought about the stories her grandfather had told, stories of a treasure, stories that involved three monks, stories of a painting he and his friend had been asked to find, in France, stories of a car chase, stories of a terrible accident, one where his friend had died, one where he had been severely injured. She had listened, had listened many times as he often would tell the story, but his mind was wandering, not totally cohesive, the start of Alzheimer's. She was never quite believing all these stories, which varied every time he told them. But she did believe two things, first, the paintings of a monk, secondly, the treasure.

Seeing that portrait come out of the garage that morning, seeing the woman place it in the van. That was the moment, she knew she had to find out more. Had to know who this woman was, how the painting got into the garage. Sixteen years old, but she was older than her years. She made herself a promise, to research, to hunt, to look, to find the truth surrounding the stories her grandfather had told her.

Sitting now, two rows behind her, Crystal was pleased. Ten years had passed, but she had discovered so much. Sadly, not so much about the stories of the three monks, but more on the existence of paintings by two Flemish masters. Crystal knew that this Miss Vitali had both but was only selling one today. Did the woman know about the secrets these paintings held. Why was she selling this one?

A Gauguin had come up on the monitor, but though there had been some bidding, the lot was not sold, obviously not reaching its reserve. A man got up, seated a little to the left of Crystal and exited the auction room as the next lot appeared on the screen. Briefly wondering why he had not stayed for the whole auction, Crystal looked at the monitor, the next painting after this one, would be the one. Stay focused, she told herself.

She had told herself that many times. Though the odd fling with boyfriends, she had, mainly due to her responsibilities at home, not acquired many friends. But over the years her focus on what she wanted to do, had not wavered. When her grandfather died, she was almost nineteen, it was a huge relief. She felt light and free, like having been cooped up in a closet for ever, and suddenly seeing daylight, the door was opened, she could do as she pleased, she had no commitments, she could breathe. Her parents had long ago vanished from the scene, had left the city under a cloud of criminal investigations and she had not heard from them again. She had been left in the house with her ailing grandfather. But she took on the role of caring for him. The freedom came with a reward, for she was left the house and a tidy sum in the bank. She had studied photography and history at school, and it was time for her to truly pursue her quest to find the truth about her grandfather's stories.

In the first two years she travelled through western Europe, particularly the lowlands. Then spent almost seven months in Italy before finding an important clue in Venice when she had followed a trail that led to the library there, where in the year 1867 the twins, Bella and Eva had compiled their children's book. It was also where Luigi Cantoni had studied the scrolls and discovered a book by Nikolai Wenschelburg.

Just as Alexa Wenschelburg made a surprise discovery, and just as Luigi made a surprise discovery, so did Crystal. For Luigi it had been in 1867, when he found that old book written by Nikolai. For Alexa, it had been nearly a hundred years later, finding out the truth about the children's book by Eva and Bella. For Crystal it was a name, that of Wenschelburg. She knew that name. Spending time on her laptop, she then connected the dots in her mind. Youseff Turan. He was in the employ of Alexa Wenschelburg, he was the immediate boss of Kazim and Huzar. He had sent them to Monaco, sent them to find that portrait of a monk, to obtain it at any cost. Well, the cost was high, Kazim had died, Huzar, her grandfather, had been severely injured, and they had failed in their task.

Crystal searched on her computer for almost two hours before she sat back, took in what she read and the cogs in her mind were whirring around, digesting all the information she had found. An inventory. Goods having belonged to Alexa. Youseff listed as the appointed administrator. She found the name of the beneficiary, Danielle Vitali, she found the address of the garage, across the road from where she lived. Also, included in the contents, were ten oil paintings. Reading through this list, something jumped out, struck a chord. Putting her laptop aside, she reached for the book that the scholar, Luigi, had found, way back in 1867, written by Nikolai, it was written in Italian, but Crystal had studied languages, Italian, French and English, she could read. It took some moments, some turning of the pages, but found what she was looking for. Have caught the gist of his writings, it seemed that this Nikolai, nephew of Alexandria Wenchelburg, had distanced himself from his aunt, had created his own path, had become an administrator in Florence, deciding to stay there. He had also, after several years of searching, found out about some of the items that had once belonged to Petrus Kastanje and his wife Odette, who was also his aunt. Among the items he found, were two paintings, both by Flemish Artist, one was titled battle on the coast, by Rubens, the other simple stated Roman landscape, by Jacob Leyssens.

Over the years Crystal had not been able to progress any further in her research of the portrait of a monk, but had discovered that the two paintings might hold a valuable secret. On the back of one of these, would be a vital clue. Earlier, having had a chance to view the painting in the viewing gallery, she had not been able to reach it so as to view the back. But now the painting appeared, on the screen, but also held by a porter on stage. Her phone camera ready, Crystal clicked and was pleased when at one point the porter turned the painting around to show the back, she clicked away some more shots.

Sitting back, she ignored the goings on in the auction room for a few moments, zooming the photo's she had taken. There were some labels, three in all, and some writing, but nothing stood out, nothing seemed of much importance. Refocusing on the auction, she noticed who bought the painting, taking some more photos, she put her phone away and thought about her next move. Perhaps, whatever clue there might be, would be on the other painting, still in the possession of Danielle Vitali. Deciding that she needed to think things through, Crystal got up and left the auction house and made her way back to the hotel she was staying at.

EPILOGUE

Saturday morning- 4th of June

Antwerpen

An hour after waking and having breakfast, Sam made his way to the museum.

On the third floor of the museum, situated on a back corner, was the boardroom. As boardrooms go, this one was not very big, a long table around which were placed eight chairs. A small counter on one wall housed cup, mugs, saucers and two thermos coffeepots. Beneath the counter was a small fridge. There was no technical equipment, no screen or projector. Three windows looked out over the city. To the left was a busy road where the tram, cars, vans and many bicycles were heading left and right. Beyond the road was a big square where the Saturday market was in full swing and beyond that the cathedral was clearly visible above other buildings. Despite it being a museum of art, the boardroom was devoid of any. The walls were a soft creamy colour, and the windows had roll down blinds. Two suspended lights hung from the ceiling over the long table.

The director and the director of the storage company had been present, but had now left, as had a woman who was introduced as the storage manager's assistant. That left four people still present. Detective Jan Schenk, Curator Emma Brood, Senior Insurance agent, Samantha Price and Art assessor Sam Price.

'Well, with the basic details having been dealt with, this leaves us here with two more items to discuss' The detective said, once the others had left the room, 'let me first of all say how happy we all are that you are safe and well Miss Price'

'Oh indeed' Emma said, her face slightly colouring, wearing the same outfit she had worn when making that discovery on the loading bay on Wednesday. With all that had occurred, most of it practically under her nose, she felt guilty not having seen that. Samantha noticed, heard it in her voice and said, 'Emma, this was a well organised plan, well, certainly it began that way, you are in no way to blame for any of it' smiling at her. She felt refreshed and vitalised, glad she had been able to spend several hours with Rico, before returning home.

Emma briefly smiled her thanks as the detective once more spoke, 'Together with Sam and which a lot of help from Sam's friend and my colleague Martijn in Rotterdam, and, also with the help, of your fiancé Rico,' he said, looking at Samantha, 'we have a fairly good idea now, having interrogated the kidnappers and two of the security team who were the inside help, as to what happened' taking a breath here, the detective then looked at Sam, and said' So, Sam, will you do the honours and sum up the events that led up to this point?'

'Thanks Jan, sure, okay, well let's return to the four days that the paintings here were being catalogued and placed into the containers. It was noted that twenty seven of these had arrived to transport the artwork, however, we discovered that thirty had indeed been made, we then discovered that two had never left the storage place where they had been built, so, in fact, and we believe that Crystal, with the help of the inside men here, brought in the twenty-eighth container. Then at some point, when you were most likely not present, during one of the nights, Crystal set to work, copied the labels from container number eleven, then moved the already loaded and catalogued one into that small room we discovered. Here she removed the two paintings and replaced the empty opaque plastic sheeting, with empty wooden frames, then she swapped the containers around again, bringing in the spare container. The idea, we learnt, was to, once the whole operation had been completed and the containers returned to the museum, to then surreptitiously wheel this container among the others to be returned to the storage facility, so that no-one would be the wiser and the plan was so that it would not even have been noticed that two paintings were missing'

Sam, gave a nod to the detective to resume,' Yes, but, and here credit goes to you miss Brood, because you changed the plan, initially it was going to be that the containers would return to the museum to be unloaded and checked, thus giving Crystal that chance to finish her plan, however, you felt it better to check the containers at the storage unit facility….'

'Yes, 'Emma said, suddenly realising that that had been a good thing to do, smiling now, she turned from one to the other as she spoke, 'I felt that something could have happened whilst in their care, I needed to make sure all was well, so yes, I did change the plan'

'This of course was not to the liking of Crystal,' Jan continued, 'and the discovery was made that two painting were missing, so now, she had a problem, how to cover her tracks how to make sure that no-one would figure out how it was done. Now, Miss Price, your discovery put the cat among the pigeons so to speak…'

'Yes, Samantha answered,' I began to get a sense of what had occurred when finding that container, but already action had been taken to take me away from reporting my find…'

It was Sam who again took up the story, 'We feel Crystal must have already been on her way, of course we do know now that the security man on duty, was one of the inside team, so, a plan was quickly made, they got to you and, well, you know what happened next…'

'I am so sorry Miss Price…' Emma began, again colouring slightly. 'Please, call me Sam, and again, it wasn't your fault…' Samantha answered, once again giving her a reassuring smile.

'I quite agree, this was all well planned, but when you came here to the museum, a new plan had to be put in place, they were desperate, though, from what we have learnt, it was never the plan to harm you Miss Price, just to delay the truth coming out…' detective Jan added.

'They did, however, shoot at me!' Sam said, 'I guess that was just their panic reaction'

'It took us by surprise too Sam, my men and I were ready, but when you came bolting out that door and this young guy was close behind and then got a shot off before we had time to react, that was such a shock, he panicked!'

'They shot at you?' both Samantha and Emma said in unison.

Sam smiled at the both, then said, 'he shot wildly, anyway, we now come to the final part of the story, Jan and his men soon had those two young guys under control and I was able to get to you Sam, funny, I still find it confusing how we are both known as Sam Price, anyhow, you were safe, the young men and the inside security men who were involved were quickly identified and arrested.'

'Confusing indeed' Jan Schenk, the detective said smiling, both of you with that same name, anyway, as Sam,' looking directly at him,' said, we arrested them all, got the whole story from them, leaving just a couple of questions left…'

'Where is Crystal' Emma said, her voice barely above a whisper.

'And where are the paintings? Samantha said.

'Oh, but we found the paintings' the detective said, smiling, because he and Sam had kept that bit of information from them to this point.

'You have?' Again, both Emma and Samantha speaking at once.

'We felt it best that the fewer people know, the better, its why we didn't tell your boss, Emma, or the boss of the storage facility, yes, we have found the paintings, they were in the building by the docks where they took you Sam, however, the mystery deepens, because although the paintings were there…' Sam said, smiled and looking at the detective with whom he had already formed a bond, giving him a nod.

'The frames were missing on both works of art, the paintings had been, certainly by the look of it, carefully, taken out of their frames.' Jan Schenk said, rounding up the story.

'So,' Emma began, thinking through what she had just heard, 'Crystal was only after the frames?'

'But then' Samantha said, also having thought it through, 'why did she have to steal the paintings? Surely, she would have had the time to do that when she created that subterfuge, take the frames off there and then?'

'My thoughts exactly' Emma added, 'It is most peculiar.'

'Thought about it too' Sam said, Jan and I feel that care was taken in taking the frames off, but I feel that maybe, Crystal wasn't exactly sure as to why these two paintings were important, perhaps she was hoping for a discovery of sorts, then realised, after receiving instructions, that it was the frames she needed, and so...'

'And so, also now knowing that we would be on her trail, she had to move quickly, still being careful in taking the frames off, she took these, when we did find that footage where Miss Kaplova changed vehicles, she had the frames, clearly seen on the film footage.'

'What on earth could be so important about those frames' Emma asked, though her voice was low, as she was just thinking aloud.

Just then a message came through on Sam's phone. 'Excuse me one second' he said, looking at the text that had come through.

'Okay,' Sam said, looking at each in turn, a further bit of interesting information, this is from Martijn, he thought the name Kaplova sounded familiar, it was, a certain Huzar Kaplova, who was seriously injured in a car crash back in 1963, chasing a woman called Natalie Umbrego, a case that we were working on recently, is the grandfather of Crystal Kaplova'.

'So, what now?' Samantha asked.

'I think it would be best if you and Miss Brood here, check the paintings, check for any damage....? But also, take a good look at the back of each, perhaps there is something there that might be relevant.'

'Yes,' Samantha answered,' good idea, though that will be down to you Emma, your expertise is in that field. I will have to relook at the insurance claim and how we can adjust that, and we also should look at those photographs again, see what the frames are like, maybe get an idea of their importance?'

'Right, yes,' Emma answered, 'where are they?' The paintings I mean.'

'Downstairs, the police brought them back this morning, whilst we were all in this meeting.'

'Also, I have just had a message from my boss' detective Jan said, looking up from his phone,' They are ruling out any involvement from your boss Emma, or from the storage facility management.'

Sam, looking across at his colleague then asked, 'This Crystal woman was surely not working alone, if your people have ruled these out, does that mean there are leads to who else might be involved?'

'Yes, we'll leave these ladies to it, we do have a possible lead…' Jan answered, getting up and nodding to the women.

Sam got up too, gave Samantha a tight hug and a kiss on the cheek, nodded to Emma and followed the detective out of the room.

Samantha smiled at Emma, thinking she was pleased that at least this part of the ordeal was over, time to now think as to why these frames might be of importance.

BOOK TWO

In the frame

PROLOGUE

Saturday morning- 4th of June

New York

'All's well that ends well' Tammy said, pouring out cups of tea for them both, 'don't you think?'

'Yes, true' Chrissie sleepily replied having not long ago woken and dressed in a light purple coloured dressing gown, sat on a stool by the kitchen counter. 'I am glad that Samantha is safe, you met her, didn't you?'

'I did,' Tammy replied, noticing that her friend, though obviously still half asleep, looked quite relieved having just over six hours ago been given the complete update on the proceedings in Antwerpen, with the phone on speaker, so that she too knew all that had happened.

'But it's not really the end, yet' Chrissie said, carefully sipping her mug of tea.

'Very true' Tammy replied, 'but with Samantha safe, and at least two criminals captured, that's good.'

'Yes, of course, I know, there is, well, I mean, it's just that I have a feeling, you know, I know Sam was very tired, but there was something, he was holding back, I'm sure'

'Well, he'll be home soon, so,' Tammy said, sipping her tea in between bites of her toast and jam, noticing the pensive look on her friend's face, 'would you like some toast?'

'Please, thanks, but what do we do now?' Chrissie asked, looking up at her friend.

'Well, to just go over the chain of events, that we know' Tammy began, 'two paintings were stolen, had it not been for a change of plan by the curator there, this Emma, it sure seems that the theft would have gone unnoticed for goodness knows how long'

'This Crystal woman had it planned to a great detail, the extra container, the copied references on the paperwork, yes, I agree,' Chrissie said, watching Tammy place two slices of bread into the toaster, 'had it all gone to her plan, then she would have been able to get the painting back into the museum in such a way as to hide the fact that two were missing'

'Right' Tammy said, turning her attention to the toast for a moment,' but then at the end, what we assumed, wasn't at all what the intention was'

'No indeed, and we were all focused on the actual paintings, with Terri looking into the Italian chap, Bartolo, who initially had them and brought them over to Philadelphia, Alison, and you and I, trying to find out more on these paintings, how they connected with Zecheriah, how they ended up back in Europe, and how they eventually came to be in the museum'

The toast popped up.

'I think the answer has to lie in the past' Tammy said, handing the toast and jam to Chrissie, 'there must be a reason why this Crystal woman wanted those particular paintings'

'Yes, I agree, and then only to be interested in the actual frames. We also know now that she was the granddaughter of one of the men who were chasing that Natalie Umbrego woman, back in the sixties, is that related to what is going on now?' Chrissie said, wondering as she spread jam onto her toast,' furthermore, we have to consider if those frames are the original ones, after all, over that period of times they could have easily been damaged or replaced….'

'True,' Tammy replied, 'that is why we really need to go back to the beginning, to when they were first painted, and find out what it was that drew the attention of Crystal, and, if it was really only the frames that she was after, why then steal the whole paintings? And where is she now?'

'Yes, good point, maybe she didn't realise that it was the frames that were important, I'm sure that she wasn't working alone, getting that extra container inside the museum, the security personnel involvement, then the urgency behind the kidnapping, no, I'm sure there was someone else behind it all, all that takes a lot of finance.' Chrissie said, then taking another bite of the roast. Then after a few chews, she continued, 'I believe that your hot friend, the guy from Interpol, Walther?'....Chrissie said teasingly, then followed on,' well, isn't he something to do with stolen art these days?'

'Shut up, yes, Walther is now involved...'Tammy said, giving her friend a look, then smiled and said, 'yes, we are in touch, good idea though, I'll send him message later...'

'And what about Rapheal?' Chrissie said, then taking another bite of her toast, smiling at her friend who would often tease her.

'Not sure, not right now, anyway,' Tammy answered, smiling at Chrissie knowing she was hoping for a response in teasing her, then, putting on a serious face, said, 'we must focus on what we need to focus on...' Tammy answered, though couldn't help but bring to mind the memory of being with Raphael Morton, the younger brother whose sister had been killed, who it was, who successfully proved, that she wasn't killed by the tornado, but by the young man, by Conrad Shelton, who, since that day, was shot and killed whilst in Rome...'

Shaking the memories away, Tammy finished her piece of toast, also took the last few sips of her tea.

'Well, I agree with what you said earlier, we must go back to the beginning, and see if we can't discover something' Chrissie said, then' I will shower and dress, then, how about we have a conference with Terri and Ally, decide how we can go about this?'

'Good thinking, I am sure that we will find the answer, in the past' Tammy replied.

THE PAST

Period 1: 1655

Off the Island of Socotra- Indian Ocean

Twenty minutes ago, Farah had wanted answers. Twenty minutes ago, the sea had been calm, the sky had been clear and as she had stood on the port side deck, she had been determined to confront him, to ask him what was going on, whose was that painting, by, she knew, an accomplished Flemish Master. Twenty minutes ago, was now a lifetime away.

She was gazing out over the sea, noticing the island in the distance. This was Socotra, ruled by the Portugues she was told, a trading route post was there. But they would bypass it, they had enough provisions now to reach their final destination of Bandar Abbas. Farah was both excited and nervous to be going home. She was determined to stay well away from her family, though having been gone for ten years, would some have passed on by now, and would anyone still recognise her? Nevertheless, she would move to a different part of the city, but she then reflected on her recent discovery. All was not as she thought it should be. The secret panel, the hidden painting, what was that all about…

Twenty minutes ago, she was close to confronting him, wanting answers.

Then there had been shouting, then there had been panic. A ship, a small ship, had suddenly appeared, seemingly out of nowhere. A two masted schooner, which was not much smaller than the vessel she was on, also a two-master. Farah turned to see what several of the men who had appeared, were pointing at. The schooner was fast, approaching rapidly. She then noticed the men, five of them, on the prow of the approaching vessel. They looked menacing, they were armed with knives and swords. A man shoved her aside, told her to get down below.

She did as was told, then heard more shouting, followed by a shot. Farah knew that there were some weapons on board, for just such an occasion. She reached her cabin as two more shots rang out. She felt the ship turn, and though the sea was calm, the ship rocked a little. She looked around the small cabin, wondered how much room there was behind the panel. More shouting, another gunshot. She heard footsteps, heard running on the deck above. The ship suddenly turned to port, a sharp turn, the ship was keeling, and Farah lost her balance, felt against the panelled wall.

She heard the click, it was a sign, she thought to herself, quickly regaining her balance, she turned, pulled one of the panels towards her, peered in beyond where the painting was and figured there to be enough room, however, the painting had to come out. Farah moved quickly, there was an eerie silence now, no more shouting, no more running footsteps. All became very quiet, and the ship was on an even keel. She pulled the painting free, stood up and placed it on the other side of the cabin, tucked it a little behind a small cupboard, then swiftly went back to the cavity in the wall and squeezed inside. Fortunately, she was of very small stature, unlike her daughter who would one day be tall, turned herself around, grabbed the panel and managed to pull it towards her. A small screw sticking out was just right to get a grip on, she pulled the panel towards her and heard the click. It was shut.

Voices, close by. Footsteps. She heard someone rummaging around the cabin. Farah closed her eyes and thought about her daughter who she had left behind. She had been smitten by her new man friend, had been so casually ready to leave everything behind to be with him. Too casually, too quickly, she was now thinking, in the darkness of the hiding place behind the panel, only the faintest strip of light penetrating through.

She could feel the ship was moving faster. Hardly daring to breathe, Farah sat as still as she could. Pirates, there was no doubt in her mind, seeing the ship approaching, seeing those men, armed to the teeth, even from a distance, she had seen their evil and their determination. Farah tried to calculate in her mind, how many crew there were on the ship she was sailing home in. Of course, her man, Babak, though she began to think that it would not be wise to pursue that relationship, providing of course, that he should still be alive, and the others? Eighteen to twenty? She had been told stories of pirates, looting and killing, and confiscating the ships.

It had been quiet for some time now. Dare she take a look, dare she come out of her hiding place? A little longer, she decided, she would stay a little longer.

Finally, having heard no sounds for some time, Farah pushed the panel open, crawled out from her hiding place and stood up, stretching the stiffness from her body. She was surprised to see that the painting she had stuck half behind a small cupboard, was still there. Puzzled as to why it hadn't been taken, she carefully opened the door of the cabin, then ever so slowly and softly, made her way along a passage, easily compensation for the gentle roll of the ship. Another door, then some worn wooden steps and she was on deck, an aft deck.

It was then that a sound came to her ears. A moaning, almost whimpering sound. Turning towards it and still ever so carefully walking along the deck, she then saw. A man, one of the crew, she recognised him. He was wounded, badly wounded. Farah quickened her steps, reached him, bent down and saw a gash on his side. The man had tried to stem the blood, but, she calculated, he must have passed out at some point, probably just as well as the pirates would have thought that he was dead and just left him.

Farah knelt down, then, again standing up and looking around, she saw the ship that the pirates had arrived in, quite some distance away now. Again, kneeling down, Farah set to work, tearing a shirt the man was wearing apart, she covered the gash, which had coagulated and no longer bleeding, so that was good. At least she hoped so. She tied the strip of shirt as tight as she could, then moved the man to a half sitting position. Leaving him, Farah walked further along the deck, then, having seen no-one else, she re-entered the ship, walking quickly now, she searched, opened cabins, opened doors, checking everywhere. She then, having found nobody inside, headed for the aft cargo deck.

Just then, before walking over to peer down into the hold, she saw another body. She recognised him also, a young boy, working in the kitchen. She reached him, turned him over and saw that he too was still alive. He didn't seem to be wounded in any way, though had a large contusion on the side of his head. Something had struck him, the lad had no doubt been knocked unconscious. He began to moan. A good sign, also sitting him upright, she took hold of his face, spoke to him. Then stood up and headed for the cargo hold. Being braver than she thought she could ever be, she descended a ladder and could see, that the cargo, she recalled having seen many boxes being placed there, were gone. It was mainly a shipment of lace, she had been told. She also saw two bodies. Sadly, both were dead.

Climbing the old rungs back to the top, she saw the boy still sitting there, eyes open and in shock. With a hand gesture, Farah told him to stay put, then, nearly losing her balance as the ship rocked in and out of a large trough, she again reached the first man. He was awake. Farah, for the first time, looked around at the state of the ship, she did know a little about ship, she saw that the mainsail was down, saw that it was slashed in several places. The forward sail, very much smaller, was flapping about, but seemed to be mostly intact. She also saw that the ship was, as far as she could tell, set on a straight course, perhaps the rudder having been set or damaged in that position. Farah focused on the man by her side, spoke to him rapidly, in her own language. He seemed to understand, with her help got to his feet and made his way to the wheelhouse. Farah went back to the other man, again, realising that he was no more than a boy, he too was now upright and was walking, more hobbling really, towards the forward mast.

Farah looked over the side, the sea was empty, the marauders, the pirates, were now nowhere to be seen, the island she had spotted when first noticing the oncoming pirates, was not in sight. Two men alive, two dead bodies in the hold, the rest most likely in the sea.

She hoped at least one of the survivors might be able to navigate. Following the boy, that was now attempting to tighten the forward sail, she approached and asked what it was she could do. He turned at looked at her, his eyes were large, still in shock, and there was a bloody patch on the left side of his shirt.

Farah knew she would just have to take charge. Strangely she felt confident and felt strongly that she had to now be strong and lead these two survivors, in the hope that they, somehow, would reach land. One thing was for sure, it was getting darker now, and at all costs, she must make sure she stayed awake.

THE PRESENT

Saturday morning-4th of June

San Francisco

She was awake, it was light, feeling very comfortable under the sheets, she thought about staying in bed a little longer.

Chantal Brewer had stayed the night, upon the insistence of Alison. The previous evening, after having earlier poured her heart out to Alison, she had been reading part of the journals written by Henry Hopkins, where, she was told, there was a part written down, where Henry had met her ancestor, Caprice. She found it, it had been in a place called Buenaventura, in Colombia…

It was in the year 1814. In a tavern near the waterfront, Henry Hopkins slowly sipped the lukewarm beer as daylight began to fade. It had been another hot day. The tavern was only half full. The situation in Colombia had been tense for some time, with Creole fighting Creole. The Spanish were on the back foot and there was talk about Simon Bolivar and his army gaining much ground in the region.

He and his team of four men had located stables on the edge of town and had stalled their horses and three wagons there. It had been early afternoon when Henry headed into the city leaving the men to rest up and guard their horses and equipment. It was the following day when she arrived.

'I didn't see her at first as I was attending to my own horse, but I heard the men whisper to each other' Henry wrote in his journal, 'Coming out to see, there she was, a rather attractive woman, judging by the condition of her clothes and the weariness of the horses, she had

been travelling a while. I put her at ease, told the men to get on with their work and took a moment to admire her horses. One was a beauty. I could see the quality of the breed. The stable master was not there at that time, so I offered to be of assistance. She spoke to me, told me she had travelled far and had no need any more for the horses, as she was about to travel by sea from here to Mexico she said. I walked around the horse, the one that was of good breeding, noticed the shotgun tucked in a special sheath attached to the saddle. It was very similar to my own, and when she asked if I was interested in buying the horse, I asked her about the shotgun, thinking an extra weapon might come in handy as my men and I still had a fair journey to undertake.

'And this shotgun?' I asked her.

'That too I will no longer need' she replied.

I spoke with her for some time, as I was calculating how much I should offer for the horses and the gun. She opened up to me, started telling her story, I had the feeling she was relieved to be able to speak to someone, and though I was a stranger, there was a trust I could see. Her name was Caprice, said she had fled from a bad situation at home, back in Bogota. This alone increased my respect for her, to have travelled that far, over three hundred miles I calculated, alone, and being a woman. She told me she was set to travel by ship, to Acapulco, the voyage having already been arranged by her man, who had gone ahead. She told me they would meet up there.

It was then that it came to me, the events of the previous day which I had partly heard about and partly observed. The sleek schooner, with the name 'Flecha' meaning arrow, was well away from the men who were pursuing it. I had heard about the theft of gold from Bogota, very likely this was her man and friends, but I said nothing, that wasn't my business. I found her to be a very likeable young woman, certainly very able and I made a deal with her. The second horse I would give to the stable master, but her own horse, I kept for myself, and the shotgun of course. I insisted I help her get to town and make sure she was well looked after until the arranged ship would take her, which, was in a few days' time. She thanked me for my helpfulness, and I wished her all the very best. The shotgun I purchased that day from the lovely Caprice, would indeed come handy a few years later, but I shall record the events surrounding that later.'

'Morning' Alison said, as Chantal walked into the kitchen, 'did you sleep well?'

'Thank you, yes, eventually, got very much drawn into this journal you gave me to read, I would like to read them all, what a fascinating man this Henry Hopkins was'

'Did you find the bit that Millie mentioned to me, the bit where he actually met your ancestor?'

'I did, unbelievable, what are the chances of that?'

'Indeed, I also found something interesting, as I said to you, our friend Tammy asked us for help, for Terri, my daughter, to investigate the provenance of those two Flemish Paintings, and I was to try and find out about this Spanish chap, Bartolo Acosta, well, what I discovered, was that, although he had those paintings that are at the centre of this theft, they were not framed!'

'Not framed…' Chantal asked, for a moment puzzled as to the significance, then, suddenly recalled, 'Ah, yes, this thief, this Crystal woman, she left the paintings behind and took the frames, so…'

'So, indeed, we must now look as to where new frames were put on, and by whom?

'Do you think that this guy at the port, this Zecheriah chap, put new frames on them, after all, didn't have them in his possession for, like, thirty years?'

'True,' Alison said, 'thinking it through, it is a possibility, I will chat with Tammy later, see what she thinks…' her phone rang, 'Great! That's Tammy, 'Hi, we were just talking about you…'

Ally listened for a while, nodded a few times, then said, 'wow, that's great news, but I have also discovered something, that is that this Italian guy, Bartolo, sold the paintings he had, well, at least the two by Flemish Masters, to Zecheriah, unframed!'

Tammy in New York, with Chrissie listening in, having just informed Ally of all that they knew and that Samantha was safe and that the paintings were recovered, though the frames were still missing, said, looking at Chrissie beside her, 'That's very interesting

Ally, so,' beginning to think out aloud, 'it can't have been the original frames that this Crystal woman was after, it had to have been...'

'Exactly' Alison in San Francisco interrupted, 'frames that were put on much later, possible by Zecheriah when he purchased them...'

'You're right, or even well after that, by that German bloke who bought them...' Tammy said.

After a pause, Ally spoke again,' I'm glad that Samantha woman is safe, is Sam flying back now?'

It was Chrissie who answered, 'Hi Ally, good sleuthing girl, yes, Sam will be on his way back here soon, the police are hunting for this Crystal woman, is Terri with you?'

'No, I'm here with Chantal, you remember I met her in Albuquerque,' Ally replied, smiling at her guest.

'Yes, I remember, you told me about her, and her connection to the gold, but could you ask Terri to keep researching the paintings? Both Tammy and I believe the answer lies in the past, anything we can find out about them could be helpful', then, thinking about the discovery about the frames, added, 'though it is very interesting, that this Bartolo chap sold them un framed, it might still be useful to look into the full history of these paintings, don't you think?' Chrissie asked.

'Of course, I'll give her the update, and I agree Chrissie, the more information we can gather the better, she's at work in the museum already, down in the archive room, it's supposed to be her day off, so she's down there without being interrupted'

'Give her my love Ally' Tammy said over the speaker phone, 'and we'll talk again soon' Chrissie added.

Whilst at the museum in Antwerpen

It was just past mid-day, and Emma Brood had been sifting through papers since several hours earlier, determined to help find any clues as to why the two stolen, though now retrieved paintings, had been selected. Taking a sip of tea, Emma stopped for a moment, holding in her hand, stapled together, three sheets of paper. She recalled this very event that she was looking at. This was when she went to the auction at the Paris fine Art Auction House. In her recent conversations with the curator at the museum in Rotterdam, who was friends with both the Dutch policeman and with Sam Price, the man who had flown across from Boston to search for their missing friend, Samantha, they had introduced themselves. But it wasn't until this very moment, that Emma understood why it had been that her name rang a bell. Reading the sheets in her hand she remembered, she had gone to the auction, with the express aim to obtain any paintings that might come up that were by Flemish Masters. For some years now, Emma felt the museum needed more works by local artists, and when she had seen the auction lot manifesto, listing a work by Jacob Leyssen, she made arrangements to go there. Emma looked at the date. 19th January, the year 2015.

About to take another sip- of tea, Emma stopped, placed the cup back onto its saucer, put the sheets down and reached for her phone.

'I thought your name rang a bell!' Emma said, when the call was answered.

'Emma?' Sophie replied, but before being able to formulate a reply, Emma continued speaking.

'January 2015, I was at the auction, in Paris, you were the manager there….'

'Goodness, yes, wait, did you say January?'

'Yes, January 19th, I purchased the Jacob Leyssen then, the Roman scene…'

Sophie was quiet for a moment, thinking back, then said,' Goodness, I do remember that day, for a particular reason, I'll tell you about that, but first, I don't have those records to hand now, though I can access them, perhaps you have the details of who sold it?'

Emma looked through her sheets, then answered, 'Yes, I made a note here, to myself, to follow up and obtain further provenance, the seller was a Miss D. Vitali, from Trieste, Italy.'

In Rotterdam Sophie was frantically searching the recesses of her mind. She recalled the auction day, forever she would remember that day, but she also knew the name that Emma just told her, Miss Vitali, from Trieste, the fact that Trieste was mentioned jogged her memory.

'Sorry Emma,' Sophie said, 'Lot's going on in my brain right now, let me, well, let me talk this through with you, its most uncanny, truly...'

'Sounds intriguing Sophie...' Emma said, thankful of this new friend who had been so supportive these past days, puzzled as to what all this might be about.

'You were there, at that auction,' Sophie began, but then said, 'No, hold on, Emma, let me call you back okay, I must research a couple of things, shouldn't be long, is that okay?'

Forty minutes later, Sophie rang Emma.

'Sorry, I had to track down my former boss, at the auction house, get his approval, but, now then, are you ready to hear what I have found out?'

'You sound positively, well, how can I say, upbeat?'

'Yes, yes, that describes it well, okay, well, listen to this, first of all, I have here the list of attendees at that auction, on that day in January, you are there, of course, as was the seller, Miss Danielle Vitali, get this though, who else was there that day, none other than Miss Crystal Kaplova!'

'No way' Emma blurted out,' for real? Did she buy anything?'

'No, she registered and listed her address in Istanbul. But did not purchase anything, but it sure must be a connection for her to be there when the Jacob Leyssen was up for auction.'

'I agree, you must be right, why else would she have been there? Now, let me see, yes, here, I have her application for her job here, she has been here for three years now, and oh yes, I see, she listed her previous address as being in Istanbul, my my, do you think she has been on the trail of this painting and the one by Rubens all this time ?'

'Considering the lengths she has gone through, including kidnapping Samantha, I think she must have...' Sophie answered, then asked, 'The one by Rubens, the battle on the coast, where and when did the museum acquire that?'

'Well, though it is signed as a Rubens, in fact this one is by Arnold Frans Rubens, not the much more famous Peter Paul Rubens, still a valuable piece, we acquired that at an auction in Cologne, let me see, yes, the same year actually, a couple of months later, late March.'

'Did you purchase it? Who sold it? It is a trail we should follow, don't you think?'

'Yes, I agree, since this theft happened, I have been searching for any reason that I can find as to why these two paintings might be of such interest, I shall find out who sold the one in Cologne, should have looked into that sooner...'

'No, Emma, with all that was going on, that was not the priority, also, I have friends in the States who are looking into the provenance of both painting, as you know, one thing they have discovered, only just picked this up myself, but the Italian guy, Bartolo Acosta, he had both paintings, but he took the frames off before taking them over to Philadelphia...probably for ease of shipping, but he definitely sold them to this Zecheriah chap unframed.'

'I see' Emma said, pondering this for a moment, again thinking how happy that she felt such a support from Sophie whom she had now only known for a few days, 'yes, that makes it even more important to trace the beginnings, why was Crystal only interested in the frames...'

'Exactly, listen, one more thing I would like to share with you Emma, and then, if you trace the Rubens, I will follow up on Miss Vitali, how does that sound?'

'Agreed, sounds good to me, so...'

'Someone else was at that very auction in Paris, the day you were there, and that was Sam, Sam Price, right now is not the time, but later I will tell you all about that, so, good hunting and keep in touch and I will do the same.'

Emma put her phone down, gulped the last of her tea down and got up from behind her desk. Though many things were now bouncing around inside her head, she pulled herself together, inwardly saying to herself, to concentrate. Who had purchased the Rubens in Cologne for the museum, and, more importantly, who had sold it?'

Writing down the details from her telephone conversation, she then set about to delve through the files, searching for purchases the museum made in the year 2015. Less than half an hour later, she had the answer. Sitting back, she was pleased with what she had found, but how would it help, she wondered, still baffled about the whole thing.

THE PAST

Period 2: 1763

Philadelphia

Bartolo Acosta was pleased with the result. He too, as had many before him, been very impressed with the Trading Post at the port. Also, he had admiration for the man, Zecheriah, who ran this little empire. He had spent well but had also sold well. Smiling to himself as he climbed aboard the wagon, nodding to the driver who was set to take him to a place almost eight miles out of town. Bartolo glanced into the back of the wagon, pleased with his goods that he had brought with him from Belgium.

The driver set the two horses in motion, and they left the shipyard, spitting out a wad of chewed tobacco, the man, quite elderly Bartolo estimated, focused ahead and said very little, which was fine with Bartolo as he reflected on these past weeks. Smiling again to himself, he thought back to when he began his run. His escape. Escape from the clutches of three brothers who were set on causing him considerable harm.

At just shy of five foot ten, he was slim in built, had very dark curly hair, deep brown eyes and a smooth and very tanned skin. Clean shaven, he was always dressed well and knew that he attracted looks from the ladies. Something he was not only pleased about but often took advantage of. Such had been the case with the French woman, Catherine.

Bartolo was born in Zaragosa, Spain, but in his early teens had set off from the family home and worked and talked his way through the journey of life, spending several years in Toulouse where he learned the trade of a cobbler. He was almost two decades old when he boarded a coastal ship from Bordeaux to Rouen, from there travelling on foot to Paris, a journey he completed in four days. Paris was good for him, for several years, with the knowledge he had easily securing a good job with a small workshop specialising in the making of women's shoes. It was then when he discovered that he was a source of interest to the ladies. Six years later he succumbed to the attention of a beautiful woman. She was as tall as he, with very long hair that reached to her lower back, had a natural wave in it and was a soft red in colour. Her eyes were a vibrant green and there was no getting away from it. She was attracted to him, but he also to her.

What he realised, too late, was that she was already betrothed. Catherine. It wasn't her husband who found out, but one of his brothers, who then summoned two of his siblings and made plans to deal with the Spanish problem, as he was referred to. Fortunately for Bartolo, Catherine picked up on this and warned him. This set him on the run and heading north he first arrived in Lille, then went on into Belgium where he decided he wanted to seek his fortune in the Americas. He needed funds.

Once again using his charm and wit, he found work with a wealthy family, now as a tutor for their three children. Living in the big house he began to plan.

A big bump in the dirt road shook the wagon and shook Bartolo out of his reverie. Turning he smiled at the old driver, who just gave him a look and spat some more chewed tobacco away.

Returning to his reminiscing and again turning to take another look into the back of the wagon, Bartolo smiled again and felt good. Not only had he outrun those three brothers, more importantly, he had outsmarted Monsieur Lavette.

He had planned it all very carefully, had booked his passage on a ship called De Waal, and had gathered his belongings, had reached a small wooden building on the dockside, the very place, where more than two hundred and sixty years later, Samantha Price would be held captive, though be it in an entirely different building.

There he sorted out his goods, there he decided that keeping the frames was too bulky. He kept the oil painting of the man beside the horse intact. He recognised the work and was quite sure that this might be a work by Titian, the other two were landscape paintings, both with a chunky frame that in both cases had already been slightly damaged, these he carefully took off. Bartolo then placed a faded wall tapestry that he had acquired, on the floor, placed the paintings, the first one face down, the second one face up, this he then covered with part of a woollen blanket. He then placed the portrait painting on top and with the rest of the blanket, he wrapped everything together, finally securing it tightly with string. Satisfied, he placed it with his other goods, ready to be shipped. The merchant vessel 'De Waal' would set sail that evening, bound for Philadelphia.

The sky was getting darker as Bartolo on board the wagon, next to the old man who said very little, was nearing his destination. He was well pleased, having sold his goods, recalling the pleasant and shrewd operator, Zecheriah Strauss, who admired the paintings he had brought, particularly the two by who he knew, were by Flemish Masters.

At the port, Zecheriah prepared to close up shop for the day, it had been a good day and there would be no more arrivals until midmorning the following day. He looked again at the paintings he had purchased. Though both were frameless, he took a fancy to them, would obtain some new frames and would then keep them in his house at least for a while, he thought to himself, having been satisfied with his deals with the Spanish man.

At closing time, Zecheriah gathered the two paintings and took them home, deciding he would have a good look around one of the rooms where he kept various odds and ends and possibly find some material there to construct some frames. The paintings would look nice in the narrow hallway of his house. Thirty years would pass before he would sell them on. Going through a door at the back of the trading post, he crossed a small courtyard and entered the building which he had made into his home.

THE PRESENT

Saturday 4ᵗʰ of June

New York

'Are you coming home?' Chrissie asked, answering the call that came in from Sam.

'Yes, do you want me to come to New York, or….'

'Yes, come over, Tammy would love to see you…'

'Just Tammy?' Sam asked, teasingly, then continued, 'Sophie and the curator from Antwerpen are working together to find out more on the history of the two paintings, Martijn has got quite a workload on which he is getting back to and the police in Belgium are following up on leads to trace the Kaplova woman.'

'Yes, cheeky, I would love to see you too, now, Tammy and I are still delving through reems of research, Terry and Alison are also working on it, and, just heard from Ally, her new friend, Chantal, she is a descendant from the folk who buried the gold, well, she is helping out too, so, any further clues come to light?'

'No, not on this end, hope you or the team in San Francisco will have better luck'

'When will you get here?' Chrissie asked, suddenly wanting to hold him tight.

'I'll get a flight tomorrow morning, will be there in the afternoon, give Tammy my love, couple of things to follow up on here, so, love you, see you tomorrow'

'Love you too,'

Meanwhile in Dordrecht in the Netherlands

It was late afternoon and around fourteen miles to the southeast of Rotterdam. The river Maas flowed slowly to the sea. Several barges were either heading to the port in Rotterdam or travelling inland towards Nijmegen. On a small carpark adjacent the river stood a white van.

Inside the vehicle, Crystal Kaplova was close to death. She couldn't move. Arms, legs, fingers, toes. No movement. She was briefly slightly amused when she realised that she could blink. She could see, she could hear, but could not speak, could not utter a cry, could not call for help. She lay stretched out in the back of the van. Her breathing was shallow, and she knew, just knew, that she was moments from dying.

She thought back to that day, the day, having been up most of the night to look after her ailing grandfather, when not having gone to school, she watched the woman fetch goods from the lock up garage. She remembers the sharp intake of breath when she had come out with that portrait of a monk. She knew about this story, from her grandfather. That day had been the beginning of a journey.

Now, all these years later, having been so proud of herself to have followed the trail and to have come across the vital bits of information that would lead to a fortune, she realised, she had trusted the wrong people. True, she thought to herself, finding it strange that although she was dying, her thought pattern seemed to be working fine, she didn't feel any panic, true she had needed them, had needed someone with the finances to put her plan in operation. She had found them, had convincingly provided the evidence needed to obtain that assistance.

Crystal blinked a few times, there was no noise anymore, no sound of traffic, no sound coming from the river that she knew was only yards away. Again, she wondered about her state of mind. Was she angry, was she scared? All those years of following clues and leads, many of them dead ends, but she knew she was finally on the right track and then successfully applied for and secured a job at the museum. Yes, she now realised, trying to focus, her hearing was gone, her eyes were now seemingly clouding over, she had been fixated on the roof of the van, seeing the faint reflections that came through from the vehicle's front windows. Shapes and shadows dancing like twinkling stars. Early on, she had figured out that this was the water from the river, casting these reflections. But now, how much later? She had lost track of time, was it only minutes ago, or hours?

Okay, this is it. Darkness came. Her sight was gone. Closing her eyes, she felt, at last, like crying. But couldn't. She had miscalculated, had not only taken into account the possible change to how the paintings were to be re-instated into the museum, but, far more serious, she had totally miscalculated the people who had financed her, who had provided assistance, supplied manpower. She had made a mistake in abducting the insurance lady. All these years, and what for? She had never married, never had children, never been in love? One thing that brought her, briefly, a sense of pleasure, the treasure was still out there, and the last thing she recalled, was, from the moment she began to understand that she was in trouble, she had taken something that belonged to them. Did she still have it? Had they discovered it?

She didn't know. She would never know.

Crystal Kaplova died.

THE PAST

Period 3: 1816

Cologne - Germany

Seventy-one-year-old Rudolph Meyer wrote. He didn't want to die, not just yet. He had a lot to write. Head close to the paper, as his eyes, already very poor from an early age, were failing. When he had so enthusiastically set out on his treasure hunt, when he so confidently felt that this would change his life, that he would be someone, mean something, he had not considered that he might fail.

Whilst his mind was still very sharp, his whole body was ailing. His gangly frame was weakening by the day. Looking over to where a small table stood against a wall in the adjoining room, seeing the treasures he had thus far accumulated, Rudolph brought to mind that day when he had arrived in Philadelphia. Having there, in that vast trading post, discovered the painting of the monk. Then, in hearing the story behind it from the proprietor, further discovered that it was not at all the painting he had been searching for, but nevertheless part of the triptych which he had been on the trail of for several years now.

Rudolph got his head down and wrote a few more notes, then looking up, thought about this fellow, this Zecheriah Strauss, a very astute businessman, with a good knowledge to boot, and the two paintings he brought from his home next to the trading post. Telling the story of how and when he had acquired these from an Italian some thirty years earlier. Closing his eyes Rudolph recollected the memory, though having been very satisfied indeed to have been able to purchase part to the triptych relating to the three monks, he recalled thinking these works by Flemish masters, would be a good investment. Smiling to himself, then re-adjusting himself on the chair as his body was beginning to ache again, he was pleased he had bought them. Although the finances he had were quite sufficient at the time, when, some years later, he sold those two paintings, the profit was very pleasing indeed. Head down once more, Rudolph continued to write.

Less than a hundred yards from where he sat hunched writing in detail all that he wanted to impart on anyone who might come after him, discover his notes and perhaps take up the treasure hunt that he had begun all those years ago, Sofia Camille Argent sat on the bank of the river Rhine.

The mighty river meandered through the city and as she sat there, Sofia was in a contemplative mood. For it reminded her that some thirteen years ago, she had sat on the bank of a river. Though some distance away, for it was the river Seine, in Paris. Then she was tearfully going through the memory of a voyage from South America, during which she had first lost a valuable item that her father had gifted her, and then, there had been that attack. By pirates. It had been her who had first spotted them, and though the captain was wily and quick, they had not been able to escape unscathed. Only one person had died. Her husband, Rene.

Sofia looked to her left. The young boy, well, not so young anymore, almost fifteen, was at the water's edge, sitting quietly and looked at all the activity on the river, the many barges and small boats. Several fishermen also were at various points along the river on both sides. Sofia smiled, young Christopher Junior had always been a very placid and quiet boy. She recalled the time the pirates had attacked, how a crewman had placed them in a safe place on board the ship, tucked away in a sort of secret space, with just a lantern. Her son had been so quiet, perhaps knowing the need to be still.

Sofia had never remarried. Since arriving in Paris, finally, after having first reached northern Spain, where it was that her husband had been buried in a cemetery mainly used for seafarers. She had focused on bringing up her son. Rene's mother had been very helpful and had a big part of his younger years. But here she was, in the city of Cologne. The reason was twofold.

Six months ago, within days of each other, Sofia had learned that her father, who had remained in Caracas, Venezuela, had passed away. Then, two days after hearing that news, her mother-in-law also died. Along with all the papers and the letter that told of her father's passing, there was a request and two small pieces of gold in the shape of a religious icon. An address was listed in Cologne where she would go and sell these. The second reason came only a few weeks ago. A surprise letter, from a lady, Kristina Solstrom. Sofia gasped when she read as to who she was. Her father's sister, writing from Copenhagen. It was to ask about her brother and was it possible to meet.

Sofia wrote back, explaining that Christopher had died in Caracas, she also wrote that she was going to Cologne and perhaps they could meet there?

Sofia called her son over, saying it was time to get to the auction house, a family run business with already a good reputation that had been in business for less than three years. Thirty years later another family would take the reins and establish it into a worldwide renowned auction house.

Sofia, her son quietly walking beside her, already a head taller, was in two minds. Was she nervous about how well the auction would go, selling the pieces that her father had sent over? Or was she more nervous about meeting her aunty, her father's sister Kristina. What would she say, her father had rarely spoken to her about his family. About his parents and brothers and sister that he had left behind when he was just seventeen. And although he had travelled virtually all over the world, she knew her father had never returned home to Copenhagen.

She was glad that she had a good command of the English language, for she could not speak Danish, and Kristina had written to her in English, opening the letter with a statement that she knew no French and hoped that the English language might be possible for them to converse. Sofia had replied in the same way and had passed on the time and place where they might meet.

Back in the Meyer residence, the gangly Rudolph made himself get up from the chair and just walk about a bit. He was almost finished with the copious notes he was carefully penning, all in relationship to the mystery of the three monks. Getting himself a drink of water from the small kitchen area, he, as he was passing the front door of his house to head back to where he had been so busy writing, suddenly thought about the woman who had knocked on his door. Rudolph stopped, arched his painful back a little to ease the stiffness and thought back.

How long ago had that been? Five, six years ago now? What was the woman's name…

…surprised as to who it might be knocking on his door, Rudolph was even more surprised to see a woman standing there.

In broken German the woman spoke 'Are you Mr. Rudolph Meyer?'….

No, it was longer ago Rudolph remembered as he made his way back to his desk. It had been in the year 1808, eight years ago, and it had been the day after he had sold the two paintings he had purchased in Philadelphia from that port emporium, from the little man, Zecheriah, from whom he also bought the painting of the monk. Yes, it was all coming back to him. Her name, what was her name? Oh yes, Monique, a fine-looking woman, Monique Lavette. She had been given his address from the auction house, for the paintings he had sold, the two Flemish Masters, had once belonged to her family.

Sitting down, Rudolph recalled that she had been told of the two paintings and wanted to know, because they had, over forty-five years ago, been stolen from her father's house by a man who had been tutoring her and her siblings. Rudolph smiled as he thought back, telling her the story of how he acquired them and that he had no knowledge of the man she called Bartolo Acosta. Briefly wondering what had made him think of that, he then picked up the pen and bending close to the paper, continued writing.

Not far away, at the old auction house, Sofia Argent met Kristina Solstrom.

The women looked at each other, realised that they each were looking for the other and both smiled and came together. They hugged. Neither of them had said anything as yet. It was Kristina who broke the silence. 'The auction is still over thirty minutes away, perhaps we could go across the street here, there is a small park, and talk?' Looking over to where she meant. Sofia agreed, it would be quite noisy inside the auction hall. Speaking quickly and rapidly in French she asked her son to stay at the auction house.

The ladies sat down on an old wooden bench. Sofia this time, started the conversation,' My father never said, why he didn't ever go home, I could see it made him a little sad?'

Kristina nodded in silence, then said,' Christopher was the youngest, I have two older brothers, very close in age, but very, competitive. Our family is a strong family, an old family, also, a very influential family, and quite wealthy. Christopher was always a quiet boy. A dreamer, but smart too. One day, when my two older brothers were again arguing, my father came from his study, and, I was close by that day, he told them, that he would disown them and give everything to Christopher. I am a girl, we don't get anything, but my brothers were shocked, really thought that this was going to happen. Christopher, well, he was, about twelve I think, my brothers began to tease him, play tricks on him, they, well I'm sorry Sofia, but they were often mean to him. Christopher was often away from the house, spent much time at the docks, at the harbour. He must have told our father about the treatment he was getting from his brothers. They stopped being mean but kept their distance. One day I was told that Christopher was going to the university in Leiden, in Holland, to study being an officer on board a ship. He said goodbye to me, then he was gone, I think he was about seventeen. I was nineteen, much involved in my own life, I think I was also not very nice to him at times. Anyway, he left, we never saw him again, and I don't think he ever wrote a letter home….' Kristina's voice trailed off and she fell silent.

Sofia took hold of her hand, said nothing and they both sat there for some time, each with their own thoughts.

Finally, in a soft voice, Sofia said,' So, that is why he never went home'

Two hours later the auction was over. Sofia had sold her items well and Kristina bought a painting. Battle on the coast, by Rubens. She liked the scene, the ships reminded her of her brother, of Christopher. She also had a little history on it, the painting, a work by Arnold Frans Rubens, was painted in about 1706. A wealthy citizen of Antwerpen, Monsieur Lavette acquired it in 1750, there it hung on the wall in the main lounge of the big manor house on the outskirts of the city, alongside another work by a Flemish artist, namely Jacob Leyssen and depicting a scene from Rome. A Spanish rogue, Bartolo Acosta, stole both paintings in 1763, removed the frames and sailed away to Philadelphia. This was later discovered by Monsieur Lavette.

More information came to light, when in the year 1806, Rudolph Meyer sold the painting through the Cologne auction house, along with another work by the Flemish artist Jacob Leyssen, both having been acquired in the American port of Philadelphia, at the trading post there which was run by a Zecheriah Strauss who had purchased both paintings over thirty years earlier.

Kristina found the history quite fascinating, the one she had now purchased, had been sold then, but had re-appeared now and she was pleased to have bought it.

Later that day, she said goodbye to Sofia and her son and would the following day travel back to Copenhagen. It would, eighty-three years later, in the year 1899, again be placed in an auction and purchased by the ambassador, Samuel Price.

Pleased with having met Kristina and understanding the reason why her father had never returned home, and also with the results of the sale of the items that her father had sent to her, Sofia and her son went back home to Paris.

THE PRESENT

Saturday 4th June

Rotterdam

'Martijn?' Sophie, the Parisian slowly adjusting to life in Rotterdam, asked as he entered the apartment.

'Qui mon cherie' he answered, smiling at his attempt to speak French, which wasn't his strong suit, he often lost track of what Sophie was saying if she burst out in her own language and rambled on so fast.

She appeared in the hallway, walked up to him, kissed him, said' look at you, I'll make a Frenchman out of you yet!'

'No way, so, what's new?'

'Well, you went and saw that Italian woman, Danielle Vitali, in Trieste, when we were looking into the mystery of the three monks, she was the one who cracked much of the case, I seem to recall also, that you thought she was rather attractive?'

'Yes, well, and…' Martijn answered, as they both entered the lounge, not sure where this conversation was going.

'I would like you to visit her again, please' Sophie said, seeing the perplexed look on his face, she continued, 'She had at least one, possibly both of the paintings that are at the centre of the theft in Antwerpen'

'Okay, well, tell me more, but first, let me fill you in on a development' Martijn said, entering the kitchen. 'They found the Crystal woman'

'That doesn't sound to good, the way you said that.' Sophie said, looking at him, studying his face.

'No, you're right, she's dead'

'Goodness, how?'

'Not conclusive yet, they found the van, the one they had captured on camera in Sint Niklaas, in Dordrecht, no sign of the frames, and they suspect she was poisoned, and actually, I do need to visit Miss Vitali again, now that we know some more about her, it is possible she could be in danger.' Martijn said, looking concerned.

Two days earlier

At the Sint Niklaas shopping centre carpark. Crystal changed vehicles. It was dark, only a few of the lights were on and the shopping centre was closed. The rain, which had been quite heavy as she drove from the dockside in Antwerpen to Sint Niklaas, a distance of about seventeen miles, had eased considerably. Fishing the keys from her handbag for the van which she had organised to be parked here the day before, she took the frames from the vehicle they had used to abduct the insurance woman, something now she knew had not been the right thing to do. She had contacted her bosses and arranged to meet in the city of Dordrecht tomorrow. Crystal switched on the engine and the windscreen wipers and set off.

The roads were relatively quiet as she drove, the rain intermittent, and she felt worried. The conversation had been brief, but she had sensed a tension and feeling that they were not at all happy with her. Still, she said to herself, I do know something that you don't. She had some leverage, nevertheless, she could not shake the feeling that all was not well.

When she arrived in Dordrecht, it was after midnight. She found the address she needed to be at for the morning, saw a suitable place to park the van and switched off the engine. Thinking through as to what she needed to do next, she got out and opened the sliding door of the van. A nearby streetlight threw light into the interior where the two frames lay on the floor. It was then when she sensed someone there.

Turning, she was shocked to see them, both of them, then felt a sting on her leg. Next thing she knew was being manhandled into the vehicle, heard the sliding door shut and felt herself getting dizzy. One of her captors had remained outside, the other was with her, then sneezed. Crystal saw her take out a handkerchief, blow her nose, then stuff it back into a pocket of her jacket as she set about to gather the frames. Crystal, already feeling her movements were difficult, noticed a corner of the handkerchief, managed to grab it, slip it from the pocket and then tucked it between the second and third button of her blouse. Then it seemed the world began to spin around her.

She heard the van door open and close. Heard the sound of another vehicle starting and driving away. There is still something you don't know, she managed to think.

Back in the apartment in Schiebroek, Rotterdam, Martijn finished a call with his boss, the chief of the Rotterdam police. Turning to look at Sophie, he said, 'Okay, he says I should go, best to go in person, so, will you help me organise some flights?'

Six hours in time difference, in New York

'Sam?'

'Yes?' Sam replied, having just walked into the kitchen of Tammy's apartment. Their friend had already left, making her way to her restaurant only a few blocks away as she had full bookings for both lunch and dinner this day, 'you find something of interest?'

'Yes,' Chrissie replied, briefly looking up at him before returning her focus to the screen of her laptop, though she did briefly think about the previous night. After Sam's arrival and the initial pleasantries, he had taken her aside, 'need to share something with you, that happened, but wanted to wait until I saw you, face to face, 'he had said. Puzzled, and with a slight tension in her stomach, she had wondered what he was about to say. 'That night, when rescuing Samantha, things that this police detective and I had planned out, well, didn't quite all go to plan, these two guys, one of them had a gun, and when I ran out of the building, to draw them out in order for the police to then nab them, he was closer behind me than I realised, but, he was panicking, he did shoot at me, but it was wild, totally missed me, and then, well, for one, I was out of his line of sight then and the police swooped in and controlled the situation, so then I could go around and get Samantha out from where they had locked her up.' Chrissie took it all in, didn't know what to say but flung herself into him and held him tight.

Seeing him arriving in the kitchen, and thinking again about the previous night, she tried to hide her smile and keeping her voice normal, she said' Do you remember, I told you, that when you went missing, Martijn and Sophie were at your old place, looking at your great grandfather's journals, looking for any clues?'

Sam checked to see that there was enough water in the kettle, then switched it on and commenced to get some breakfast. He too was thinking of the previous night, thinking of when he had arrived from Amsterdam and the pleasure of seeing Chrissie.

'Sort of, yes, they were looking into a painting by Jan Steen, 'the feast of St. Nicholas, I seem to recall, why?'

'Had an idea this morning, wanted to check on something, you know, when we first looked at those fabulous journals, we first, or rather you did, looked into the purchase of the Gauguin painting, the woman on the shore, the one he, your great grandfather, purchased form Gauguin's wife, Mette, when he was in Copenhagen'

'Yes, it was then, finding that out, why I had been a bit concerned about that painting at the Paris Auction house, the day....'

Chrissie looked up, realising what he was thinking, 'Yes,' she said, her voice soft, 'I know'

The kettle came to the boil and Sam made himself a coffee, asked if she wanted one, which she didn't and poured some cereal into a bowl, then said, 'go on.

'Well,' Chrissie replied, looking once more at the screen, 'then there was the time when we found out, or rather, this was what Martijn and Sophie found out, about the Feast of St. Nicholas, and how it was hanging in your great grandfather's residence when he was in Cape Town, and they worked out some scenario as to what might have happened to the diamonds which had been stolen'

'Yes, good sleuthing by the pair of them, pretty well right on the button, and?' Sam asked, taking a spoonful of the cereal and briefly again thinking about the previous night, before paying attention to what Chrissie was saying.

'And, well, yes, so, then there was the time that I looked through his journals and found out about another painting, also by Jan Steen, the lovesick maiden, and the box that featured in the painting, anyway, Sophie, bless her, later she made a whole report on your great grandfather's acquisitions over the years, what he bought and what he sold, we never looked for anything else in particular, but he knew his art, no doubt it's where you get it from, passed down the generations, well, this is what I found, are you ready for this?'

Sam ate some more of the cereal, then, bowl in hand, came closer to where she sat by the kitchen table, 'Yes, I'm ready, what have you discovered?'

'When the ambassador was in Copenhagen, when he bought that painting from Mette, the woman on the shore, by Gauguin, he also purchased another painting, about a week or so later according to Sophie's findings, and, you'll never believe it, the painting was by Rubens, titled, battle on the coast!'

'Never!' Sam said, placing the bowl back on the kitchen bench, then walking over to stand behind her.

'See?' Chrissie said, pointing to the screen. His closeness made her once again think about the previous night. She had been so relieved and happy that he had come home safely, having been shot at! She understood his reasons for not telling her sooner, then, he proceeded to tell the whole account of what had happened in Antwerpen to her and Tammy, before saying goodnight to Tammy who said she would be leaving early in the morning due to a very busy Saturday.

'Wow, that's amazing,' Sam said, quickly placing a kiss on her neck, then said, 'look, he bought two that day, the other by, haven't come across that name before, Jan Baptist Weenix,'

'Indeed,' Chrissie answered, her neck tingling wonderfully. And an interesting title, Dutch ambassador travelling to Isfahan, wonder where that is?'

'Sound Persian' Sam answered.

'Now' Chrissie said, determined not to be distracted at this time, this means that we need to go home,'

Sam pondered for a moment, then understood. 'The journals are at home,' he said.

'Yes, and we know he, the ambassador, took pictures of all the paintings he purchased'

'We can check out what frame it had' Sam said, completing Chrissie thoughts.

Chrissie looked up at him behind her, then reached both hands upwards and circled them around his neck. Sam bent forward and kissed her. The wonderfulness of the previous night still very much with him.

THE PAST

Period 4: 1898

Copenhagen - Denmark

The previous British ambassador had died.

Samuel Wilfred Price looked around the office and smiled. He would get his camera and take some pictures. The wood panelling, the deep plush carpet, the paintings on the wall. The fabulous desk. The decorators had done a fine job. When he had first arrived two days ago, had been welcomed and shown to his office, he had been disappointed, for it was a mess. His new assistant had been appalled, for it seemed that burglars had entered somehow and had defaced the wall, broken some of the furniture and there were several rips in both the carpet and the rugs that now lay in crumpled heaps on the floor.

Samuel had noticed her total surprise, had seen that she was on the verge of tears in shock and disbelief. He comforted her, glad that his own possessions had not yet arrived and wondered why this had occurred, this wasn't just a robbery, this was vandalism, seemingly done in a rage. He was later informed, once the police had been and gone, that his predecessor had left under a cloud, but had then apparently committed suicide.

His own personal belongings arrived, and a crew was quickly employed to clean, redecorate and mend, and then to place his collection of artwork as he instructed.

Samuel was pleased, they had cleaned and tidied the lovely wood panelling, totally replaced the flooring and had put down a plush carpet and had brought in a different desk and chairs. And they had neatly hung the paintings as per his instructions. He was fond of art. Placing his leather case on the desk he looked around the office, then smiled his thanks to his new assistant and nodded his head in approval.

His first appointment as an ambassador. Samuel was born in the year 1870, in London into a well to do family. He was the second son and already at an early age showed sign of being quite intelligent. He was only just thirteen when he was enrolled in Eton and came away with a master's degree in art and politics. Now twenty-eight he had arrived at his first post as ambassador to the United Kingdom.

Samuel sat down behind his desk, a lovely old oak one that his assistant, whose name he was trying hard to pronounce had so quickly sourced from who knew where, along with three comfortable chairs. She came in and placed a stack of folders on the desk, smiled and in broken English asked if he wanted a drink.

'I would like a..kaffe… please Miss Gunbiorgh,' Samuel said, hoping he was close to the correct pronunciation.

She smiled at him, said, 'please, call me Laerke,' then turned and left the office. Samuel smiled and looked at her name on the sheet of paper, noticed the spelling and thought that how she had said it, was nothing like how it read. Sounded more like 'Lurka' he thought, then focused on the stack of papers she had placed before him.

Twenty-five minutes later, having consumed a coffee and some sort of Danish pastry, Samuel stood up and walked over to the large window overlooking the street below. Observed the many, orange-coloured tiled rooves of the houses along the street and again smiled, happy to be here. To the left of the window, hung a painting he had picked up at an auction about a year ago, the scene, according to the information that had come with it, said, it depicted a Dutch ambassador travelling to a place called Isfahan. It had appealed to him. The place, he had to search for information on it, was a large city in Persia, it looked to be an interesting place. The painting was by a Dutch artist, Jan Baptist Weenix, from Amsterdam. Walking back to his desk, Samuel wondered where his career as ambassador would take him. On the wall behind his desk hung two more oil paintings, both by the Dutch artist Jan Steen. The lovesick maiden and the feast of St. Nicholas. He could not even begin to imagine, as he focused on the paperwork in front of him, that both these paintings would have a connection with his great grandson many years from now.

Four days later Samuel met Mette, she was a teacher of the French language, was a well know figure in the political scene, having taught ministers, other ambassadors and company directors over the years. Furthermore, she was the wife of the French painter, Gauguin and Samuel would, in the near future, purchase one of the paintings that her husband had sent to her from Tahiti where he was living and painting at the time. A painting that would eventually be instrumental in a career change for his grandson and name's sake.

It was early in the year 1899 when Samuel, on a very cold and frosty Saturday morning, strolled through the various rooms of a large mansion house. It was the Rosenborg residence, a family whose roots went back many centuries. The economic climate along with the reckless spending of several of the male inheritors over the years had put the family estate into serious debt. Goods and possessions had to be sold. In less than two hours, an auction would be held in one of the lounges of the large house. Samuel had his eye on a couple of paintings, one in particular drew his attention, a battle scene, a coastal confrontation, well painted. He made a note of the lot number and saw that it had been purchased in 1816, in cologne. Deciding it would not only add to his collection but that it would look good in his embassy apartment, Samuel would do his best to obtain it.

Time, as it does, passes and Samuel received his first transfer. Quite a journey, quite a distance away, for his next post was to be Cape Town in South Africa. And so it was, that in 1901, after a journey by ship that took him from Copenhagen, via Amsterdam to Cadiz. From there via a second ship, he crossed the seas, never too far away from the east coast of Africa, to arrive on a very warm day in the city of Cape Town, marvelling at the beautiful scenery and the unmistakable sight of Tabletop Mountain.

Victoria Thompson sat, legs crossed, in a chair on the other side of the desk, making notes as the Ambassador, Samuel Price, spoke. He was explaining that he needed to go to a conference in Johannesburg, asked if she would arrange the flights and that he would be away for several days and that a problem had been found in his residence. A vicious variety of woodworm, apparently. Three rooms had to be cleared for the fumigators to do their job. He was asking her to oversee the project and that the courier, Jan Smettens, would be in charge of all the workmen.

Victoria wrote down all the details, then reminded the ambassador of the agenda he needed when getting to Johannesburg. He thanked her and Victoria got up and headed for her office, that was adjacent to the Ambassador's study. She was very pleased. He had arrived in Cape Town in the summer of the year 1901. As the secretary of the previous ambassador had left, an advert had been placed. At only twenty, she did feel that she might be too young but had secretarial skills and applied for the job. She recalled being the youngest person there awaiting an interview, the other three at least twice her age, she thought.

With nothing to lose, she entered and began to explain her credentials.

Preparing himself for the trip to Johannesburg, Samuel smiled as he watched his assistant leave. Recalling when she had applied for the job, recalling when she had burst into this very office and had with gusto, related her knowledge and credentials. He had to wait for some time before she eventually took a breath, and he could speak. He instantly liked her. She had been the last to be interviewed, the previous three had been accomplished, had good references, had certainly looked the professional part. But he had found them rather stiff and boring. Here now was a breath of fresh air. Before he had even a chance to think of some questions to ask her, he had already made up his mind. She would do nicely.

Victoria sat behind her own desk, quickly typed up some notes and was thinking to herself that she would keep an eye on this courier, this Jan Smettens, whom she had met on several occasions. There was something about him that she didn't like, sure, he was friendly, and chatty, always courteous. But there was definitely something about him that bothered her. Yes, she would keep an eye on him.

The embassy and the ambassador's residence were in one building. It was the residence part of the building, which occupied the whole of the second floor, where, according to the findings, the woodworm was prevalent. Workmen came, shifting furniture and taking paintings off the wall, something Samuel, being fond of his art collection, was adamant about. No spray anywhere near them. Jan Smettens organised the crew, watched over the proceedings as the paintings in the main lounge were carefully taken down. It all seemed to go to plan, he was thinking.

Victoria also kept an eye on the work, being careful to be surreptitious, often walking around and with papers in her hand, pretending to be sorting out some administration, whilst watching the courier. She was very glad that she did.

Jan Smettens was the diplomatic courier for the British Embassy. He was also a thief, a conman and a smuggler. He had bided his time, he had carefully researched and had manipulated the way for him to be taken on for the post of courier, a vacancy that he had made happen. It had been the first part of his plan. The second part had been successfully completed. The final part was happening now. The fumigation. Little could he know, that a twenty-year-old would scupper his carefully made plans.

Entering the ambassador's office, he took a quick look around, spotted Victoria sitting at her desk in the adjacent connecting room and asked her' Any correspondence to go out?'

She said there wasn't, and as Jan left the office, he briefly noticed a black journal on the ambassador's desk, frowning he thought how he hadn't recalled seeing it before. Mentally shrugging, still feeling buoyant that his plans were going so well, he left the embassy, deciding he would treat himself to a nice dinner, and knew just the right restaurant to go to. All he had to do now, he thought to himself, once seated and studying the menu, was to be very patient and above all be careful.

THE PRESENT

Sunday 5th June

Rotterdam

'Promise you'll be careful' Sophie stressed, then kissed him.

'Of course,' Martijn answered, then opened the door to their apartment and left. He had a plane to catch, two in fact, the first flight would be to Rome, then his second flight, two hours later, would take him to Trieste. Sophie had arranged all the transport, his boss had agreed the need to visit this woman, this Danielle Vitali, not only to hopefully provide more information, but, and more importantly, to ensure her safety.

Although he thought about giving miss Vitali a call first, he decided against it, though he didn't exactly know why. He recalled the last time he saw her when he visited her in connection with the mystery surrounding the three monks. He had found her to be most helpful and had listened to her story of the discovery she had made after her mother had passed away.

Meanwhile, in Dordrecht, despite it being a Sunday, the coroner had examined the body of Crystal Kaplova, also her clothes had been checked, and a discovery was made. A female assistant, upon stripping the body ready for the examination, was suspicious of a small lace handkerchief, that had been tucked into the blouse. Not a normal place to place it, almost haphazardly shoved and she decided to test it, noticing the saliva up[on it. It wasn't that much later, that it was discovered it wasn't the dead woman's DNA. The local police inspector was called, informed and subsequently a call was made to the chief of police in Rotterdam.

He, in turn, called Martijn.

'You need to watch your back' he began, as Martijn, now on the flight to Trieste, answered his phone, 'we have a connection with the Kaplova woman, possible culprit in her murder, a woman, she, along with her brother, are known criminals, both in the system, I'll send you the details, but moreover, it is likely that they could be on their way to Trieste, so, keep an eye out, there will be a detective to meet you when you get there.'

Martijn took in all that his boss was saying, agreed he would be careful and to look at the information on this brother and sister duo. He recalled the conversation with Sophie when he left, when she had asked him to promise to be careful. He would certainly watch his back, he said, inwardly to himself, his destination was twenty minutes away.

Martijn clicked on the email and began to read. The report had been written up by his Belgian colleague Detective Jan Schenk. It was detailed. In their search for the Kaplova woman, they had investigated where she lived. Upon the discovery of Crystal's body in the van in Dordrecht, they had found no house keys. Entering her apartment in Antwerpen, the police realised that, although the door wasn't forced, someone had definitely been there and searched the place. Several drawers had been opened, cupboards had been emptied, and though much of Miss Kaplova's computer equipment was there, like a printer, various leads and cables, the actual laptop had been taken. This brought about some detailed search to gather more clues that the burglars, or no doubt the same people who had been responsible for the death of the woman, might have missed. Jan himself had come to the scene whilst forensics checked for prints. He found notes that were relevant to the case and hit the jackpot when he found a diary.

The plane began its descent towards the airport in Trieste. Martijn digested all the information in the report and when he had read the contents of the various parts of the diary that Jan had discovered, he began to get an idea as to why Crystal had been on the trail for so many years. She had been on the hunt of a very valuable treasure. But the clues she had found in her search, were vague in some areas. She had dimension written down, 92 centimetres by 60 centimetres. She had written down the two paintings, which had the same dimensions, had then written down the year 1903 and the initials BO-13.

With a bump the plane landed. Martijn got ready to disembark. The one thing that was now also certain, the brother and sister criminals, had taken a flight out of Brussels and were very likely already in Trieste. Danielle could well be in danger.

Whilst in Antwerpen, Emma brood, also deciding to come in on a Sunday, had found the paperwork she was looking for and made a note of her findings. The painting, by Arnold Frans Rubens, titled 'battle on the coast, had been sold by Danielle Vitali, this had been in the February, so, Emma calculated, she must have first placed the Jacob Leyssen for sale in Paris, then had travelled to Cologne to sell the Rubens, also, as she had sold two pieces of art in Paris, the other being a work by a Turkish artist, she had also sold two pieces in Cologne, the second one being a painting by the Italian artist, Bernardo Bellotto. Emma also found a photograph of the painting that the museum purchased, the Rubens, then checking it with the information she had, was sure that the painting and the frame were exactly the same as back in 2015. Whatever it was that Crystal was looking for, must have been some information she had gathered about the painting, before this Danielle woman had acquired them, where were they prior?' Emma decided she would call her counterpart in Rotterdam, Sophie.

Walther Bouvier arrived by private plane at Trieste airport. He made his way to the arrivals lounge and checking the board he sat down. He had not met Martijn but knew of him, through Sophie. Walther, seeing he still had some time to wait, reflected on his career as a detective from Interpol. He first met Sophie, then the auction house manager, back in 2019, assigned to her protection detail and involved in a stolen art case and a South African woman who was wanted for attempted murder in Cape Town. Since then, he had been involved in other such cases and was also present, a year later, when he assisted Sophie in bringing two people in from the States in search of the mystery of the monks.

Walther smiled at the memory, when he first saw the blond woman from New York, a very attractive lady called Tammy. Who had come along with a younger woman, Terri, an art curator from San Francisco. Later he had escorted the three women to a bookstore where they were following up a lead on the trail of the three monks.

Walther checked the board as it ticked over the various arrivals and departures, saw that the plane he was awaiting was due in fifteen minutes. He was assigned to observe and support, but not to interfere with the Italian police, unless necessary. Glancing to his left, he saw the detective that was here also to await detective Vogel and get to a woman called Danielle Vitali who was possibly in danger and probably had some information that would be valuable.

Checking his pocket, he assured himself he had the keys ready for a car that was waiting just outside. Walther, who, for some years now, had the nickname PPK, had a French father and Austrian mother and was named after his mother's father, a grandfather he had never met and knew little about. He was very much a loner, was happiest by himself and joined Interpol over ten years ago. Dark hair, clean shaven and standing a solid five foot eleven, he was fit and agile and though often noticing women looking at him, he was shy when it came to romance. Again, he thought about the blond New Yorker, she was petite, and he was quite attracted to her. Perhaps he would have an opportunity to speak to Martijn about her. The flight from Rome arrived.

Martijn, carrying a small carry-on bag entered the arrival lounge and was immediately greeted by the local police detective who rapidly introduced himself, then said,' she left the house, went shopping, big shopping centre, in the centre of the city, she was followed'

Martijn nodded, picking up on what he was saying in quickly spoken and sharply accented English. 'Okay, let's see if we can find her, before they do, were there two of them who followed?'

'Si, a man and a woman' he replied, 'car over here'

Martijn threw his baggage into the back seat and then jumped in the front, having just secured his seat belt when his Italian counterpart sped away. 'You know what the woman looks like' he asked driving above the speed limit and weaving in and out of the traffic, miraculously missing the many scooters that seemed to be everywhere. According to his earlier research, the city centre was about twenty miles away. He prayed that the woman would be safe, surely if she was in a shopping centre, a public space.

'Yes, I have met her' Martijn replied, impressed with this man's driving skills.

Martijn began to think that he should have called her after all, forewarn her of a potential danger. But he reckoned as he could see they were approaching the city centre, they needed information, they weren't going to harm her, at least, not until they had whatever they think she might know.

The radio in the police car came to life. A message came through. Martijn could not understand the rapidly spoken Italian, and neither he, not the Italian detective noticed the car following them.

'The man and the woman, the ones you say are a brother and sister, our man has their car in sight, the driver, the man, is still inside the car, the woman has gone into the shopping centre. Miss Vitali's car is only three vehicles away from where they have parked'

'Is this a big shopping centre?' Martijn asked

'It has two floors, quite big, many shops' was the reply, and although the traffic was getting heavier, he didn't slow down. He did however, put flashing lights on, which helped clear the way somewhat.

Tyres screeching, he drove into the carpark, then stopped abruptly and said' here stairway to shops, you look, I park in section C'

'Right' Martijn replied, got out and headed for the stairwell, ignoring the lift he bounded up the stairs two at a time and opened the door to arrive on the first floor.

As fate would have it, Martijn spotted her almost immediately, coming out of a clothing store, she was heading towards him, but he then spotted a woman closing in on her, from the look on her face,

Martijn had no hesitation in thinking that this was the woman who along with her brother, were after Danielle.

Deciding to call out, Martijn shouted' Danielle! Watch out behind you!

Danielle Vitali heard the shouting, heard her name and saw him, she recognised him, the Dutch policeman, she also understood what he was saying and was quick to turn around, noticing the woman who was fast approaching. But sensing trouble, she turned and began to run the other way.

'Oh no you don't' Danielle thought, dropping her shopping bag, she went off in a sprint.

Martijn couldn't believe how quick she was, and as he reached where she had dropped her shopping bag, he also noticed what was happening ahead.

Danielle was fast, quickly caught up with the woman, then leaped into a flying tackle, grabbing the other woman by the waits and took her down.

From the other direction Martijn saw his Italian counterpart arriving, noticed that Danielle had the situation well in hand and stopped to pick up her shopping before heading to the scene where Danielle had now stood up and looking down on the tackled woman, then looking at Martijn as he arrived. Shoppers were stopping to look and then the Italian police detective spoke, showing his badge and that all was well and under control, to please carry on.

He bent down and lifted the woman back onto her feet with one hand, the other holding a phone into which he spoke rapidly. Martijn reached the scene, smiled at Danielle, said, 'Hi, I believe you dropped your shopping, which is not all you dropped, goodness me, that was quite the tackle!'

Danielle smiled back, could find no words to say and reached towards him and embraced him.

'I guess my sporting background proved to be helpful,' she replied, a little out of breath, 'who is she?'

Martijn hugged her, was somewhat amused as there had been several people who had applauded the rugby tackle move and said, 'I will explain all, best to get you home first though'

'I agree with that' a voice said. Then, as both Martijn and Danielle looked at who had spoken, the man said,' I am Walther, I know your lady friend Sophie, she may have mentioned me?' But before Martijn could formulate an answer, he said, 'best you go with this lady, I will get your baggage from the local detective, they have the man, the brother, in custody also, then I will meet you at miss Vitali's home, by the way, that was quite some tackle, I am from Interpol, following a lead on stolen art, Martijn here will explain, I must go and liaise with the local police, I will see you both later' and with that Walther left them to it and followed the detective who was escorting the woman down the escalator.

Martijn raised his eyebrows, nodded and said to Danielle,' Sophie knows him, he was part of a security detail, back in 2019, protecting her, then again was helpful last year, whilst I was visiting you here, he was in Paris helping Sophie, Tammy and Terri whom I have also spoken about if you recall.'

'Yes, I do, I remember the story, and wasn't Sophie also at one time the manager at the auction house in Paris, when I sold one of my paintings ? Is that what this is all about? 'Danielle answered as she was walking towards the escalator, then saying, 'I have my car in the basement, I think I need a strong coffee, my house is not that far away'

'A strong coffee is a great idea' Martijn said, still carrying her shopping as they descended to the ground level.

Meanwhile it was just before seven o'clock in the morning in Boston.

'Here, this is it!' Chrissie called out. Sam came out of the kitchen where he had been making breakfast, surprised to discover that she was already up. She was on her knees on the floor, by the coffee table where one of his great grandfather's journals was open. He stopped briefly, realising how much he loved her, her hair tangled and swept to one side, exposing her lovely neck.

'This is what Sophie and Martijn discovered, remember, and their speculation as to what may have happened?'

Sam placed himself next to her and looked, recalling the findings of their friends when the journals were still at his old apartment in Rotterdam.

'That's seems like ages ago now' he said, looking at where she was pointing.

He could see why they had come up with the speculation that the frames of two paintings had been swopped, likely, they had thought at the time, by this woman called Victoria Thompson, personal assistant to the ambassador.

'I know, it sure does' Chrissie answered, though having got up early to start to investigate the journals, she had only briefly showered and had put on a dressing gown, wanting to get started, both having felt too tired the previous evening when they got back home from New York.

Chrissie kissed Sam on the cheek, then said,' But it's not what we are looking for right now, but this is, wait, let me show you' she said, turning several pages.

'Here' she said, turning to look at him, then back at the page she had opened, 'This is where, in Copenhagen, he purchased the Gauguin, the woman on the shore, the very painting that was a pinnacle in your life, you told me, it makes sense though, you obviously have the genes from him, the love and feel of art, anyway, he also, whilst in Denmark, bought another piece, this was a work by the Flemish artist Rubens, the title, yes, indeed, the battle on the coast.!'

'Wow, that's amazing, the fact that he once had the very painting that has caused so much attention, but we are still in the dark as to why, he took photos of all his paintings, is there one?'

'Oh yes, my dear Sam,' Chrissie said, turning the page.

They both looked at the picture in the journal. Underneath the ambassador had written, 'Battle on the coast' by Arnold Frans Rubens and a date, 1706.

'The frame looks quite plain, basic really' Sam observed.

'Yes, it sure does, I wonder, this could be the very frame that Zecheriah put on, he did purchase them from that Spanish guy without a frame.' Chrissie suggested

'It is quite possible, Zecheriah liked the painting, he kept it for over thirty years, for him it was all about the scene, the painting, not the frame, hence it's plain constructure. 'Sam figured.

'Yes, you're right,' said Chrissie, then began to turn some more pages, saying, 'let's see when, or if, he sold it'

'When did he buy it?' Sam asked, trying to remember when his great grandfather was in Denmark.

'He bought it the year after he bought the Gauguin, in 1899' she answered, continuing to look through the journal.

'So,' Sam said, sitting himself upright and deciding to place an arm around her waist,' Zechariah sold it, to the German chap, Rudolph, back in 1803, meaning Rudolph must have sold it on, there's nearly a hundred years to check on.'

'Got it' Chrissie said, enjoying his close proximity and his hand around her waist,' wow, he sold it at an auction in The Hague, in 1909'

Sam bent forward to see where she was reading, the sat back again, thinking it all through.

Chrissie sat back as well, leaning into him and placed her head under his chin.

'Tell me what you're thinking,' she said.

'Well, the frame doesn't appear to have any special value, when he purchased it in 1899, we can assume that nothing changed for the next, nearly, ten years so, we now need to investigate to whom it was sold in 1909, then, hopefully trace it forwards and maybe find out why the frame of the painting when it was in the museum in Antwerpen, was so important.

'We can easily find out when the museum got it, and from where' Chrissie suggested, 'that would narrow it down'

'Agreed, I'll call Sophie on that'

In Rotterdam

Sophie answered the phone, having only just finished speaking with Martijn who had a lot of information, not to mention relating the rugby tackle performed in the shopping centre. Apparently to applause. 'Oh, hi Sam, I have so much to tell you…'

'That's great, for I have a question for you that you might be able to get an answer to.'

'Okay, you first then, what's the question?'

'Can you find out when the museum in Antwerpen purchased the battle on the coast?'

'I already know the answer to that' Sophie replied, 'It was bought at an auction in Cologne, in March 2015, Danielle was in Paris first, where she sold the Jacob Leyssen, and we know, that Crystal Kaplova was there as well, and, of course, you were there too!'

'Really?' unaware of this information, 'you mean, that day, in January...'

Sophie realised the memory that it brought to Sam, 'Sorry, so much has been going on, what with you being shot at, Samantha being kidnapped, and that Crystal woman being killed...'

'What??' I wasn't aware of that either' Sam said, wanting to say more, but Sophie spoke again,' Sorry Sam, you were on your way back to New York, then, what with the time difference, well, Martijn felt it was important to head out and see Danielle, thinking that perhaps she might be in danger, if nothing else, she might also have useful information, so, your friend the police chief agreed and he left for Trieste, I have just finished speaking with him, let me tell what action happened in a shopping centre...'

In Boston

'Goodness me' Chrissie said, after Sam had finished the call with Sophie, as she had listened in on the conversation via the speakerphone.

'Indeed, quite the woman, this Danielle, I wonder what else she might be able to reveal as to how she acquired those paintings' Sam wondered

Chrissie shrugged her shoulders,' who knows, I guess Martijn will fill us in soon, right now though, I think I had better get changed.'

THE PAST

Period 5: 1903

Caracas, Venezuela

It was the month of October and late in the afternoon. The tide was high and about to go out and the sun was still keeping the warmth upon the ships that were moored in the harbour and upon the large trading post that served the port. Almost exactly a hundred years earlier, the former tin miner from Cornwall, Henry Hopkins, arrives and for the first time sets foot on the South American continent. His stay was brief, as he was on his way to Colombia where he would find work in the silver mines. Little could he have even imagined or guessed, that over two hundred years later, someone would be reading the journals, that he would not even begin to write for another nearly fifty years. He had arrived rather sunburned, purchased several hats as well as a beautifully painted miniature on ivory. He would spend the next seventeen years in South America and not knowing any Spanish at all when he arrived, he would be very proficient by then.

This day, in the afternoon of a weekday in the middle of October, a ship was about to set sail. A three masted Spanish galleon, named Alicante Atlantica. Carrying an assortment of freight, from sugar and tobacco, through to stoneware pots and crafted blankets, to guitars and ornate wooden picture frames. Her destination was Cadiz. From there she would sail to Gibraltar and then on to the port of Antwerpen. The voyage was marred by a severe storm that would demand repairs upon arrival in Cadiz.

January 1904

In a changing world, there were more changes for Ambassador Price. Though having enjoyed South Africa, he was okay and ready for another change and received a letter and documents to say his next appointment would be Paris. He recalled smiling when he read the news, for it would mean he would be able to practice the French he had learned from Gauguin's wife Mette, when he had been in Copenhagen. What made him smile even more, was that Victoria was determined to go with him.

Someone else who was smiling when he heard, was the courier, Jan Smettens. It meant the ambassadors belongings would leave the country. Perhaps the ambassador would sell a few paintings in Paris as Jan knew that he would now and then sell in order to purchase some new works. Jan started making arrangements for him and his accomplices, his nephew and niece, to relocate to Paris.

Prior to the ambassador leaving, Jan handed in his notice, explaining he had a family commitment to attend to in Johannesburg. Arrangements all in place, he, along with his niece and nephew, left Cape Town by ship. A freighter that would take them onto Gibraltar, from there the ship would travel on to Italy. Jan, his older sister's children, Albert and Karla, found accommodation in Gibraltar until they found passage that would take them to France. The Spanish galleon ship, the Alicante Atlantica, arrived, much delayed after repairs in Cadiz and though its destination was Antwerpen, Jan and his niece and nephew bought a passage. Eventually they arrived in Paris only four days before the ambassador arrived to take up his new appointment.

Jan kept an eye on the comings and goings of the ambassador. Often reflecting on that day, when he had, successfully, pulled off that diamond heist. The largest of its type, the papers were full of it, for days on end, police baffled, border patrol intensified and Jan making sure that he went about work as normal, instilling that on his nephew and niece also, to go about your life as normal. And above all to be patient. Often when he though back, he would smile, pleased with all the planning that had gone before it, pleased with the result, pleased with how the transfer of the diamonds into the frame of the Gauguin painting had gone. Smoothly, all having gone exactly as he had planned.

Jan, knowing that the ambassador would from time to time sell a painting that he had admired for some time to then purchase something new counted on this. But, if all else failed and the ambassador did not sell it, that too was no problem, the crucial factor in all his planning, was for the diamonds to leave South Africa, and with diplomatic status, the ambassador was the ideal candidate for his plans.

Time passed. He, with the help from Albert and Karla, committed the odd residential robbery here and there, to keep some money coming in and pay for their daily bills of rent and food. 1904 ticked over into 1905. No sign of the Ambassador heading for the auction rooms. His niece and nephew were losing their patience.

Ambassador Samuel Price thoroughly enjoyed Paris. There were many functions, there was lots to see, and he was pleased to be working with Victoria every day. But, for Samuel too, timed passed and he received a new appointment.

January 1908

His new posting was to The Hague, in the Netherlands. He was thrilled when Victoria insisted, she came too. It was also a great opportunity to sell the Gauguin, thinking it would sell well here in France, prior to his move. He entered it in the auction, the woman on the shore by Gauguin, would be under the hammer just before he was due to move.

Jan Smettens was very happy. At last, the painting was coming up for sale. He had funds ready, enough to make sure he would become the new owner. His nephew and niece once again became excited, having become almost resigned to the fact that they would never see the diamonds again. The auction was well attended, Jan, wearing a disguise so as not to be recognised by the ambassador, waited patiently for the right lot to appear. The bidding was strong for a while. Three rows in front of where Jan and his niece and nephew sat, the ambassador, who had brought his assistance Victoria along, was pleased.

Having spent a bit more than he anticipated, Jan was nevertheless pleased that he was the new owner, not only would he retrieve the diamonds, but at some point, would be able to sell the painting on, knowing it would be in demand. Later that day, in the small dining room of the apartment he had rented, Jan carefully dismantled the frame from the painting, then equally carefully looked for where he had plugged the drilled hole. But it wasn't there! Totally dismantling the frame then, almost in a frenzy, he was completed stunned and shocked. No diamonds! Albert and Karla looked at him, looked at each other, then began accusing their uncle of double crossing them.

Two days later they left Paris, leaving Jan, still quite dumbfounded as to what could have happened, behind and saying they never wanted to see him again. Jan was uncertain as to what to do, he felt the best thing also, was to leave Paris. Certainly, for now, he could not dare to sell the painting, the diamonds were gone, how? Was he being watched, was the police on to him? No, two days had already passed, nobody had come knocking on his door. Still. He decided to leave Paris. He carefully put the frame back on the painting and never noticed that Victoria Thompson had written her name in the bottom corner of the painting. He also had not noticed that the ambassador's assistant, Miss Thompson, had, despite his disguise, recognised him at the auction.

Four years later

Four years in the Hague had gone rather quickly and he was happy to receive his next appointment. London.

It was now the year 1912

It was wonderful to be back in London, but Samuel Wilfred Price hadn't been back in the United Kingdom very long before he received orders to take up an appointment in Vancouver. He felt a little lost. Moments earlier he had said goodbye to Victoria. Pacing around the front room of the house he had been taken to upon his arrival in London, he let his mind wander and thought back. London is where it had all started, his studies at Eton, joining the Diplomatic corps and relishing the opportunities that he was sure would come his way. By all accounts he had been, at the age of twenty, a wealthy young man. Both his parents had succumbed to gas poisoning, when a leaky pipe had caused a leakage affecting several houses in the suburb where they lived. Though naturally quite shocked and upset, it hadn't taken long for him to focus on his studies and was determined not to let his inherited wealth stop him from his ambitions.

His first appointment as ambassador had been in Copenhagen. Samuel stopped pacing, for a few moments looked out the window onto the street and watched for a while as several carts went by and he noticed a small group of boys playing in the field opposite. He had never been much of a sporting type, had not often played with other children and had mainly concentrated on his studies and his piano playing, turning away from the window he thought back to the recent conversation with Victoria, smiling he again paced the large room and remembered when he had hired her. He had arrived in Copenhagen in 1898, three years later he was posted to Cape Town in South Africa, quite a journey. Here it was, with the previous assistant having left together with the previous ambassador, that he interviewed several women who had applied for the vacancy. Victoria, young, freckles, long hair tied in a ponytail, quite the breath of fresh air. But she was knowledgeable, keen, enthusiastic and he had not hesitated in giving her the job.

In the year 1904 he was posted to Paris. Victoria Thompson went with him. Samuel broke away from his thoughts, decided he must further prepare to get ready for the next stage of his career. She decided not to come this time. His time in Paris had been good, nearly four years there, then onto to The Hague in the Netherlands in 1908, from which he was recalled three weeks ago. Tension was rising in the lowlands, and they needed him elsewhere. Elsewhere being Vancouver.

Eleven years. She had been a faithful assistant for eleven years. But only a week after having arrived in London, she met a young man, this at someone's birthday party she had been invited to and had fallen in love. Sorting out his clothes as to which to pack on the journey and which to ship over, Samuel wondered why he had never fallen in love. Maybe it was time to focus on that, he said to himself.

From an early age Samuel had been interested in art. Often going to museums or exhibitions when he could. Having the finances, he regularly purchased a painting or a sculpture, though he mainly stuck to paintings, which, he would have for a while, then sell, so that he could purchase something else to adorn the walls of his rooms or office. All of these were still packed in crates, and he was looking forward to redecorating his new residence, though that was still some time away as he had planned a long journey, mainly overland, to get to Vancouver in British Columbia.

Samuel placed a diary into a case. He did have journals, well-kept journals, meticulously written, and with photographs, of all the painting he had purchased and sold over the years, along with other details about the surrounding circumstances he found himself in. Journals that his great grandson, many years from now, would read, as would a few others in order to solve several mysteries. But the journals were still packed in crates. The diary would have to do to record his upcoming journey to Canada. Also, what he could not possibly foresee, was that Victoria would, at some point in the future, become part of his family tree.

Two days later, Sunday 7th July

Liverpool. It was busy on the docks. Despite it being a Sunday, despite it being less than three months since the sinking of the Titanic. Work goes on, travel goes on, life goes on. Two months later there would be chaos in the city, protests, uprising, clashes. All to do with the battle for home rule in Ireland. Samuel feared that something had to give at some point, being very much aware of the political situation of the time. In as sense he was glad to be leaving, leaving these shores and discovering new lands. Papers all perused and stamped, he walked up the gangplank carrying one large and one small case.

The ss Armenian, just over 8000 tonnes, with a length of five hundred feet had three decks and was a designated cargo liner. Already Samuel had noticed the beauty of the four masted schooner and felt quite exhilarated as he walked on board. He was greeted by the captain himself and was, along with the first mate, led to and shown his cabin. Once settled in, he ventured onto the deck and watched the loading. The weather was great, the sun shone warmly, and Samuel looked over the city and briefly wondered if he would ever return to this country. First stop Boston. Then quite the journey overland from there. He wondered about the letter that Victoria had given him, on the day she had come to say goodbye, he mustn't read it until he was on board the ship, she had said and made him promise. He promised.

Victoria Thompson watched the ss Armenian leave the docks. Many others were around her, waving goodbye. Victoria didn't wave. She stood, and watched for quite some time, then turned and headed away. She had come, had been early, had seen him embark. Walking back now, heading for the railway station, she wondered when it would be that he would read the letter. What would he think? How would he react? She asked herself, as she walked along with the throng of people who had seen off their loved ones, their family, those who had chosen to leave, chosen to settle and live their lives elsewhere.

Not much later, as she sat herself down in the train carriage, heading back to London, she thought about the letter she had written, the details she had put down in words, not just how she felt, but, more importantly, what she had done, what she had seen and considered the consequences of what he would discover.

She sat back, oblivious of the passing landscape, and took herself back in time. To a time in the year 1903, to Cape Town. The ambassador was away, a conference in Johannesburg, he would be away several days. He had informed her of the need to have several rooms fumigated, informed her that the courier, mister Jan Smettens, would see to it all. Whilst the man, who had been the courier for the past two years, was amiable and always courteous and friendly towards her, there was something about him she felt uncomfortable with. Deciding to keep a close eye on him whilst the ambassador was away, she was glad she had done so……

The fumigators, two of them, wore white overalls, had hats and masks and equipment that created a lot of noise and dust. Furniture had been moved, paintings had been taken off the walls and many dust sheets had been placed in the rooms they were working on, to eradicate this particular type of woodworm, she had been told. But it was soon apparent to her, that all was not as it seemed as she watched the goings on, being careful not to be spotted. It was one afternoon, the second day of their arrival, that, hearing the noise of the machinery, she decided to take a closer look and wondered where the courier had disappeared to as the two men in coveralls were working away, their, vacuum style of machine, making quite some noise. But she detected another sound, that of a drill.

Victoria knew the embassy building, knew the ambassador's residence on the top floor, knew her way around and following the new noise, she made her way towards it. What she discovered took her by surprise, what she saw puzzled her. She watched Jan Smettens, sure that he would not see her, watched him as he was drilling a hole into the top part of the frame that held the painting of the woman on the shore, a painting by Gauguin, the ambassador had told her, that he had purchased in Copenhagen, from the wife of the painter. She knew all of his paintings, knew he was quite a collector and often he would tell her about them. She watched Jan the courier, as he drilled a long thin drill into one side of the frame, then, he turned to the other side, drill again, she could see what he was doing, drilling a small hole right through the centre. Thinking about the purpose of this, she remembered something that had been on the news recently, it had been a headline story. A diamond theft, an audacious theft, the largest of its kind apparently.

Standing from her vantage point, barely remembering to breathe, she watched as Jan inserted a straw like tube into the hole, then he carefully placed, what she was sure were diamonds, into the tube. Then he had some kind of putty, sealed the holes and each end and with a brush he painted these plugs and even from the distance she was away from this scene, it was clear, as he used a cloth to rub and clean the frame, that it would be hard to detect. Sensing he was nearly done, she quietly withdrew, headed back downstairs, noted the two men were still using their loud machine, though still more or less in the same place as they were before, and returned to her office, sitting herself behind her desk. Moments later the courier suddenly appeared, smiled at her and said that they would be finished soon, and he would see to it that all the furniture would be put back.

She smiled back at him, nodded and pretended to focus on her work, glad that he could not hear her heart beating loudly.

It was early evening when Jan and the fumigating crew packed up and left. Making sure they had gone, she then walked around the rooms, the main reception lounge of the embassy and then upstairs to the residence and saw that all was neatly back in place and tidied. She had thought it through as to what to do and having then decided to put that plan into action, she got ready.

She was now the only person left in the building, other staff had left, kitchen staff had left. She had a small apartment at the back of the embassy on the ground floor where she very happily lived. It was small but as she might often be on call, it was ideal. Deciding that the best place to work at what she had planned would be the main reception lounge, where there was a large table, and where often functions would be held, it was also here in this room, that the paintings were hung.

Grabbing a small ladder, gathering a variety of tools and placing two large blankets upon the surface of the table, she started. First things first, take the paintings of the wall, there were two, side by side, it was when studying these that she had formulated her plan. Climbing up the ladder, she lifted the painting by Gauguin. It was heavier than she thought it might be, but managed to get it down She placed it face down on the table. Studying the frame closely, she could just make out where Jan had drilled and made the hole. Already beginning to perspire, she then moved the steps, then took down the adjacent painting. This was a work by the artist, Jan Steen, and the title of it was, The Feast of St. Nicholas. This too she placed face down on the table. Studying the back of these works, she worked out how to do what she intended. To swop the frames.

Working carefully, she first managed to work the frame free from the feast of St. Nicholas, she carefully took out the actual painting, placed it equally careful on the floor, then began to work on the Gauguin. Having then after quite some time, worked that one free, she then picked up the Jan Steen work and inserted it into the Gauguin frame, both paintings were almost identical in size, often artists would use a certain style and size of canvas, and the frames, she had noted, were also very similar. She smiled and wondered if the ambassador would ever notice. Feeling the need to have a little rest, seeing on the wall clock that it was already well after midnight, she drank some water, then put the feast of St. Nicholas, now in the Gauguin frame, back on the wall.

Next, the woman on the shore to be put into the other frame. Satisfied that she had completed her plan and that all looked fine, she hung this back on the wall, stood back and looked at them both, smiling and wondering one day what mister Jan Smettens might think as to what had happened. To further tease the man, she had, in tiny writing, prior to putting it back in the frame, written her name on the back of the painting. Who would discover that, and what would they make of that. Tidying up, making sure she had left no evidence behind, she then went to bed. It was almost four o'clock in the morning......

Victoria broke away from her reminiscing and saw that London was not too far away now. She wondered if the ambassador had kept his promise not to read the letter until he was sailing away. For not only had she told him how she had feelings for him, but more importantly, she had described in detail all that she had done whilst they had been in Cape Town, the switching of the frames, imagining the look on Jan Smettens face when he would discover the diamonds missing. Just prior to their move from Paris to The Hague, Victoria had an opportunity, the ambassador had decided to sell the Gauguin then, but not the Jan Steen feast of St. Nicholas, which Victoria knew was one of his favourites. But in the readiness of the impending move, Victoria decided to see if she could get to the diamonds, having then obtained the right equipment, had managed to open up the hole that Jan had drilled, poured out the diamonds, which sparkled beautifully as they rolled onto the dark red table cloth which covered the table upon which she was working. Victoria replaced them, all except one. She kept one diamond for herself. Then resealed the hole, used some varnish to cover it up and was pleased with her work.

The train was approaching the London station. She opened her handbag to retrieve her train ticket, then unzipped a side pocket, felt into it, drew out a velvet cloth bag, and, making sure that no one was in the vicinity, she poured out the content into her hand. She smiled for the diamond glistened and sparkled so wonderfully. Putting it all back she wondered what the ambassador would think of her having done that.

The diplomatic status was very helpful for Samuel as he processed through customs. Two small crates and two leather suitcases, which had arrived three days earlier, were ticked off and loaded onto a cart. Samuel signed a few documents and placed his luggage with the other goods and stepped onto the seat next to the driver who would take him to the railway station not far away. Making a sound with his mouth, the horses, two of them, set off. It was quite busy. It was Friday, the eighteenth of July. The journey from Liverpool had taken twelve days. Mid-morning and the sun was already increasing the ground temperature. Samuel sat quietly, apart from a quick nod to the driver, he had not spoken to him. The station was close by, and the train was scheduled to leave in just under two hours' time. As the horses and cart drew closer, he could hear and smell the steam of the train's locomotives. Whilst the crossing over the Atlantic had been an experience, it had also been uneventful. Samuel had already several sea journeys under his belt. When leaving Copenhagen, he had travelled by ship all the way to Cape Town. Then in 1904 he had again travelled by sea to Paris. He had now crossed the Atlantic and for him, the adventure was now to begin, a long overland journey, the first part, by train, all the way through the valley that ran between the Catskill and Adirondack Mountains to Syracuse and Buffalo, then onto Cleveland, from where he would travel by sea, through the lakes, all the way through parts of Lake Eerie, Lake Huran and Lake Superior, to finally reach Thunder Bay. Then it was again going to be a railway trek to Vancouver.

Samuel made sure the crates, and his luggage was loaded, thanked the cart driver and settled himself into a luxurious compartment. Then getting his diary, he began to write. A steam whistle and then with a jolt, the train set in motion. A letter slipped from within the back of his diary. The letter from Victoria.

He picked it up, then for the second time thought about it, and for the second time he tucked it back into the diary. For some reason he was not ready to read it. He had been surprisingly affected, when she had told him she had fallen in love and would not travel with him to Canada. He blamed himself. He should have told her how he felt a long time ago. But felt it would be inappropriate. The news had rocked him, had made him realise that he cared so much more for her than he had ever admitted to himself. But it was all too late. She had fallen in love. Samuel looked out of the window as the train slowly began to pick, up speed, then sighed, and focused on what he wanted to write in his diary. Right now, he did not want to read a letter from someone he was, of this he was sure, in love with.

He did briefly wonder, why it was that she made him promise not to read it straight away, but casting those thoughts aside he watched as the American landscape rolled past the window.

THE PRESENT

Sunday 5th June

Boston

'Well, that all ties in, I can see from these other notes that he wrote, in this diary, which he used whilst his journals were packed in crates, that he was in Paris, from 1904 to 1908, then was posted to The Hague, where he was stationed until 1912. He sold the battle on the coast there in 1909.' Sam said, reading notes from another part of his great grandfather's journal.

'He had no idea the trail of intrigue he left behind' Chrissie said, thinking how the Gauguin had been the catalyst that helped Sam change his career, the same painting had then been used to smuggle diamonds on, except that never happened because the ambassador's assistant, Victoria, had changed the frames. And now this second painting, the one by Rubens, causing much mystery. Why was it so important, was this painting also used for some kind of smuggling? 'I hope Sophie calls soon, can't wait to hear the full story of what Danielle can reveal.' She said, looking up from the journal that contained a photo of the very painting.

Across to the west coast in San Francisco

'Goodness, it's so early Terri' Alison said, 'have you been up all night?' Letting her daughter in, she closed the door behind her and followed her into the lounge.

'Sorry mother,' Terri answered, sitting herself down on the couch and placing a stack of folders on the coffee table,' best make us a cup of tea, so much to go through, is Chantal still here?'

Alison, dressed in her pale blue bathrobe walked into the kitchen and said, 'Yes, she is still here, I will get some breakfast sorted, and some tea, then, I'll wake her....'

'No need, I'm up,' Chantal said, arriving in the kitchen, like Alison, wearing a bathrobe, 'heard the front doorbell...'

'I'm so sorry, I didn't realise it was quite so early...' Terri said, getting up and walking over to Chantal,' I'm Terri, so nice to meet you'

'Listen, I can tell you're excited to share some information, but how about we, that is Chantal and I, get dressed, then we'll breakfast and I for one will be more awake by then, glancing at the kitchen clock which showed it to be a quarter to seven.

'Okay then' Terri said, nearly thirty minutes later, finishing her cup of tea, then looking up at both of them sitting opposite on the two-seater couch, she began to explain. It was now a quarter past seven. Both Chantal and Alison still drinking from their cups of tea.

'Just to fill you in on something that happened last year' Terri said, looking at Chantal, 'I was held at gun point, all to do with a mysterious painting of a monk, so, together with a lady called Sophie, from Paris, and a lady called Tammy, from New York, we followed a trail that led to Florence.' Pausing briefly, seeing that she had both their attention, carried on, 'what had led us to Florence, was a children's book, written by twin sisters Bella and Eva Umbrego, anyway, when I started looking into the history of the two Flemish masters, Jacob Leyssen and Arnold Frans Ruben, to see why the two paintings might have been so important, or, as we subsequently found out, why it was the frames that were of interest, I came across these twins again, who were, at the time, in Venice. Following that line, and the history a little bit, I then came across another name, that of Luigi Cantoni...'

'I know that name!' Chantal said, interrupting Terri's flow, 'sorry...'

'No, not at all, how?'

Chantal put her cup on the table, then closed her eyes briefly, trying to recall, then said' Yes, okay, well, Terri, you know of course about the gold, and the mosaic tiles, a mystery that your mother helped to solve, it is, of course how I met your mother, at the exhibition in Albuquerque, anyway, I had been following a trail, on my ancestor, her name was Caprice, named after her grandmother, who had, together with her husband to be, Juan Castagnet, liberated the gold coins out of Columbia, anyway, it was this granddaughter, Caprice, who sold a painting in Boston, and from what your mother told me, this all connected with a mystery to do with a Spanish woman, Letitia, but there was something else in my research on her that I found, when she was selling the painting, which was a Titian, she came across some scrolls, and was intrigued, apparently, according to her writings which I found, these were Hebrews scrolls, or rather, they were translated Hebrew scrolls, and they were by a scholar called, Luigi Cantoni'

'Wow' Terri said, then' That's right, he was a scholar, a very well-known scribe, most interesting, about those scrolls, worth looking into, but not now, because the connection I found, was that this Luigi, was following up on what the Umbrego twins had been writing, and, presumable, talking about, you see, he was there, in Venice, in the library the same time as they were, but, that is also not what made me come here so early in the morning, I found something late last night, and that is, a woman called Alexandria Wenschelburg, she came from Trieste, and, knowing of course that this Danielle woman was also from Trieste, who had both the paintings at one time, and sure enough, I connected the dots, this Alexandia woman had a daughter, Alexa, and this Alexa, who, by the way, was shot and killed in Istanbul, something that also connects to the mystery of the three monks, but, more importantly now, connects to the woman from Trieste, Alexa had a daughter that she gave away for adoption, and she, is the mother of Danielle....'

Terri stopped speaking, looked at both women in turn and smiled, as she could see that they were taking it all in. Terri sat back in the chair, still smiling, pleased with her findings, and thinking what she had to do next, who to call first.

THE PAST

Period 7: The year 1939

London

On the second floor of the old hospital in the suburb of Edgware, north London, Victoria Thompson looked out of the window. She stood there for some time, wearing a light blue coloured dressing gown over a white nightdress. Not far away she could see the roof of the Boosey & Hawkes instrument factory and wondered if that might be used for different purposes now as the war seemed imminent. Taking in a deep breath, she sighed and fought away the tears that were welling up behind her eyes.

War. Again, she thought, when many felt it wouldn't happen again. Her daughter would be arriving soon. Her thoughts took her back, back to the day she had travelled to Liverpool. The day she had last seen the ambassador. Frowning, she was puzzled, though not for the first time. The letter. The letter she had written to him, the letter she had specifically asked him not to read until he was at sea, until the ship had left the port. A letter from which she never received a reply. Hearing the door to her room open, Victoria turned and smiled as her daughter entered. _

'Hello mother' said Jane, wearing a nurse's uniform.

'Come, sit on the bed, I need to tell you a few things' Victoria said, pulling back the sheets, taking her dressing gown off and getting into the bed, then said 'are you on a shift soon, or have you just come from one?'

'Next shift in an hour from now' she answered and sat on the bed once her mother had settled, 'what do you mean, tell me a few things?'

Victoria looked at her daughter, smiled, then said, 'a love story'.

Smiling at the puzzled look her daughter gave her, Victoria said, 'I fell in love with your father, it surprised me' she began, then shifting herself to a better sitting position, continued' you see Jane, for many years I had been in love…'

'With ambassador Price' Jane said. She knew that, she also, having received confidential information regarding her mother's health, was concerned, though trying hard not to show that.

'Yes, with ambassador Price,' Victoria said, giving her daughter another broad smile, sensing that she would have found out about her medical condition. She was truly blessed to have such a lovely daughter. 'Yes, but I did love your father, just before you came in, I was reminiscing, thinking about the war that is looming, remembering how James, not long after we were married, went off to war, never came back….' Victoria's voice trailed off.

Jane watched her and waited, she had never known her father but did know her mother had loved him. Had never re-married.

'But, as I have just said, before your father, yes, I was in love with Samuel, he was such a kind and caring and rather knowledgeable man, yet, although I'm sure he had feelings for me, he never said…. Anyway, I wrote him a letter, in it, I confessed to a couple of things, one of them, was that I had been in love with him… I had given him the letter before he set off for Liverpool, and said he mustn't read it until he was at sea, perhaps I thought that he might have stayed otherwise, maybe, I don't know, but I never heard from him again, often I would wonder, had he read it? But I never did get a reply.' Victoria took a deep breath again, the illness that was affecting her brough about waves of a dull ache that affected her breathing.

'Mother?' Jane said, seeing the discomfort, 'should I…'

'No, no I'm good, thank you dear, now, I did eventually, write to him, several years later, found his address in Vancouver. He wrote back, much to my surprise and joy, but also with a question unanswered, you see, he wrote back, saying that he was now married, a lady called Elizabeth Claussen, and, that he had a son. But he never mentioned anything about the letter I had given him before he left, so, this did seem puzzling, why didn't he refer to that, had he read it, had he lost it? Anyway, over the years we wrote occasionally, I did however just recently, sent him a letter telling him of my illness...'

'I am sorry mother' Jane whispered, 'I was talking with the doctor yesterday, having had the results of more tests, there is...'

'I know, there is nothing that can be done now....' Victoria finished, then leaning forward, took hold of her daughter's hand, 'It's alright, I am okay with it all'

Jane moved herself forward and hugged her mother, then both of them began to softly cry.

After a few moment Jane puled herself back upright, saw to her tears and looked at her mother and said,' wait a minute, I have just remembered, you said you confessed to a couple of things...that you had been in love with him, yes, this I already knew, so, what was the other thing?'

Victoria dried her tears, smiled, turned to take a look out of the window and briefly wondered about Samuel Wilfred Price...

Former ambassador Samuel Wilfred Price had moved from Vancouver to Kamloops. Not long after having received his appointment to British Colombia, he had met, fallen in love and began a relationship with Elizabeth Claussen who he later married. He never did open that letter from Victoria but did send a reply to a letter he received from her several years later and informed her of his marriage to Elizabeth and that they had a son, born in 1919 that they named Samuel Junior....

'At home' Victoria said, once again looking at her daughter, 'there are two diaries, two different years, find them, read through them, they hold important information'

Jane looked at her mother, again a puzzled expression on her face, but before she could say anything, there was a knock on the door and a man entered, armed with a small bunch of flowers.

In the bed, Victoria smiled, Jane, who had stood up and facing the man could think of nothing to say and the man, looking from one to the other, then resting his gaze upon Victoria, said, 'Father sends his love'

The second world war began.

Victoria dies in the hospital. Samuel Junior joins the war effort and Jane continues nursing, and together with so many other nurses and doctors they are soon inundated with wounded.

Samuel Junior is wounded and is sent to England where, as fate would have it, he arrives at the hospital where Jane works. The initial look they gave each other, that day in the hospital where Victoria was, was rekindled, they each knew that they were meant for each other. Jane said so, and Samuel, though feeling it was perhaps a womanly thing to say, admitted, they indeed were meant for each other. They married in 1943.

The diaries that her mother had left her, were never read. And, Samuel Junior, having never returned to Canada where his father and mother now lived in Kamloops, received a box with his personal belongings, but also his father sent him a letter, one that Victoria had written and one that he had never opened. Putting this together in a box along with the two diaries, one from the year 1903 and the other from 1908. It was put away.

A son, James Samuel was born in 1946 and a year later a daughter came into the world, they named her Victoria. Though it was still a tough life after the war, it was a new beginning, new hope, a new life.

Such was not the case sixteen years later for Hugo Visser and Alexa Grossman, for their lives had ended.

The year 1963- Istanbul

Youseff stood by the bodies. He was thinking about what to do next, or even what to do first. The gunshot, the one he heard, the one that was very loud, though it reverberated around the building, no one from outside would likely have heard it amid the noise of the traffic. He looked down the body of the man, Hugo Visser, noticed the small calibre bullet mark, right under his heart. A big gun was lying close to his right hand. This was the gun that he had heard. He looked down at her body. His employer, Madam. The damage was severe.

Youseff concluded that she must have shot him first, then he, likely falling to the floor, had somehow produced a gun and had shot her. He hadn't, as yet, touched anything, but realised that he had to do something quite quickly, a coroner would be able to calculate the time of death pretty accurately.

He moved fast, went to Madam's office, noticed the keys and the painting that Hugo Visser had brought with him, as well as a stack of papers and documents. Gathering these up he then recrossed the large room, headed for his own office, there he then rang the police before opening a wardrobe, getting out a holdall in which he stuffed the papers and keys. He then shifted the wardrobe a little, placed the painting of the monk behind it, and shoved the furniture back in place. The holdall he, by standing on his desk chair, placed upon the top of the wardrobe. Then Youseff Turan composed himself and went downstairs to await the arrival of the police.

Three days later and Youseff was by his desk, a police detective was sat in his chair, reading through various papers and now and then looking up at him.

'Kazim Oblensko's body is in our morgue, I have details of what has occurred, Huzar Kaplova is badly injured and in hospital, I have spoken with him, so, Youseff, you now need to tell me all that you know, unless I take you in for further questioning at the station?'

Youseff looked at the detective, then glanced at the wardrobe, noticing that the bag was still there. No doubt the painting was also still behind the wardrobe. Deciding that it was best to play as ignorant as possible and tell as little as he could, Youseff began to speak.

The detective made notes, now and then looking up at him. He then mentioned the family. 'Madam has a daughter' he said, 'She would no doubt inherit? I mean, the paintings, some are quite valuable I believe'

Youseff knew of the daughter that Madam had given up for adoption but saw for himself a way of hopefully gaining some of

Madam's wealth. He shrugged his shoulders in response to the detective's question.

Four weeks passed. Kazim's body was released for burial. Huzar was discharged from hospital and would be now cared for in his home, by his daughter. The lock up garage across the road from where he lived, was used to store Alexa's belongings, as the officials tried to trace her next of kin, the daughter she had given up for adoption. Youseff, realising he was not likely to benefit in any way, chose to leave the city.

Papers and documents were sent to an address in Trieste. There was no reply and due to a fire in a section of the council building where many documents were kept, much was destroyed, arson was suspected, possibly by criminals who were intent of destroying evidence against them. No culprits were found.

Forty-two years later Danielle Vitali would arrive in Istanbul and open the lock, up garage. Observed by the sixteen-year-old granddaughter of Huzar Kaplova.

Danielle would pack everything and take it all back to her home in Trieste.

THE PRESENT

Sunday 5th June

Trieste.

'I was surprised how much stuff there was' Danielle said, 'I just packed it all up and brought it here.'

'Yes, I remember how you said you had come by the painting of the monk, and those keys, which turned you into that great sleuth, figuring it all out' Martijn said taking a sip of coffee and watching her across from him.

'And now I am in the middle of another mystery' Danielle said, rubbing her knee which had begun to throb after her lunging tackle in the shopping mall.

'You sure gave a performance that will be remembered, likely even feature in the papers tomorrow!' Martijn said, smiling, seeing her rub her knee.

Danielle blushed, but then composed herself quickly and said, 'right, mister Dutch detective, tell me again, what is going on and how can I help?'

'Well, the man from Interpol, Walther, should be here soon, I'm guessing he has a lot of information too, oh, I think he's here now' Martijn answered, seeing a car pull up outside the house in a lovely suburban area, remembering it from when he had visited her before.

A few minutes later, Walther, declining a drink, formally introduced himself to both Danielle and Martijn, and then sat down, 'please, allow me to begin, then, if you, Martijn can add your side of the story and then you Miss Vitali...'

'Please, just Danielle.' she interrupted.

'Okay, although I do have a limited knowledge of your language m… Danielle, I am glad to be having this conversation in English….'

'As Am I…' Martijn said, smiling.

'Right, well,' Walther began, looking from one to the other, then said, 'Since that case with the South African lady, who called herself Steffi Baertjens at the time, and on whose trail your Sophie was on,' looking at Martijn, 'I have been reassigned to focus on stolen art, something that is well organised throughout Europe, keeping tabs on various museums, art galleries and auction houses. News of the theft in Antwerpen caught my attention, by the way, Martijn, you and the team in Belgium did a great job, rescuing the insurance Lady'

'Rescuing?' Danielle interceded.

'It will all become clearer' Walther said, then going on,' I was keeping an eye on the events, then, with intelligence I had received, suddenly it became clear as to who was behind it, then, when news came through about the death of this Crystal woman…'

Someone died?' Again, Danielle said, trying to make sense of all she heard, 'sorry. Carry on'

'Quite alright m… Danielle' Walther said, then continuing, 'I felt, like you did too Martijn, that you, Danielle, not only might have crucial information, it was also possible that you might indeed be in danger.' Walther paused here for a moment, then said, 'I flew by private charter to Trieste, already aware that you were on your way Martijn, awaited your arrival and then followed you, back up, in case you or the Italian police needed it, my instruction were not to interfere, but to speak to you, Miss …sorry, Danielle, at some point…'

'I'm glad you are here, 'Martijn said, then, looking at Danielle,' okay, let me tell you then, what has happened' looking briefly at Walther who gave him a nod to proceed.

'Yes, I am still, quite, well, shocked I suppose, so, do tell'

Martijn told her all that had occurred since the insurance woman, Samantha Price, mentioning that she was an acquaintance of theirs, was informed of the theft, and the subsequent kidnapping, rescue and discovery of the paintings without the frames. He then told her about the police then finding the body of the woman, Crystal Kaplova, who had been behind the theft, but obviously in cahoots with these two criminals, the brother and sister who have now been arrested, thankfully, can you tell us more on those two?' Martijn asked looking at Walther.

'I will tell you more on those two in a moment, but, Daniele, how about we hear how you come to have been in possession of the two paintings that were stolen, what can you tell us about them?

Danielle looked from one to the other, felt her heart flutter and hope she wasn't showing any colour in her face as she, just now, realised that she had two rather handsome men sitting across from her. Slowing letting out some breath, she then closed her eyes briefly, composed herself and began to talk. 'This was all in 2005, my mother, had, after a lengthy illness, passed away. Though it was not a surprise in one way, she fought her battle for a long time, it was still a shock, anyway, a few days later, after the funeral, after I had replied to the many cards and well wishes that had been sent, I was in my mother's bedroom, making myself go through her clothes and personal belongings, having to decide what to keep, what to give away and so on, anyway, it was then that I discovered something, it took me by surprise, it shocked me, because I had no inkling, she never told me, but I found papers, documents. My mother was adopted. She never told me who her father was, and now, I discovered that the grandmother I had briefly known, for she had passed before I was a teenager, wasn't my biological grandmother at all. I remember sitting there, on mum's bed, looking, staring at these documents.

Back then, I was a divorced woman, no children, and I wondered about my own life, about who I was, and suddenly sad that I had no family left to speak off.' Taking in a deep breath, Danielle again looked up at each of the men, then, realising they were both very attentively looking at her, she continued,' There and then, I decided I needed to know, I needed to know my heritage, where I had come from. It took some time, lot of research, but I found it who my biological grandmother was, a woman called Alexa Grossman. Well, I was totally engrossed of course, at that time I was a senior nurse in a private clinic, and due to the nature of what I had found out, I took time out from my work, because I discovered that this Alexa Grossman, had been shot and killed in Istanbul.'

The men looked at each other briefly, then refocused on Danielle, neither saying a word at this time. 'I delved deep, looked up newspapers items, and police reports and this eventually led me to a man called Youseff, who was, apparently, Alexa's secretary or something, but he had died and with the help of the police in Istanbul, I contacted a relative, an elderly sister, and she had a little information, but more importantly, she told me about a lock up, a garage, and that she had the keys.'

I flew down, met with her, she was sweet, very frail and told me she was nearly a hundred. She also told me her brother was not a very nice man. I explained again who I was, and she then gave me a bundle of papers and the keys and address of this garage. Well, that's where they all were, as Martijn knows, it is also where I found a portrait of a monk and the silver keys that he and his friends were on the trail of, anyway, that's a different story, what you want to know, is the paintings, well, there were ten of them, various artists, some rather lovely. I shipped everything there was back here. Then, oh gosh, must have been ten years later, I decided to travel, left my job, and planned to sell a few paintings to bring in some finance. I sold two in Paris, then another two in Cologne, by the way Martijn, I went there because that's where the elder monk went, just for curiosity,' Danielle said, smiling.

Walther then spoke,' the painting you sold in Cologne, back in, 2015, is one of two that are involved in the theft we are investigation, one of the paintings you sold in Paris, was the other one, do you still have the other six, and do you have any more information as to where this Alexa woman, your grandmother, got them from?'

Danielle looked across at Walther, smiled at him and thought back, to that day, when she had made that discovery in her mother's bedroom.

THE PAST

Period 8: The year 2005

Trieste

Danielle Vitali shrugged her shoulders, then took a deep breath and entered what had been her mother's bedroom. Time to sort things out, time to clear things out, time to bring some sort of closure. Deciding to start with the wardrobe, Danielle took everything out and placed all the garments on the bed. She would organise to get some cardboard moving boxes and had already made up her mind to donate most of her belongings to a charity organization that had been set up through the church her mother had worshiped at.

Her long auburn hair was tied in a ponytail. She wore pale jeans, a white blouse tucked into them, and her feet were bare. The thirty-five-year-old, who was a senior nurse in a private clinic, decided to work quickly, wanting it to be done as soon as feasible. At one point she stopped as she caught herself in the long mirror. She looked at herself for a few moments, studying her slim figure, wondering briefly about her own life. Her mother had been the one to raise her, she never knew her father and her own marriage had failed after less than five years. She had no children. Shaking her head briefly, Danielle carried on sorting through her mother's things. Coming across a shoe box, that contained several sheets of papers and some documents, she took out the top sheet and froze. It was an official document and Danielle stared at it for some time, before sitting herself down in the edge of the bed.

How had she never known this? Her mother had been adopted. How had she never told her, shared this information? She had never revealed who her father was, now, it seemed that she never told her many things. Sitting on the edge of the bed, Danielle looked around, looked at all her mother's clothes that lay on the bed, looked around the room, where, when a small child, she had often spent time with her mother. Thinking back through her teenage years when she had been quite rebellious, but her mother had been always patient and kind, but had never shared about her own upbringing, though, Danielle admitted to herself, she had never asked.

Sitting there, she made a decision, she would find out, she would learn about her mother, her background, where she came from, who her ancestors were. It would be a new beginning, of sorts, re-invent herself, wanting to not just be someone who lived and died and never left a trail.

Four days later she had dealt with all the funeral arrangements, had placed the house, now belonging to her, up for sale and had taken some time of work. In her own apartment, along the shore looking out over the water, Danielle sat by her dining table and looked at the various papers and documents that lay spread there. She had read them all. Using her skills on the computer she had discovered much about her mother, had discovered the person who might possibly be her real mother, but, most interestingly, had discovered who her real mother's biological mother was, her true grandmother. She was Alexa Grossman, and after some searching, Danielle discovered that she had been shot and killed, back in 1963. In Istanbul.

This information had not only taken her by surprise, but had so intrigued her, that she promised herself to search for whatever happened, and why.

After countless hours of research and perusing through document, some of which she had to translate, Danielle found out that Alexa had purchased the complete first floor of an old historical building, with all its contents. The previous resident had been an ambassador who had left the city very much in a hurry, pursued by the family of a woman he had been secretly seeing, a married woman.

Among the contents of this building were the ten paintings, and she had a list. She also found out some contact numbers and then discovered that she had been left some of the belongings, housed in a lock up garage in the city. To Istanbul she must go, and it was only a few days later that she packed a suitcase and had organised travel arrangements.

THE PRESENT

Sunday 5th June

New York

Tammy shut the suitcase, checked her phone, then pressing a few numbers, spoke briefly and then gathered the suitcase, along with a cabin bag and a handbag. She had made up her mind. In her mind she mentally ticked off all the things she had to do, recalling a time, seemingly ages ago, when she had arrived back from Yonkers, back to her old apartment, when she learned of her inheritance, learned of the finances she was to receive, she had, in preparation to travel to Paris, checked things of in her mind.

She had organised cover for her restaurant, had arranged all the flight details and had once again contacted Thomas, the pilot. The one who had, a little over a year ago, been so instrumental in collecting Terri from San Francisco, then had collected her from New York before taken them to Paris. Tammy smiled. That was when she had first seen him. Walther.

She placed her cabin bag on top of the suitcase, then trundled them down to corridor and with her handbag across her shoulder, she opened the door and left her apartment. Again, she smiled to herself, remembering when they had arrived in Paris, and the plane was taxiing towards the hangars, how young Terri had spotted him, observing what a' hunk' he was. She had thought so too. The taxi arrived and Tammy gave instructions.

Thomas Klaassen, smartly dressed in navy blue trousers, a crisp white shirt underneath a blue blazer, stood in the doorway of the small jet. He had just picked it up from a nearby hangar, had completed the necessary checks and had then taxied it across the apron to a nearby small terminal, where he had then opened the door and lowered the steps to give access to Tia.

Cynthia Barnes trundled her suitcase towards the waiting jet. It was a warm morning in Portland, Oregon. Her long dark tresses, smartly connected in a ponytail, she wore pale blue jeans. Her feet in a pair of low heeled blue slingbacks and carrying a lightweight jacket across the shoulder of a silky patterned blouse, predominantly in shades of red. Carrying her handbag in the other hand, she smiled as she approached, thinking how dapper he looked. She was looking forward to meeting Tammy. Though Thomas had met her previously, he didn't know her that well, however, young Claire, who had met the New Yorker, was full of praise and admiration for this woman.

Tammy had called the previous evening, even though Tammy, who was financially a very wealthy woman, could have easily hired anyone, but as she knew Thomas, had asked if he would fly her to Paris. Could Cynthia come along, he had asked to which she had replied that of course she could and looked forward to meeting her, having heard so much about both of them from Claire when they had met in Albuquerque. Cynthia, known to her friends as Tia, climbed the steps, Thomas came down to assist her by grabbing her suitcase, then kissed her, before turning and entering the sleek craft. Fifteen minutes later they were airborne, heading for an airfield near Yonkers, New York.

It was when the jet was twenty minutes out from New York, that Tammy arrived at the small airfield. She was glad that Samantha was alright, she had met the insurance lady when she had travelled to Antwerpen on the trail of her grandmother, and she had been with her when they visited a house where Rosemary Quinton had once briefly lived. She had, prior to her decision to travel to Paris, spoken at length with Sophie, both speaking in French, which Tammy was good at, having lived in the French capital or several years, and a delight for Sophie who mainly conversed with Martijn in English as he found it difficult to follow her when she spoke rapidly. Sophie had brought her up to date with what had occurred, from the time that Samantha had been kidnapped, to when Sam, with the help from local police had rescued her. Then told her of the culprit, a Crystal Kaplova being found dead and how her Martijn had flow over to Trieste to see a woman named Danielle, who Tammy knew by name as she had been instrumental in the solving of the mystery of the three monks, to the part where the Interpol officer, Walther, was now also involved and with Marijn at the very present. It was then, after that lengthy conversation, that Tammy had sat down, had thought it through and had made up her mind. She liked Walther, she was going to see him. As he was due to fly back to Paris, she had emailed him. Coming to Paris, can you meet me at the airport? She had asked.

His reply had been an emphatic 'Absolut mon cherie'. Sorting out all the travel arrangements had been fun, speaking with Thomas had been good, it was comforting to have someone with her she knew, then his girlfriend, Cynthia coming along too, excellent. Claire had told her about them, especially about Cynthia, or Tia, as she had been the woman who had rescued her. She watched as the jet approached for landing.

Meanwhile in the small town of Myrtle Creek

Claire drank some water from the bottle, swivelled the chair in the study to face the computer and then began to type. Thomas had explained to her about the circumstances surrounding the kidnapping and rescue of Samantha, how he and Tia were off to take Tammy to Paris and would she mind holding the fort, so to speak. Though a little jealous about not going to Paris, or seeing Tammy who she had instantly liked, she put on a brave face and said of course she would. It had been Robert, now sadly passed away, who had been the initiator of the search programmes, first in the hope of tracking down his former girlfriend, Holly, who had simply vanished, but had then totally absorbed himself into the tracking down of missing persons. It was he had had located her, and then Tia who had rescued her from her captors. The various programmes Robert had installed into his computer system were very technologically advanced and covered the global network of similar programmes. This had enabled her to navigate her way through various forms and documents that had enabled her to successfully find Robert's former girlfriend Holly, and all about a very hush hush event called the Ontario Project.

It was whilst doing this research, she came across a name, a name that linked to a place, that in turn linked to another name and another place. Claire loved doing her research, she loved the detective work of following trails and figuring out into a grid system of timelines, as to where and where everything fitted. She was also good at listening and retaining information, though often making sure she would note these down, in case further references were needed. So it was, that in the case, the first case that Thomas had got involved in shortly after inheriting the house after Robert's death, Claire recalled how she had been so impressed when, he, Thomas, had set off to help a situation that had appeared on Robert's computer system inbox.

It was during that case that she had come across a chap named Desmond Peter Janssen, a former police detective. It had been he, who had discovered relevant information with regards to a missing man, a Roger Sutherland. It was this name, that then brought a connection to a Hugo Visser, who had been the thief that had stolen articles from Roger's house in Eastbourne, England. Having then taken it upon herself to follow that link in order to discover why these articles had been so important, that she found out about this man's life and, that he was subsequently shot and killed in Istanbul. And it was this place, that sprang into her mind, when Thomas had mentioned that he was off to pick up Tammy, to take her to Paris because her friend, Walther, who he had briefly met, was on his way back from Trieste, where he had met a woman in connection with some missing paintings that had once belonged to her biological grandmother, who had been shot and killed in Istanbul.

Drinking another swig of water, Claire scrolled through some pages, and it wasn't long, before she discovered a great connection. This Hugo Visser had been shot by a woman called Alexa…. Who herself had been shot and killed by Hugo.

Thinking how she might be of help in this investigation, remembering how Robert had always said to her, can't have too much information, it all counts. Claire decided to delve deeper.

Meanwhile, on board the private jet, Tammy and Cynthia were in deep conversation as they flew high over the Atlantic Ocean.

'So, you actually met this Samantha woman?' Tia asked, having for several minutes now spoken about her involvement with Robert Pentegrass and the rescue of Claire, which Tammy had asked her to explain.

'Yes, it was all to do when we were involved in following up on the search for an intricately painted piece of ivory, a miniature….' Tammy said, recalling the event in her mind, thinking back to that day in Antwerpen, already a little over three years ago…

She saw her arrive, knew it to be the woman she was awaiting, knew it to be Samantha Price, 'Hi, I'm Tammy,' extending her hand, 'thank you for coming'

'My pleasure' Samantha answered, shaking the offered hand, 'So, you're Rosemary's granddaughter and I'm guessing this is about the missing miniature? Sam asked me to meet you, but didn't exactly say why, other than possibly being a translator?'

'My grandmother fell in love, chap's name was Bastiaan Bouten. He travelled with her to New York, though there was no mention of him in grandma's letters. But Sam discovered who he was and that they shared a cabin on the boat that left here for New York. Now just recently I discovered a letter from my grandmother's father, Percivald, a very brief and more business-like letter, stating that he, Percivald, had found out that this Bastiaan was married and send him packing, presumably back to here' Tammy said, indicated the house to where they were heading.

Samantha knew the house, Sam had told her about it, 'and you know who lives here now?' she asked.

'Yes, his grandson, Adriaan, I spoke with him yesterday, he doesn't live here yet, has only recently inherited it, but agreed to meet me, Sam suggested that it would be good if you came along, thank you, I do appreciate it'

'So, what are you hoping to find? 'Samantha asked as Tammy knocked on the door.

'Answers' Tammy replied…

'Yes,' Tammy said, smiling at the woman next to her, 'A lovely lady, engaged to be married, I am glad she's safe now, though, it's still all a bit of a mystery of what the thieves were actually after'

'Maybe my friend Walther might have some answers' Tammy said, after a few moments of silence as the jet flew across the cloudless sky. Then, again turning to Tia, said 'So, now, do tell me, Claire told me quite a story, about you and Thomas, escaping from this Spanish hacienda, by plane?'

Tia smiled, already forming a bond with this New Yorker whom she had heard so much about, 'Yes, we'll I can imagine Claire telling you the story, we did leave her in dark at times as to what was going on, which, of course, drove her mad. By the way, thank you, she was so glad of your company when she went to Albuquerque, spoke so highly of you, Thomas and I do appreciate that, so yes, anyway, the escape, an idea that came into Thomas's mind, like in the middle of the night, we had just managed to rescue the English lady, Victoria, and managed to get away from the hacienda, when Thomas suggested we return there! To steal the plane. We needed to get away, out of Spain, and that, seemed to be the only option.' Tia began to explain, recalling the adventure with fondness, then, seeing how Tammy was keen to know more, continued the story as the jet flew almost silently through the sky.

THE PAST

2015

Paris

Sam Price had needed to get away, needed to breathe, needed to take in the reality of what had happened. Finding himself in Paris that day, have travelled by train from Rotterdam, he had wandered into the auction house. Had been puzzled by a painting by Gauguin. The flurry of activity that subsequently happened was, really, a welcome distracting. He sat now as a painting appeared on the rostrum and also on the big screen. A well know Turkish artist was explained by the auctioneer and Sam glanced at his catalogue. Hikmet Onat. He had not come across that name before and he was often found in museum or reading books on artists and their works. He would not long after having been to this auction, be offered an opportunity to put his knowledge of art into the role of an art assessor. Much later, this event would prove to be the catalyst that changed his life.

Seated five places along from Sam, Danielle Vitali was focused on the auctioneer. This was her first lot. She was pleased with the sale and awaited her second lot, which, according to the catalogue, would appear in three lot's time.

Two rows, directly behind Danielle sat Crystal Kaplova. She was specifically waiting for Miss Vitali's second lot to appear. Listed as 'Scene of Rome' by the Flemish master, Jacob Leyssens. It was her reason for being here in Paris, having spent many years in researching the property of Alexa Grossman. Initially on the trail of the portrait of a monk but had then switched her attention to the ten paintings

191

that had now come into the possession of this Miss Vitali, it was to ascertain who would end up purchasing it.

Three seats to the left and a further row behind Crystal, Estelle Cabal was making notes in the margins of her catalogue. At that point she knew nothing about Sam Price, nor about Danielle Vitali. She was, however, interested in the young lady to her right, who, she would discover was Crystal Kaplova. In years to come, she would know about all three.

After the auction, Estelle watched the young woman she had been observing, walking down the street, heading for what she assumed, would be the railway station. She would obtain information on her from the auction house records. Looking up at the sky, figuring it might rain soon, she too then moved and checking her watch, headed for where a row of taxi's were parked. Her flight was still three hours away. Using her latest model mobile phone, she pressed some numbers as the opened the taxi door, giving instruction to the driver to go to the airport. Once on her way, and having left a quick message on her phone, Estelle sat back and thought back as to how she got to this point in her life. It had all begun when her younger brother and her had inherited the farm...

...'on the other side of this river, are the Teremos Orchards. Big company, old family, very influential, they ordered the dam to be taken down that your grandfather had put up to create extra water flow on our fields' the old man said. He was the current manager of the farm. Whilst they grew several fields of cabbages, they also, first cultivated by the man whom the farm manager had referred to as their grandfather, had begun to grow poppies, under netting and in a secluded area of the farm, surrounded by low bushes so as to keep the area from being easily seen. Drugs were lucrative, drugs brought in finance.

Estelle and her younger brother Filippe looked over the rapidly streaming river. She knew about the poppies, knew about the part of the second barn where they harvested and prepared the drugs for distribution. A small venture, but Estelle knew it could grow bigger, bring in much more money, but they needed a better water supply. 'I will contest their claim' she said, looking at the farm manager, then at her brother, before saying, 'I have studied law, I will get that dam reinstated'

Filippe smiled at his sister. The twenty-one-year-old was almost six foot in height, and though very slim, was incredibly agile and much stronger than he appeared. He loved his sister, a sister who had always looked after him, for he had been born partially deaf and with a speech impediment. He was slow in learning, could not understand or grasp many things, but was almost always in the company of his sister for whom he would do anything. He didn't understand about the land ownership deals, or the claims, or the business that was operated here. He only knew his sister and merely did as was asked of him by her.

Estelle headed back to the farm. Just having turned twenty-three, she was about three inches shorter than her brother and kept herself very fit. She had been surprised when the documents had arrived, informing her of the deeds of the farm which now belonged to her and her brother. She had packed and had explained to Filippe that they were now leaving their small cottage on the outskirts of Madrid and head north, to live on a farm.

He had nodded and complied, as he did not speak very often, he had remained silent and had gathered his belongings.

Estelle and her brother had arrived, had settled in quickly, and the young woman had quickly taken control, had spent several hours reading through many papers and documents, had a grasp of the business, had spoken to every member of the staff that managed the farm, had spent a considerable amount of time with the farm manager, Stefan, and felt very much in control, knowing who she could trust and work with.

First, she would ensure that the farm ran as smoothly as possible, then she would follow up on a side business that her grandfather had set up and had documented for her, she knew he had faith in her, rather than his own daughter, who had, more than five years ago now, left the family and had not returned. After this, referring to a trip she needed to make to Paris, to an auction house and to observe a young woman who had come up in some research she was undertaking, she would then take a look at how best to contest the neighbour's land rights. A woman named Letitia Teremos, the boss of the Teremos Orchards…

…Estelle took a taxi to the airport, she needed to get back home, back to her brother whom she rarely left alone, but the trip to Paris had been necessary, and very important, for information had to be found regarding the ancient notes she had found in her grandfather's study. Notes from her ancestor in Colombia, a man, they called the Patron, a certain Jose De Garagoa. Notes that mentioned oil paintings and emeralds, as well as the young woman, a Crystal Kaplova.

Heading for the boarding gate to fly to Bilbao, Estelle didn't notice that she was being observed. Crystal Kaplova had earlier in the day noticed the Spanish woman, had seen her name in the register at the auction house and had seen her when leaving the hotel before that. Crystal just knew that this woman was observing her, but why? Now, as she watched her board her flight, Crystal decided to further investigate who she was, and why the interest, then turned and headed for her own boarding gate, for she would soon be flying to Cologne. For she knew that Miss Vitali was heading there. Now she knew who had purchased the first painting, the one by Jacob Leyssen, she now wanted to find out who the buyer might be for the second Flemish painting that Miss Vitali was about to sell. She knew this because she had been monitoring the movements of the Italian lady for some years now. The search for the treasure attached to the portrait of the man had failed, the trail, meagre at best, based on hearsay and the rambling of her grandfather, had not amounted to much, but in her research, she had come across some other information, regarding two paintings by Flemish masters, a story she had picked up about the possibilities of a trail that might lead to a cache of Emeralds.

She had made copious notes and also knew about a family that lived in Spain, a family that had connections with Colombia and Crystal wondered about the presence of the Spanish woman, sensing that she perhaps, was also in search of this treasure, a treasure that had to do with a precious emerald necklace. Furthermore, as her funds were beginning to run low and she still wanted to continue her quest to find the treasure that was rumoured to be connected to one of those two paintings, she made a decision, she would contact her. Her name, again this from the register at the auction house, was Estelle Cabal. Crystal would, in her research, confirm that this indeed was the family connected to the Columbian necklace, wondered how much she knew, and the possibility of working together, as she felt she had more detailed information that would enable her to strike a satisfying deal. Little did she know that it had been her own investigation into the connection with the necklace, that had been discovered and had created an interest in the very person she was hoping to strike a deal with.

THE PRESENT

Sunday evening 5th June

San Francisco

Terri Hudson was alone in her apartment. She had left her mother's house, had said goodbye to Chantal who was soon to travel back to Boston, and wanted to focus on the research that Tammy had asked her for. Her mother had already researched some information on the Spanish guy, Bartolo, but she wanted to continue looking into Flemish artists. Though initially wanting to know more about the artists and the two paintings that had been at the centre of the theft, in her earlier research, there was something else that caught her attention, something that seemed strange to her, something that appeared to be most unusual.

Unscrewing the cap of another bottle of water, Terri would drink at least eight a day of these, she sat herself down behind her desk in the second bedroom of her apartment which she had turned into her study. Various clipboards were hung on the wall. A large map of the world covered almost an entire wall.

Typing a few lines on her keyboard, she found the place that had caught her attention earlier. A company in Bogota, Colombia, that specialised in creating picture frames. All sorts and sizes, from plain to very ornate. Reading more on this company, she noticed it was a family business that had started a long time ago, a craft that had been taught from father to son, or to daughter. As well as frames, they also made guitars. The wood they used was the Mexican Cypress, a softwood ideal for carving. What had caught her attention the most, was that they exported their work to Spain, France and Belgium, from as early as the late 1800's.

Working from this information, Terri then scrolled and searched for companies that used these products, that imported these frames from Columbia. Half a bottle later and already well into the evening, she needed a break from the various documents she had perused. But sat back and afforded herself a quick smile. She had found a connection. A business in the city of Antwerpen had bought a small shipment of assorted frames in 1903.

It was another two hours later, Terri drinking the last of the bottle of water, that she switched of her computer, looked at the notes she had made and decided that it was time for bed. She had made a connection with the frames from Colombia to a business in Antwerpen, to a studio in that city and to the fact that several of the paintings done by the old masters had been reframed by these ornamental frames so as to create a better sale potential. Terri's eyes were very tired from having read the sometimes almost illegible writing, but she had a list of actual works that the studio, which in fact was also a place which sold art and supplies, had been reframed. The list consisted of various artists from different periods, but two names stood out for her among the fourteen that she had written down. One was a work by Arnold Frans Rubens, titled 'Battle on the coast' and the other a landscape by another Flemish master, Pieter Bout. The dimensions of both paintings were exactly the same.

Myrtle Creek

Just over 600 miles to the north, Claire had also just switched off the computer system in the well-equipped study that Thomas had dubbed the search engine room. Sitting back in the desk chair, Claire was pleased with herself, though she could feel her back was stiff from sitting for a long time. Taking in a deep breath, she got up, stretched and arched her back and left the room. It was time for bed, but as she closed the door of the study and headed for her bedroom, she smiled to herself, because she felt quite certain she now knew why it was that the frames of the stolen paintings might have been so important.

Would she be able to sleep, she wondered, knowing what she knew, but also realising that it was the middle of the night in Paris, so couldn't call either Thomas or Tia at this time.

Fifteen minutes later she pulled back the covers and slid into her bed. Turning off the light she lay there, thinking through what she had discovered. Like Terri, she too had found out about the framing business established in Colombia, but she had taken a different turn from there and made a connection with a powerful landowner called Jose de Garagoa. She had come across some historical accounts about a chest of gold coins that had been liberated from this landowner, apparently the robbery had taken place in the night at a house in Bogota city belonging to the patron. According to the account, they had chased the robbers to the city of Buenaventura, where it was assumed, the gold was taken aboard a ship bound for Mexico. Though it made for interesting reading, there was another account she found, from around the same time, the year being 1814. It had to do with the patron's wife, a woman named Dacha…

…Dacha, having been married to Jose for over twelve years, was not terribly overcome when the news reached her ears, that her husband had been shot and killed. He had not been the most attentive husband, has spent a lot of time running the business, running the group of men that were in constant battle with the Spanish and aside from all that, had made time for a mistress. When the gold coins had been stolen from the town house, she recalled his fury. But that was nothing compared to when he had heard the news and confirmation, that it had been his own daughter, that had planned and executed the robbery and had subsequently disappeared. Most likely to Mexico. He had been livid. Had blamed her, had yelled at her, had been very close to striking her. But Dacha had remained composed, calm and defiant. She had a loyal and strong family behind her. She felt confident that he wouldn't dare touch her.

She had been right. Over the next few months, she had hardly laid eyes on him, then, when he and a group of his men had encountered a band of outlaws that had begun to operate in the region, he had gathered a posse of men. No-one encroached on his territory. But a battle had ensued. He had been wounded and had died only hours later…

Dacha had inherited the family ranch and business, and it had been the name De Garagoa, that had piqued Claire's interest, for when she been to the special exhibition held in honour of Professor Parker, for her work in the field of Geology and archaeology, for it had been her team that had discovered the buried gold coins, stolen so long ago from Colombia, she had heard that name. A family that was now contesting the fact that the gold coins belonged to them. A case that was quickly dealt with in a court of law. A name that was now connected to the stolen paintings, of that she was sure, and Claire turned on to her side and fell asleep.

THE PAST

2019

London

Glendale Auction House, situated in Hammersmith, was a small family business. Not anywhere in the same league as Christie's or any of the other top auction houses in the city of London. But they had connections, they knew people, friends who supported the business and as some preferred to deal with what was commonly referred to as a boutique establishment and certainly with a reputation for being discreet, the business, though not thriving, did succeed in maintaining a presence.

Peter Simpson, the manager, looked at the sheets of paper on his desk and perused over the various items due for auction later in the day. One thing that he was good at, was making sure of the best provenance possible for each item they sold. What stood out for him that morning, was a painting by the Flemish Artist, Pieter Bout.

This work of art had quite a fascinating history. Painted in around 1650, it had disappeared, for many years, eventually turning up at an estate in Shropshire and, having read through as to how it had turned up there, Peter read of how it had been found in a barn in Yemen by a journalist, who had sent it home to his wife. This intrigued him, so, he decided to delve into the history of it.

Peter was badly injured on his right side, he was one of the eight hundred who had been injured when suicide terrorists had detonated several bombs in London, on the seventh of July in the year 2007, referred to now as the 7/7 bombing where fifty-two people from a range of nationalities had died. It had taken months of rehabilitation and counselling to get Peter to a point where he could get back to work. His uncle was the owner of the Glendale Auction House and offered him to work there.

Peter loved the challenge, began to study art and was soon very much part of the team that researched the articles that came in for auction. The painting that came in from the estate in Shropshire, caught his attention. The lovely rural landscape was certainly painted by an accomplished artist. Not having come across this Flemish painter before, Peter did some research, then, having read through the documents provided by the family, the Powell-Hunters, a well-established family in the region, Peter was then totally engrossed in how the painting came to them. A journalist named Thomas Powell had discovered it, and had been given it, when he was in Yemen, covering the riots and chaos there, which, he found out, also cost him his life.

It was an interesting research, he felt admiration for this journalist who, he had found, had been working for an American Newspaper at one time in his life. But Peter's appetite had been wetted, he wanted to find out more. Often, he would still have shivering bouts, moments where he was unable to focus, moments when he trembled and shook. Moments when all around him went silent. These episodes would, thankfully, not last long, he knew, after all the counselling he had gone through, why they would occur, he also knew what to do, and how to reset, was the phrase used. Doing research was a way when he would be at him calmest and when those episodes were far less frequent.

Though the research on the journalist was interesting, Peter wanted to try and discover how that painting, by this Flemish master, had found its way to Yemen. It was during this research that he came upon a story. A story originally written in Arabic, but, a scholar, by the name of Bert Ham, had translated this, back in the early eighteen hundreds, the story of a Persian woman who was travelling back to her homeland, a story of piracy and shipwrecks, Peter, once he had started reading, was completely drawn in…

…Farah did manage to stay awake for many hours. Constantly checking on the boy and the man. The boy, still very much in shock as to the violence of it all, at the encouragement from the woman, worked the forward sail, having managed to pull it back up the mast, he had then, with guidance from the injured man handling the wheel, manoeuvred it in the directions to catch the wind. Farah brough them food, brought them water. Of the two, the man who was handling the wheel, was the most injured. Farah could see he was getting weaker by the hour and daylight was fading. Thankfully the sea was very calm, and though not much of a breeze, there was enough to keep the battered ship sailing. But in what direction, Farah wondered and would they ever reach land.

The night sky was clear, the stars were bright and the man at the wheel knew that the direction they were heading in, was the right way. The boy had tied the sail to a set position and Farah could see that he had lain himself down and had fallen asleep, she also noted, that the cut in his chest, had been bleeding again. Kneeling by the boy she sat there for a while, sensing that sadly, he might be dying. For the first time since the pirates had boarded, ravaged and killed most of the crew, Farah began to softly cry. Letting the tears flow, letting them roll down her cheeks, she thought about her daughter, about Bibiana.

Then three things happened. The first was that she heard a falling sound and turned to see the man at the wheel had collapsed. Just as she was about to get up to see to him, the boy made a sound, then briefly fluttered his eyes open, before his last breath left his body. The last thing was that she, in her attempt to get up, seemingly lost all balance, had no strength and simply collapsed…

Peter wondered, who this woman was, that had travelled from Antwerpen, he found out, to sail to Persia. A woman, according to the notes he found written by this scholar, had been the wife of a Dutch sea merchant, and who had left her ten-year-old daughter behind in Rotterdam after the death of her husband who had been captain of a ship that had sunk in violent weather. The notes were originally written by an inhabitant of the city of Mukalla, a port on the Arabian Sea. A young man, who, when setting out to go fishing at the break of day, saw the wreck, saw the two masted schooner, saw the damage and went over to investigate. The only survivor was a woman, whose name was Farah Maas.

This research gave Peter a great provenance. The painting had been signed and dated by Pieter Bout in 1653. The ship that Farah had sailed on was shipwrecked on the coast near Mukalla in 1655, the painting then had somehow from there landed up in the port of Mocha, where, in 1752, nearly a hundred years later, the journalist Thomas Powell discovered it in a barn, from there it had come to England, to Thomas Powell's widow, who died in the year 1804. The painting remained in the family for the next, nearly, hundred years and was sold in an auction in York in 1903, bought by a Belgian gentleman who had it cleaned and restored and reframed before then selling it on in the same year.

Marilyn Montrose was celebrating her fiftieth. To have flown business class from San Francisco had been a treat, to spend her birthday in London was also a treat. She enjoyed some of the sights, many of the shops and the luxury of the hotel she was staying in. The only thing that kept going through her mind, was the fact that she was alone.

Getting into a black cab and giving the driver the address, she reflected on her life, how it was that she was here and moreover how it was that she was going to an auction. Her mind took her back to when she had been asked to check through the apartment of a known criminal, this being Josh De Garagoa, a distant ancestor of a former ruling Patron in Bogota, Colombia. Smiling to herself, whilst also thinking about the volume of traffic that was all around and how she would surely not want to be driving here, she remembered the documents and deeds she had found that day, relating to property in Colombia. These however led to disappointment. The search for any possible claim on the gold coins that had been stolen from the De Garagoa family also resulted in a negative way. But, knowing that Josh was still in prison and for several years to come, she had once more gained entry into his apartment, this at the request of Josh's lawyer, Isaac Javed, who wanted to know what valuables might be there in order to sell them for needed funds.

It was then, when she discovered some old letters, this time mentioning Dasha, the widow of Jose De Garagoa who had been killed in battle. Able to read the in Spanish written letters, Marilyn remembered her heart skipping several beats. Looking out the window as the taxi drove along, she was momentarily distracted and wondered how the many cars even managed to get from one place to another as they went round this large roundabout. Then, returning to her thoughts and the very reason she was now in London, the emeralds. Dasha, died in the year 1862, she had a younger sister, who had a daughter, Dasha's niece Rebecca. It was to her that an exquisite emerald necklace was bequeathed. The niece, when in her twenties decided to travel to Spain, not wanting to carry the valuable necklace, she arranged, through her uncle's frame and guitar making business, to get those emeralds through by inserting them into one of the frames. The frames were shipped to Antwerpen in Belgium, however, before Rebecca was ever able to collect the frame, she became very ill on the crossing and sadly died.

After weeks of research, Marilyn had eventually tracked down the shipment number, cross checked the dates and finally, made a connection. She knew, or was certainly quite certain, that the frame, having arrived in the early 1900's, was fitted to a painting in 1903. She had vague details about a stencil, with the letter BO- and the number 13. A painting by the Flemish artist Pieter Bout fitted with all the information she had. The right measurements and the fact that it had been reframed at the very studio where the frames had been exported to. It all dovetailed as far as she could see. and it was coming up for auction, today. Would she have enough funds to buy it? Marilyn arrived at the auction house, paid the taxi driver and entered the building where she registered. She felt confident and smiled as she entered the room where various paintings were on display prior to be auctioned.

THE PRESENT

Monday 6ᵗʰ June

Paris

Tammy couldn't help but smile as she looked out the window of the jet as it taxied towards the hangar. She recalled the last time she had arrived at this small airport close to Paris, when young Terri had spotted, 'the hunk' standing next to Sophie. Beside her Tia was also looking. 'So,' she said, not much more than a whisper,' that's Walther?'

Tammy felt herself blush, not turning around, she answered,' That's Walther' happy that her voice seemed normal and under control.

Thomas shut down the engines and switched off all of the many dials before taking of his headphones and getting the plane ready for disembarking. When he came out of the cockpit he nodded to Tia who then set about opening the door. She had always wanted to do this and got Thomas to show her the mechanism before they had set off from Portland.

'Thank you for flying with us madam' Tia said, smiling broadly to Tammy as she approached. Tammy gave her a mock scowl and then descended the steps that Thomas had now lowered into position. Walther was approaching and Tammy noticed the grin on his face. He was happy to see her. She was happy to see him and her heartbeat noticeably quickened.

Fifteen minutes later, whilst the plane was being refuelled and Tammy's luggage was taken off, Walther had finished speaking, completing his update from the journey to Trieste, informing them, a very attentive Thomas, Tia and Tammy, of his involvement in the world of art theft and forgeries and how the woman from Trieste, Danielle had supplied a great deal of information about the very paintings at the centre of this case. Including the events at the shopping mall and the rugby tackle that had received a round of applause. He then mentioned the names of the brother and sister duo, known criminals from Spain, when Tia interrupted him.

'I know that name' she said, 'Sorry Walther,' but I know about Estelle, haven't heard about her brother, but Estelle Cabal is the neighbouring family to where Letitia Teremos has her orchard business, it was her who tried to take Letitia to court in order to overturn a land right about building a dam on the river. Thankfully they lost, apparently, they have connections with drug people in Colombia.'

'Yes, miss Tia,' Walther answered, 'Yes, that is right, so, did you ever meet her then?'

'No, I helped Letitia with the legal stuff, we presented it to the court, were ready for the hearing, but she was a no show, so, that all petered out.'

'Well, she and her brother will be no trouble now, facing lengthy prison terms.'

'And why were they after these paintings?' Tammy asked, 'and this Crystal woman, did they kill her?'

'Yes, when Crystal Kaplova decided the need to kidnap the insurance lady, this Samantha, whom you've met Tammy?' Walther said, getting a nod from Tammy, then continuing, 'they felt it drew far too much attention on what they were after, but, although we have them on a number of crimes, now including murder, we still don't know…'

It was Thomas's phone who alerted him to an incoming call at that moment, 'Its Claire, must be important, excuse me, Thomas said, then 'Claire?'

Thomas stood up, looked out the window of the small lounge and seeing the jet being refuelled, listened for some time, then said, 'Wow, you are a very clever little researcher, well done you, I will call you back soon, okay?' then ended the call and rejoined Tia on a two-seater couch.

'Incredible' he said, looking at Walther and then Tammy, who sat in single chairs opposite them, 'Claire has, very likely, found out why these paintings might have been so important, or, to be precise, why the interest in the frames. However, this brother and sister team, this Estelle and Filippe, didn't have the correct information, they should have been searching for a different painting, a different frame...'

Then it was Tammy's phone that rang. She saw who it was,' Its Terri, got to be important, let me... Terri? '

'No, its fine, you have obviously discovered something to do with this case, I know how clever you are, so, spill...'

After a few moments, Tammy said, 'Wow, listen, thank you so much, now, do you remember when I told you about young Claire, from Myrtle Creek, she works alongside Thomas and Tia, who are with me right now here in Paris, along with Walther, I'm sure you remember him!' she said teasingly and smiling at Walther who, Tia noticed, coloured slightly. 'Well, hang on, you and her need to get in touch with each other, I'll pass you onto Thomas, he'll give you her number, hang on...'

Thomas gave the number, handed back the phone and all eyes were now looking at Tammy.

'Terri, just like Claire, both have delved into the past, both have discovered the reason for the interest in the frames, and both have also discovered that they stole the wrong painting, the wrong frame...

Meanwhile, across the Atlantic and over in the west coast of America, Terri called the number that Thomas had given her.

'Claire?' 'Hi, I'm, Terri, Alison Hudson's daughter and...'

'You went to Florence, with Tammy and Sophie' Claire interrupted, 'Hi, so nice to hear your voice, I've heard the stories of how well you al did, goodness, sorry, has something happened?'

Terri smiled, she had heard about Claire from Tammy, knew a little of her back story, was pleased to be speaking with her and really knew that they should get together one day,' No, no, it's all good, Thomas gave me your number when I called Tammy just now and you had just spoken with him. You see, you are a clever researcher, and apparently, we have both discovered some fascinating facts about the paintings, the frames and the fact that they, being this Crystal woman, and this brother and sister criminal duo, have been chasing the wrong painting, the wrong frame, so, let's compare notes and see if we, together, can paint a complete picture.'

Whilst back across to Europe, in Rotterdam Martijn updated his boss on the proceedings in Trieste and the involvement of Walther from Interpol.

Sophie's phone rang and she answered. 'Terri?' recognising the voice instantly having not connected her with the number on the screen of her phone, 'Hi,...'
'Hi Soph, listen, right now Tammy is in Paris, she's with Walther and Thomas is there too, he flew her across, his girlfriend, Tia, she is there as well, anyway, earlier Thomas heard form Claire, and I rang Tammy. Then, Claire and I spoke at length, between us we have figured out the mystery of the paintings, or, I should say, the mystery of the frames, so, pin back your ears and I'll tell you...'

In the evening-
Thursday 9th June

Antwerpen.

The museum was closed. Emma Brood stood on the polished wooden floor in the centre of three adjoining galleries. A section of the museum dedicated to Flemish artists. She stood and looked at the wall where three paintings were hung in a row. The one on the left was the coastal battle scene by Arnold Frans Ruben, the one of the right the Roman scene by Jacob Leyssen. Both had been cleaned and reframed. The painting in the centre, was by Pieter Bout. Emma stood for a while, looking at those three works of art, having instructed her team to place them here, the central focal, point. There were two small two-seater benches behind her. Taking two steps back, she sat down. Visitors will come. The newspapers would be covering the story. A story about a kidnapping, a death and about two criminals caught. A story about three paintings, a trail of intrigue and mystery. A story that was set in motion by a theft, but a story that had begun over a hundred years ago.

Yes, it would capture the imagination of the readers, it would bring visitors to the museum. Emma smiled. Her director was very pleased with the outcome, though had been mostly away these past few days as his wife was about to give birth to their first child. Sitting there, Emma took in the paintings, her mind taking her back to the day she had discovered the theft, unbelievably only just over a week ago.

In the kitchen of her apartment, Samantha finished tidying up, setting the dishwasher to go and preparing a tray with coffee to bring through to the lounge, where Rico was stretched on the couch, leg in plaster. He was glad to be out of hospital, even more glad to be back with Samantha. He smiled at her as she brought in the tray and was grateful that the kidnapping ordeal was over, remembering that he hadn't, as yet, personally thanked Sam for coming to the rescue.

'You seem deep in thought there' Samantha said, smiling at him. 'What are you thinking?'

'I must call Sam, haven't thanked him yet, feel bad about that'

'It has been a rather hectic time, he'll understand, no need to worry' Samantha said, placing a cup of coffee within his reach.

'Can't wait to see the newspaper tomorrow, a complete story, you said?'

'Yes, the detective who was, alongside Sam, so helpful in my rescue, apparently helped to make sure that all the details and facts were known, yes, I'm looking forward to reading it'

Rotterdam

'So, it will be in the papers tomorrow?' Sophie asked, pouring two glasses of red wine and bringing them into the lounge where Martijn was finishing up writing his report on his laptop. He looked up at her, smiled, took the offered glass and said, 'Yes, the full story, quite a piece I understand, my new friend and Belgian colleague, Jan, has dealt with it all, a reporter, a journalist, who is actually his younger sister, quite the coup for her, she has all the reports, from Jan, from myself, from Walther, and of course the stories from Samantha and Sam, and from Danielle. With references to the thorough investigation and research by Tammy, Chrissie, Allison, her daughter Terri and Claire, from Oregon'

'I should think so too' Sophie said, sitting opposite him.

'Of course, there is stuff in the story about you and Emma too, after all, it sure was a team effort to have reached the conclusion it has.'

'Is that your final report for the chief?'

'Yep, it has to be quite detailed, including all the expenses paid as well, not to mention the assistance of the Italian police and the help from Walther, the Interpol man.

'Well, my dear Martijn, here's to a happy ending' Sophie said, reaching forward to clink her glass with Martijn's.

'Cheers, mon cherie' Martijn said, smiling and closing the laptop having finished his report.

Paris

Tammy, dressed in a fluffy red bathrobe, stood by the window that overlooked a narrow street, one of several that all came out to where the opera building stood, which she could see from where she stood. Arms folded, she thought about how she felt. It was, unlike she had ever felt before. She felt sort of tingling. It was getting darker outside and she caught sight of her own reflection in the window, realised she was smiling, well, grinning really, she thought to herself. She was glad she had made the first move, glad she had taken the lead. He was so very shy.

Walther appeared, wearing just a large towel wrapped around him, noticed her standing by the window and said, speaking French, 'This newspaper article, it will be in just one newspaper?'

Tammy turned, admired his physique, then, remembering the question, answered,' No, it will be in the Dutch newspaper, as well as a paper here in Paris, and the story has been taken up by a paper in America, in Philadelphia actually, with a particular reference to Zecheriah's Ledger'

'Of course, a great source of information' Walther replied, then came over to her, she took a step towards him, and they embraced and kissed.

Boston

'Okay, come on now, you are the best at recapping, I know it's early in the morning, but with the article coming out later today, I want to hear the story, I want to get my head around all that has happened, and especially why, and they stole the wrong paintings? so, my husband to be, talk'

Sam smiled, it was early in the morning, but having spoken with Martijn the previous day, the story was now complete, they had found what the criminals had been looking for.

He sat in his now favourite chair. By the window and Chrissie sat herself down on the couch, looking at him expectantly.

'Okay then, well, here goes….the theft of the two paintings set off an investigation, one that Samantha started, when she went into the basement of the museum and discovered that extra storage cage…. However, the reason for those two paintings to have been stolen, started quite some years ago, I went through the whole story with Detective Jan, who's sister is writing this whole story, so together we made sure we had all the information, all the facts….now, it partly begins with the Crystal Kaplova woman, putting the information together with what Danielle told Martijn and Walther, Crystal knew about the painting of the monk, this from her grandfather who, if you recall, was one of the guys chasing Natalie Umbrego and ending up severely injured in the car crash, anyway, Crystal was only about sixteen at the time, but several years later, she starts to investigate, this after her grandfather had died. She however failed to find out more about the three monks, you know that Danielle was the one who uncovered the most on that, but, during her research, Crystal, who, by the way was quite a clever girl, sadly, took a wrong turn in life, sadly also, took a wrong turn in her investigations, for one, she was following a story of another hidden treasure, this time, to do with paintings of Flemish masters, she also then, because she needed financial backing, chose the wrong partners, contacting the brother and sister team, this Estelle and Filippe Cabal, she had found out about them, found a connection and knew they would be interested with what she had discovered, but, when she reacted to the discovery, she panicked and kidnapped Smantha, that was her undoing. Now, it was the brother, this Filippe Cabal, who, once arrested, sang like the proverbial canary. '

'So, this Crystal, was on the trail of two paintings, but neither were the ones that might lead to a treasure?' Chrissie asked.

Myrtle Creek

Claire Symonds was pleased to be the centre of attention as she spoke to Thomas and Tia who had only hours ago, returned from Paris. They informed her that Tammy had decided to stay a while, with the man from Interpol, Walther. And had told them to head back home.

They had arrived, though a little tired, but had not been able to curb Claire's enthusiasm as she was itching to tell them all, and how she, together with Alison's daughter Terri had solved the last piece of the puzzle.

Walking, pacing the lounge almost from one end to the other, she talked, sometimes animated with hand and arm gestures, informing them the sequence of events.

Thomas, sitting beside Tia on the two-seater couch, was impressed and somewhat proud of this young lady, who had so quickly become part of his life, who had so diligently been the assistant of the late Robert Pentegrass, whose nickname had been the searcher. And Tia, recalling the time she had rescued Claire, and the incredible help in her research qualities since that time, was equally impressed.

'So, this Crystal woman, well, she must have been quite patient, being on the trail for such a long time, then getting a job in the museum, but she got it wrong?' Tia asked.

'Indeed she did, she was first under the impression that there was something, a clue of sorts, on one of the paintings, either the battle on the coast, the one by Ruben, or the Jacob Leyssen landscape, however, we don't know how, but she must have learnt somehow, that was she was looking for, was in the frames.'

'But not in the frames of the ones she stole?' Thomas said, getting his head around the whole story.

'No, and sadly, she trusted the wrong people, and when she kidnapped Samantha, that was in desperation, it was then when it all fell apart for Crystal, and they killed her, took the frames, which they thought were the one they were after, but, of course, they weren't'

San Francisco

Alison's daughter, Terri, was also relating the facts, telling the story, though not quite as exuberantly and Claire, but more in a matter-of-fact tone, much like a journalistic report. Ally sat and listened, briefly feeling so thankful that she had her daughter back in her life.

'So, these criminals, this brother and sister, they were captured in Trieste?' Ally asked, proud of her daughter and she sat and explained everything.

'Yes, and they also found the frames back in Spain, where they live, broken to bits, they must have been so livid, and having put their finances into it all' Terri answered.

'But you, and Claire, discovered the right painting' Ally stated, smiling.

'Yes mother, I must go and see her, between us we figured it all out, following various import documents and shipping documents, the secret was in the frames sent from Colombia, they were shipped over land to Caracas, from there sailed to Antwerpen. Now, the person in charge of recovering the frame, which was coded with a special number, never got there. So, the frame was used and put on the painting by Pieter Bout' Terri said, smiling back at her mother, also pleased that her mother, who she once had been told had died, was in her life.

'So, back in 2019, this painting then came up for auction in London, it was purchased by a private collector from Antwerpen. Apparently, there was a bit of a confrontation at this auction, according to an account that Claire found, this American woman, Marilyn Montrose, who had been one of the bidders, confronted the buyer, anyway, she left and both Claire and I wonder, if she knew something about that painting, but we couldn't find out any more.'

'So, the painting then went to Antwerpen?' Ally asked.

'Yes, and the amazing this is this, it was in the museum all along, the private collector gave it on loan after he purchased it in 2019.'

Friday 10th June- Philadelphia

Chantal Brewer had decided to see Zecheriah's Ledger that was in the Seaport Museum. The ledger was in a glass case and was open. Chantal saw that the writing was neat and legible. Taking a few steps back, she sat down on a small bench and opened the newspaper she had earlier purchased. The story was there, a story that was made complete with the help of several people, with the help of research and with the help of information that had been written in Zecheriah's ledger all those years ago.

It was the second time she was reading the report, written and compiled by Marijke Schenk, a journalist investigator, who, Chantal knew, was the sister of detective sergeant Jan Schenk. She had titled the piece, 'Flemish Masters in the frame' and had very nicely written up the story that was easy to follow and drew the readers into the very adventure that reached its climax in the very museum, where two paintings had been stolen from. It mentions a kidnapping and a death. It mentions the capture of known criminals and the connection of a number of people who investigated and followed a trail that had begun centuries ago.

It had a couple of photos as well, and the main picture showed several people standing around a landscape painting that was done by Pieter Bout, the people were the museum curator, Emma Brood, the detective, Jan Schenk, and the insurance woman who had been kidnapped, Samantha Price. The second photo showed fourteen beautiful green emeralds that had been smuggled from Colombia to Belgium inside a wooden frame, which, having not been collected by the smuggler, had, un beknown of the contents, been put on the Pieter bout painting when it was reframed. The emeralds were estimated to be worth close to a million Euros. The story mentions the research done by a number of people, but in particular two young women, Terri Hudson and Claire Symonds, who research discovered the truth and the fact that the criminals, a brother and sister who had connections with Colombia, had the incorrect information and were following the research done by the woman who had planned the theft and was subsequently poisoned, who had been following the wrong paintings.

Chantal stood up, once more looked at the beautifully written ledger in the display case, thought about the journal she had been given by Alison, written, also in neat writing, by Henry Hopkins. History of the past bringing the truth to light in the present.

Smiling Chantal left the museum. She would head home, to Boston, making sure to visit Sam Price and his fiancé Chrissie. She wanted to find out more about her own ancestry, especially about Caprice, who's diaries had begun her own journey into the past.

THE END

9 781967 279661